150

THE ADVENTURES
OF BEN GUNN

DONATED
BY
PATRICK D. (PAT) ALMOND
2016 SEPTEMBER

D0896625

The Adventures of Ben Gunn

R. F. Delderfield

NEW ENGLISH LIBRARY
TIMES MIRROR

First published in Great Britain by Hodder and Stoughton Ltd., 1956
©R. F. Delderfield 1956

*

FIRST NEL PAPERBACK EDITION DECEMBER 1973

*

Conditions of sale: This book is sold subject to the condition that it shall not, by way of trade or otherwise, be lent, re-sold, hired out, or otherwise circulated without the publisher's prior consent in any form of binding or cover other than that in which it is published and without a similar condition including this condition being imposed on the subsequent purchaser.

NEL Books are published by
New English Library Limited from Barnard's Inn, Holborn, London, E.C.1.
Made and printed in Great Britain by Hunt Barnard Printing Ltd., Aylesbury, Bucks.

45001671 4

CONTENTS

For
VERONICA AND PAUL
who demanded
"What then—What then?"

HOW THIS BOOK BEGAN

I REMEMBER so well the occasion I first read *Treasure Island*.

It was one of those grey summer evenings that sometimes escape from November to May, and I was alone in the house.

Treasure Island, of course, had been piously recommended to me by countless adults, but our home copy had no illustrations and adult literature taste is gravely suspect to the thirteen-year-old. My prejudice was at length overcome by a chance perusal of the School library edition. A glance at the illustrations therein was sufficient to convert me on the spot.

I began reading, I recall, about 6 p.m. Two hours later I was summoned from the embattled stockade by a repeated knocking on the front-door downstairs. I descended to open it, half expecting to find Bones, or Black Dog on the doorstep, but it was only a stray aunt and uncle, on a surprise visit from London.

The aunt was a favourite relation but, despite this, and the certainty of a half-crown tip on her departure, I wished the pair of them at the bottom of North Inlet, alongside Hands and O'Brien. All I desired, all I demanded of life at that moment, was a chance to get back to the stockade.

Since that far-off day I have re-read *Treasure Island* at least once a year. I never tire of it and I now know that I never shall. It is, indeed, one of the great consolations of life, like hot tea, tobacco, and Italian cheese. It is a justification of life, a compensating factor, as it were, to the chance that brought us here in time to survive two world wars and the threat of extermination by guided missiles.

Last year, when my daughter Veronica was ten, and my son Paul was eight, I read *Treasure Island* aloud to them.

The night I turned the final page, I had to go back to the beginning and start again. After the third reading the questions began, a spate from each of them.

Paul's were routine questions. What happened to the three mutineers marooned on the island? Did anyone ever find the arms and bar silver? How did Ben Gunn stumble on the treasure by accident?

Veronica's were less direct. What *made* a promising man like Silver bad in the first place? Did it hurt when his leg was 'ampytated'? Who owned the old wreck in North Inlet, where 'flowers bloomed on deck like a garding'? Why did good friends, like Hands and O'Brien, fight to the death in the cabin? And, above all, how did a dear harmless creature like Ben Gunn become a pirate in the first place?

These questions were by no means new to me. I had been pondering them nearly thirty years and had even sought the opinion of fellow Treasure-Islanders, without obtaining any satisfactory answers. At forty-plus there was only one thing to do; answer them myself.

This book, therefore, is not a sequel to *Treasure Island* and not, I most earnestly hope, a bad imitation of it. It is more of a supplement and one, I feel, of which Stevenson might have approved, at least in principle.

At all events, I like to think he would approve, for he certainly loved these pirates of his very dearly. How else could they have become so dear to so many readers of successive generations?

R.F.D.

PART ONE

THE PARSON'S SON

Set down by James Hawkins Esq. at his home, the manor of Otterton, in the county of Devon, in the year 1805.

BEN GUNN, onetime pirate, died eight months since, at the advanced age of 80 years.

We laid him to rest in the little churchyard of East Budleigh, the parish in which he was born in the year 1725. He lies not twenty yards from the mother who gave him life and whose heart, he claimed, he broke in two, but I have always felt that Ben was one of those unfortunates who take upon themselves a heavier load of guilt than they need.

Ben's mother, as the wife of East Budleigh's sexton, was a hardworking soul, with a family of eleven, and Ben, who came somewhere in the middle of the brood, ran away to sea, in somewhat unusual circumstances, before he was out of his 'teens.

If the pious Mrs Gunn did mourn him it was not for long, she had so much else to do, and she was mercifully spared the knowledge that her son, throughout his young manhood, was a professional cut-throat, roaming the western seas in the company of hardbitten scoundrels like Flint, and John Silver. She had been at rest many years when Ben at last sailed home on the *Hispaniola.*

For myself, I could never see Ben Gunn as a pirate. For that matter, I could never see him as anything other than I saw him that first terrible afternoon on Treasure Island, when he accosted me in the broken ground north of Kidd's Anchorage, and talked what was to me, at that time, a spate of gibberish.

He had undoubtedly played a minor part in some terrible crimes between the time he left home, in company with that

10

curious, swashbuckling surgeon-philosopher, Nick Allardyce, and the moment he renounced his evil life in the cabin of the terrible Flint, when that monster lay a-dying at Savannah, but I have had the better part of forty years to learn the details of his wanderings from his own lips and I have no doubt that Ben, weak and easily-led as he doubtless was at all times, inherited a marked streak of piety from his mother that was proof against the active evil of his companions.

To my knowledge he only killed one man in cold blood and his victim on that occasion was a mutineer, pledged to murder his Captain and employer. Moreover, Ben committed this murder with the joint object of ingratiating himself with the loyal group, and reducing the fearful odds that faced our party at the outset of the mutiny.

For the rest, he was much more of a piratical servant, like Darby McGraw, than a real buccaneer, and his shipmates treated him with a sort of derisive contempt.

He was, however, by no means the fool he would have one believe, and possessed a measure of calculated cunning and canny resource that stood him in good stead on more than one occasion during his chequered life.

Left alone on the Island he fended for himself for more than three years and, had we not arrived in the schooner, would doubtless have survived among the goats and the bones of dead seamen until he succumbed to old age.

His lonely sojourn on Treasure Island made a new man of him, at least spiritually, for he never again turned his hand against those in authority.

Money he could never keep and, like so many of his former companions, strong drink was his evil genius. Yet, drunk or sober, Ben was quite harmless all the years that I knew him, and I am not ashamed to relate that I shed a tear or two when we laid him in the churchyard where his father had dug graves for half-a-century.

Long before Squire Trelawney and Doctor Livesey died, Ben and I were on terms of great intimacy. Because I was the one who first located him he always reserved for me, man and boy, a warm corner of his heart. He would tell me stories out of the past that could never have been wrung from him by the Squire or the Doctor, and I, for my part, do not betray his trust by passing them on, having obtained his permission to set them down on paper after his death.

I think he regarded this promise on my part as a kind of

11

post-mortem confession on his part. Until the day he died he had a morbid fear of the bloody past recoiling on his grey head. I could never really persuade him that his admirable behaviour during the mutiny substantially atoned for his life with Flint, and he died, I feel, in the expectation of severe punishment from Almighty God.

In spite of this, or perhaps because of it, I am sure he received mercy.

At first it was my intention to set down his story in the words in which he told it, but such a task would require skill beyond that of a mere narrator. Ben never told a story with a beginning, a middle and an end. He began one, went off at a tangent, spiced his theme with a wide variety of pious reflection, and finally led his listener into a morass of irrelevant detail.

It has taken me many years, and much sifting of notes, to marshal his reflections into some sort of order, and even now I am obliged to supplement the narrative with guesses. This inadequacy of sober fact has obliged me to recount his life story, and the stories of Silver, and others of his companions, as a straightforward sea-yarn, speaking of myself (in those passages of which I had first-hand knowledge) as a third person, and a minor actor.

It has been a difficult task indeed but it has had the merit of being continuously interesting to the author.

It was, as I say, impossible to set down Ben's narrative exactly as he told it but it would have lost something if I had recounted it in anything but the first person singular. Accordingly I compromised, using my own judgement in marshalling Ben's thoughts, and putting them down in the way he meant them to be heard and understood. I am sure that he held nothing back from me once the Squire (of whom he stood in great awe) had passed to his rest. He gave me his complete trust and I hope I have done that trust full justice.

Sgd. Jim Hawkins,
Otterton Manor.
1805.

12

CHAPTER ONE   THE PARSON'S SON

I WAS no more than seventeen when Parson Allardyce and his
family moved into the East Budleigh manse, and took the living
offered by the new folk up at the Big House.

We had had time enough to get used to changes by then,
for the parish had been at sixes and sevens since Old Squire
died, childless, and the big estate went to the Custers. The
Custers were cousins of the Squire's, from up-country, somewhere in the Bristol area, and none the better for becoming
big landowners overnight as it were.

The living was vacant on account of the treatment they had
meted out to the tenants and small-holders round about. Parson
Gibbins, who my father remembered from the time he was
sexton's boy at East Budleigh, had been a bachelor, long of
heart and short of sermon, as the saying is, but he uprooted
himself less than a year after the Custers moved in. He told my
father he couldn't match up the Sermon on the Mount with
the persecution of village folk driven to poaching by hunger,
or the orders the Custers had issued to their keepers to let fly at
trespassers on sight, as they would at rabbits in the flower-beds
of the Dutch gardens west of the Big House. He went off as
a private chaplain to one of the Beauforts, and Parson
Allardyce, his wealthy wife, and their son and daughter
moved in.

The Parson's wife was some sort of relative of the new Squire
and held similar views so I heard, though she seemed friendly

13

enough from the little I saw of her before me and her boy had to run for it.

At that time I was part-time gardener and odd job man at the Manse, and helped father between times, when the winter rains kept him specially busy with his gravedigging. I spent about half my time with the Allardyces and they paid me in fruit and vegetables from their garden. There were almost a dozen of us at home and my mother was glad of anything I was able to bring home; the young ones took a deal of feeding those days, particularly after the new squire forbade gleaning.

They were good to me, the Allardyces, especially the daughter Miss Dulcie, a fine upstanding girl, two or three years older than Nick, the son, who was at College, learning to be a sawbones they said. Miss Dulcie was devoted to him and prattled on about how clever he was, and how great a man he would be, as I weeded the beds in her corner of the big garden. At that time I didn't pay overmuch attention to her talk. If I'd known how close our courses were to run together in years to come, I should have asked more questions about Nick.

Parson was a hard, unforgiving man, just and a powerful enough preacher – there wasn't one of us that understood more than a word here and there of his sermons, he was that educated – and his wife wore the finest clothes I ever saw, before or since, and talked with a kind of sleepiness in her voice that was very genteel, and how the quality in London talked. She took no part in her husband's work and lived for her son, whom she had spoiled and cosseted from babyhood. Miss Dulcie helped out with Parson's rounds, and everybody came to love her within a month of her coming among us. There was nobody sick or in trouble but what Miss Dulcie wasn't on the doorstep in no time, and she was good to my mother, and sent her medicine for her cough that came of a damp cottage under the Church wall that the Custers would never shore up. The waste from the churchyard ran right through our back in winter, and sometimes the bedding was wringing wet, and had to be dried in front of the fire before we could dispose of ourselves in the two rooms for the night.

As I say, things were at sixes and sevens all across the Estate, what with the Custers set on enforcing the game laws, and enclosing land that had always been reckoned common geese pasture in Old Squire's day.

Basil Custer, the Old Man's heir, was the chief instigator, so they said. He was a tall, pale-faced ferret of a man, about

14

twenty-five when I first ran across him. He had stubbly red hair and a sort of wetness about his complexion that never dried off. He was determined to be the real Squire and rode big horses, sitting them loosely and getting pitched off every now and again. He was a good shot with a fowling-piece and winged Abe Gooding at two hundred paces one evening when Abe was setting traps on the edge of Baker's Brake. Abe got clear but had to leave home and enlist for a soldier to escape transportation. It was soon after that my Uncle Jake poached his last pheasant and began the chain of events that started me off halfway across the world, but let me tell about that in my own time. First I'd best explain how Nick, the Parson's son, came into the story.

Some months after the Allardyces had settled in, home comes son Nick in black disgrace. He had thrown up his studies in London for the gaming clubs and worse, and had run himself so far into debt that he would have been lodged in a debtor's ward if his mother hadn't paid off enough to his friends, and tradesmen, to keep the Sheriff at bay. He owed his tailor the better part of fifty sovereigns, and his father decided that he had better cool off in our district before he started him off on another career in the city where he could run into bad company all over again.

Nick wasn't what you would call a natural scapegrace. He was big, broad-shouldered and open-faced, with thick curly hair and blue eyes that were always laughing. He had hands as white and soft as a woman's but was as strong in the arm as Ned Summer, our blacksmith, and could throw Ned three times out of four when they practised Cornish wrestling on the green on summer evenings.

He was a gentleman of course, and always spoke like one, but he had a way of becoming one of us when he was with us, and I remember my father saying how different it could have been if Nick had been Squire Custer's heir instead of that wet-faced Basil, who settled on the countryside like a gingery leech, and sucked all the joy out of our lives.

Nick and Basil soon fell foul of one another and my family got caught up in the quarrel, for it began over Uncle Jake, the poacher, whose manner of dying made Basil the best-hated landowner from Axe to Tamar.

Jake was a great favourite of mine. He was a cider-drunkard, and a ne'er-do-well by most standards, and I don't recollect him ever doing an honest day's toil in his life. My father and mother wouldn't give him house-room but we boys learned all our woodcraft from Jake and were always ready to spend a night with him in Custer's coverts, staking our hides on the shilling or two we hoped to earn when Jake sold his catches in the Exeter market on Fridays.

Nearly all the poulterers within miles relied on Jake to add to their stock Christmastime, and Jake did his best to supply these at Custer's expense. It was wrong of course, and slap against the law, but that didn't justify Basil Custer setting man-traps in the coverts. Keepers are one thing – it was them or us, and victory to the liveliest – but a man-trap, with saw-edged teeth, and a bite like a hungry shark, that's the sort of thing as breeds murder in a man's heart.

Jake didn't come home one night and his wife left it a day or two before she let on he was missing. Oftentimes Jake spent seventy-two hours in the open, either poaching, or lying up in one of his hideouts after an extra-long spell at the cider-jug. When he had been absent the better part of a week she came to my father for advice and we organised a search-party, beating the coverts as far south as the cliffs, and hallooing across the whole stretch of pasture and ploughland between the Otter and the Exe Valley.

On the second day my brother found him, stone-dead from loss of blood and exposure and fast in one of Custer's new traps not two miles from the village. His mongrel Tufty was crouched beside him, half-dead with hunger and whimpering soft as a child in its cradle. If Jake hadn't trained the dog to keep so quiet when abroad he might have lived to come up before the Assize Court. As it was we reckoned it had taken him a day and a night to die.

There was a big funeral. Almost everybody from as far away as Poppleford there, and a lot of muttering and black looks in the direction of the Big House, but it came to no more than that. How could it with the Custers owning every foot of thatch and every fowl-run of all the mourners, and ready enough to raise rents or evict the first man to make a protest?

There was one man present however, who had nerve enough to speak his mind and that man was Nick Allardyce, the son of the man who committed Jake's ill-used remains to the ground. Nick hadn't attended the funeral in person but when my father and I had started filling the grave and the crowd had begun to disperse outside the yard, Nick strolled over and watching us, puffing a long Virginian cheroot, and looking mighty thoughtful.

Presently he rolled his cheroot to one side of his mouth and said, quietly enough:

'You won't be looking for settlement of this score I suppose, Gunn?'

My father looked up and down the yard to make certain no-one else was within hearing.

'Jake was always a waster, Master Allardyce,' he said, bending anew over his mattock. 'I live in a Custer cottage and your father pays me with Custer tithes. There's thirteen of us all told, and all to be fed and clothed, through winter. Why would I be looking for settlement, Master Allardyce?'

He was a soft-spoken man was my father, and knew his place before God and man.

Nick grinned and moved away with a nod in my direction; he knew what I thought of the business, but I judged he also knew my father spoke commonsense.

At that moment there was a clatter of hooves under the wall, and Basil Custer stumped up the steps and across the mounds to where we were working. Nick stayed still a yard or so away, and let him pass, without so much as moving an eyebrow.

Basil stood for a moment beside the half-filled grave tapping his lean thigh with the heavy, ivory-headed crop he always carried. Finally he laughed. He had a harsh, grating laugh, that made you think of a chain-harrow being dragged across gravel.

'Well, Gunn,' he said, as father straightened up and touched his forelock, 'that's one the less, and the cleverest of them if everything I hear is true!'

'If the people here had a spark of spirit, Custer, they'd pitch you in on top of him!' said Nick, speaking level, and never taking his eyes off the Squire's son.

Basil Custer gave him a quick, snakey look. His pale face flushed, just a quick glow, and then went dead white again. I don't think I'd ever realised what an ill-favoured face God had given the man, with his fishbelly cheeks, and long ferrety teeth pushing back bloodless lips.

'You keep your observations for the drabs of Covent Garden, Allardyce, and don't stay here putting your father's living in jeopardy!' he said in his thin, reedy voice.

Nick never moved, nor took his steady eyes off Basil. For a

long half-minute they looked at one another over the heaped-up clay. Then Nick spat out the cheroot butt.

'Any time you bait one of your traps for me or my family I'll call you out for a feudal bully,' said Nick finally. 'Fists, quarterstaff, pistols or rapiers, it's all one to me!' he added, 'for I'm not one of your lickspittle tenants, Custer!'

I thought Basil would have fallen on him there and then. He took half a step forward, hate crackling from every line of his body, but he stopped, suddenly, turned on his heel, strode down the steps and flung himself into the saddle. Nick watched him gallop away, his mare's hooves striking sparks from the cobbles. Then he gave a short laugh and, with a satisfied nod at me, lounged off in the direction of the Manse.

That was the first time Nick really took hold of me. He planted something in my heart beside Jake's grave that was to grow big enough to shut out everything else for years to come and was still growing when that big frame of his was long bones – bones as you've looked upon, Jim.

CHAPTER TWO   THE PARSON'S SON

FOR some time after that I watched for a visitation of Squire's
spite on us, as onlookers of the quarrel. That's a queer thing
about quarrels – folk who overhear them always run foul of
the losing side, but nothing much happened beyond Squire
stopping winter fuel collection in Hayes Wood, and making
us village folk buy kindling at a penny a sack.

The next time Basil and Nick crossed swords I only heard
about it in the run of village gossip. It was the night of the
Hunt Ball, given up at the Big House, a few days before Christ-
mas. The cause of the strife on that occasion was a woman,
pretty Miss Fairfield, from Axminster Hall.

There were rumours before that of a match between the
Custers and the Fairfields, but Miss Anne was a fine figure of
a woman, and kept half-a-dozen of the local gentry hoping and
hovering.

It seems that Nick used his good looks and his spry dancing
pumps to good advantage at the Ball, and Miss Anne played
him off against Basil, the way a pretty woman will if she's
given half a chance. The upshot of it was high words in the
conservatory, and a straight challenge by Nick to fight it out
on the spot. By this time he must have been spoiling to see the
colour of Basil's insides.

The duel of course was stopped before it began. Old Man
Custer saw to that. He did more. He called on Parson Allardyce
and stated his terms bluntly. Either the Old Man packed his

boy back to London or, better still, across seas, or the living would be withdrawn and given elsewhere.

There was a family conference over it at the Manse and, working there as I did, I picked up odds and ends of the arguments. Miss Dulcie, of course, was for appealing to the Bishop, and brazening it out, and Nick's mother, who was a high-spirited woman, was for putting out feelers for another living Oxford way, and cutting the ground from under the Custer's feet and was, as it were, heart and soul beside him. In some way he had become our champion and there wasn't one of us among the younger set who wouldn't have rejoiced to see Basil carried away on a hurdle. It never occurred to us that Nick might be the loser of an encounter.

Parson Allardyce, however, put his foot down. He wasn't going to be winkled out of a comfortable living by a son who was already the talk of the country, what with his mettlesome temper and roistering ways, and he told Nick to fit himself out for a new start in the Colonies, and keep clear of Basil Custer in the meantime.

Nick didn't take kindly to the decision. I daresay his mother and sister egged him on to defy the Old Man, but weeks went by and, although there were no more encounters with the Custers, Nick hung around hunting and drinking and gaming as far afield as Dorchester and Plymouth. I suppose he must have been generously supplied with money by his mother for he spent freely and his dissipated life soon began to show on his face. His eyes were often bloodshot and he was sometimes around daytimes in stained and dirty linen.

I saw a great deal of him these days. After the incident beside Jake's grave he took a fancy to me, and kept me with him as a sort of horse-holder and body-servant. The most important of my duties was to get him home o' nights from tavern and supper-parties, and a main tiresome job it was when he was dead drunk, and could barely sit a saddle.

Sometimes I got drunk with him for company and then it was worse than ever, the two of us careering about the turnpike clinging to one another, bawling scraps of songs into the night wind and sleeping out, time and again, in barns and outhouses, with the horses tethered alongside.

Once we were nearly run down by the Plymouth mail, and came in for a good all-round cussing by the frightened passengers. Another time we turned a herd of Custer's cows loose on seeded ground, and had the watch out looking for the culprits.

A third time Nick had us in crêpe masks, posing as highwaymen at Yettington crossroads, and stopping a chaise for the devilment of it. Nick stripped a Sidmouth notary and his wife of purse, trinkets, and watch but sent the spoil back by marketcart the following day with a note saying he had seen the light, and was for an honest, sober career from now on.

This sort of junketing continued for, maybe, three or four months. Then my mother stepped in and called on Parson Allardyce, saying it was to cease or she would be obliged to get advice from Squire. It was a bold thing for mother to have done, to face up to Parson in that manner, but she did it and it had its effect. The Old Man posted off to Plymouth the following day and booked a passage for Nick on a brig, Charlestonbound, coming home to give his son a hundred guineas for a fresh start and three days to leave home with or without the money.

Nick decided to leave. I don't think he was enjoying this vagabond life but lived it because he had nothing better to do. He was full of plans for becoming a planter in the Carolinas. He had learned something of the Colonies from his London friends and he told me that America was a place where a man wasn't fenced in by greedy families like the Custers, and was free to take as much land as he'd a mind to and could make a fortune in a brace of seasons if he had enough capital to buy a dozen slaves. I don't know whether Nick Allardyce intended to plant cotton, tobacco or farm in the English way, but as it turned out his plans came to nothing, because when we did arrive off the Americas it was in the company of men who had their own ways of picking up a fortune and did all their farming on the high seas.

He was to leave the last week in April and his mother and sister went about sniffing into handkerchiefs all that week.

A few days before his sailing date he was given a farewell party by some cronies in Exeter and I rode over with him, the pair of us finishing the evening in our usual condition, he in the supper room and me in the servants' hall.

It was a mild spring night when we rode back over the common under a full moon and passed the Custers' mansion two miles east of the village, with the moon shining full on its sweeping front and pillared portico, and the home-farm woods dark and silent to the west, where the ground sloped away to the sea.

We were only partially sobered by the ride and my ears were still singing from the spirits I'd taken.

Nick must have been more fuddled than I was to propose taking the mad course he took that night.

'Ben,' he said suddenly, 'let's ride in and give the Custers a rousing good morning! This day week I'll be on the high-seas, and I'll never have such a chance again!' And without waiting for my comments he spurred his mare through the lodge gate and went whooping up the main drive like a savage, firing his pistols into the air and calling the Custers every name he could lay tongue to and none of them much of a compliment as you might say.

I was scared, I can tell you! His horse was a far better animal than mine and he was a furlong away before I had wits enough to go after him. Before he reached the second lodge lights were showing up at the House, and a keeper ran out of the lodge behind me and loosed off a fowling piece at my back, the scatter-shot whistling all round me, and a pellet lodging itself in my pony's hind quarters if his sudden leap was anything to judge by.

There was a sharp bend in the drive about half-way up and I lost sight of him for a moment. When I came pounding round it I saw two or three men run from the side of the house and head straight for us. One was tall and spare and I judged it was Basil Custer himself.

Nick must have been more sober than he seemed for he saw them and swung his horse to one side and dashed off the drive into a narrow ride between two clumps of rhododendrons that led off towards the Big Covert.

I would have turned then and bolted back the way I had come, leaving him to talk himself out of his own folly, but the armed man behind me was barely fifty yards off and I saw he was reloading and standing square in the centre of the drive, so I took the only escape route open and spurred after Nick, getting into cover a few yards ahead of the group from the House.

It was dark as a bag in under the trees and I had to slow down. I could hear Nick ahead of me and guessed he would make for the west boundary wall where there was a low gate he could jump and make for the village over open ploughland, but when I got to the gate he wasn't anywhere to be seen in spite of me having a clear view right across the moonlit fields to the church tower.

The sounds of pursuit had died away and I thought the party

must have gone back to the house, so I decided to tether my pony and hunt around for Nick before he could get up to any further foolishness. It was a reckless decision, and one that cost me dear, but I was only a youngster and I'd grown to love Nick more than I can tell.

There was a by-path leading deep into the covert and I followed it, moving slowly and carefully, as Uncle Jake had taught me to cross coverts in our poaching days. I'd gone about two hundred yards when I heard voices ahead and doubled into the undergrowth just in time to see two of Custer's keepers coming down the path in my direction. They were both carrying guns and I knew they would run right into my pony. That made me feel pretty low, for I guessed the pony would be recognised, and this night's frolic was going to run up a big account. I stayed under cover until they were past and then took to the path again, pushing on as far as a little glade, where the keepers had a small hut they used for patrols, night-times.

I was about to cross the glade when the moon sailed out over the tree-tops and there was Basil, his gun thrown forward on his left arm, standing motionless outside the hut.

At that moment Nick, leading his horse, came slowly into the brilliant moonlight at the far end of the glade and Custer swung round and fired, without bringing his gun to his shoulder.

Nick cried out and staggered a little, his horse rearing up, with Nick still hanging on to the bridle. I saw Basil run forward, throwing his gun to the ground, and then thick wisps of cloud shut out the moon leaving the glade in deep shadow.

I ran forward at full pelt and right ahead of me I could hear a gasping and the fierce crackle of trampled undergrowth. By the time I crossed the glade the moon was out again and I saw Nick leaning against a tree, his horse shivering some distance off. Basil Custer was on his knee between horse and man, with his hands supporting him and his head bowed.

I called out, 'It's me, Mr Allardyce – Ben!' and as I reached him Basil gave a sort of cough and fell forward into the bracken where he lay still. I looked round at Nick and saw him slithering down the trunk of the pine, clutching feebly at the twigs for support. Even in that light I could see the front of his shirt and cravat was dark with blood and that he still had a sheath knife held in his right hand.

There wasn't much time for reflection. Back along the path I'd followed I could hear shouts and another outcry, further off, in the direction of the house. I knew we were both finished

23

if we didn't get clear of the grounds and catching Nick's mare I led her over to the trees where Nick was sitting, slumped up against the bole.

'Can you mount?' I shouted, bringing the horse right up against him.

He didn't answer but struggled to his feet and groped with his left foot for the stirrup. I guided it in and gave him a powerful hoist. He swung up and fell forward on the mare's neck. I twisted his fingers into the mane – they were already sticky with his blood – and then, seizing the bridle, set off at a jog-trot into the woods behind the hut.

My poaching past saved our lives that night. I knew Custer's estate like the palm of my hand and it wasn't long before I had foxed the nearest keepers and jumped out through a gap I knew on the Colyton Raleigh side, striking a bridlepath up to the old fort and getting clear on to the cliff path just as the first pink glow of morning showed in the sky over Otterhead.

I stopped in a fir coppice and gave Nick a long swallow from the brandy flask he always carried at the saddle. The spirit revived him enough to ask where we were, and how we had won clear.

I had a closer look at him and saw that Basil's ball had torn through the fleshy part of his left arm and that the wound was still bleeding freely, soaking his left side and running down his breeches to his boots. I reasoned he must have left a spatter of blood all the way from the glade, and that, as soon as it was properly light, they would be able to follow the trail with the naked eye. He must have thought the same for he said:

'You'd best put on a tourniquet, Ben. If I don't bleed to death they'll be on top of us in no time.'

I followed his directions and they were clearly given for a man in his condition. It didn't take me five minutes to cut a branch and twist his cravat into a knot that checked the flow. It was cold up there at that hour of the day, and probably this helped to check the bleeding. He had another swallow of brandy and tried to grin.

'It was him or me, Ben. You saw it, didn't you? He fired without a challenge and was running in to finish me off!'

'We've not time to talk of it now, Mr Allardyce,' I said, 'we've got to get somewhere for you to lie up while I go for help.'

'I'm in your hands, Ben,' he said, and his knees buckled. I

24

caught him, hoisted him up again, and went right on racking my brains for a plan.

It was almost light now and we had ten minutes at best to find somewhere to hide.

Then I knew my instinct had been right in heading for the cliffs. Not a mile from where we stood was a gully that led gently down through a landslide to the beach. If we could get into the gully, and under cover of the gorse we had a good chance of reaching it unnoticed, we could strike one of Jake's hideouts, a small cave in a sandstone bank a few feet above the stream-bed, and perhaps a quarter-mile from the tidemark. I'd been there once with Jake and I felt sure I could find it again. It was a slim chance but the only one open to us.

We came out into the open again and crossed the scrub for the head of the gully, reaching it without seeing anyone and, as far as I could guess, without being seen.

Once here we had to turn the mare loose. She could never have got down the gully and in any case, her tracks would have been too easy to follow. I dragged Nick down and gave the mare a couple of good welts with a hazel switch. As she cantered off towards Otterhead I got a firm hold of the folds of Nick's breeches and an arm under his unwounded shoulder. In this way we staggered in the gully, clinging together and with him bearing rather less than half his own weight.

It was the sea-mist that saved us. It came creeping in with a damp, south-west wind, and settled on the cliff edge like a grey blanket, but I knew we had little enough start, even if the cave did prove a temporary refuge.

We took to the stream-bed all the way and were sometimes knee-deep, for the Spring had been a wet one, and a big volume of water was coming down on to the beach. Nick fainted twice but each time he was ready to struggle on and in this way, an hour or so after we abandoned the horse, we made Jake's cave, a snug enough crevice, with a sandy floor and its entrance cunningly draped in bracken and ivy.

The effort had all but killed Nick and he lay like a dead man while I cut away his coat and bathed his wound, easing the make-shift knot and bandaging his upper arm with strips torn from the lining of his jacket. He didn't come out of this swoon so I let him lie. After an hour or two of watch-keeping I dropped off myself, and we slept side by side, while Custer's pack ranged the whole cliff-top without us so much as knowing they were near.

It was about an hour before dusk when I woke. I peeped out and saw the sun, blood-red, and masked in heavy purple cloud, sinking down over the Haldon Hills. I listened and heard a distant scraping sound, coming from the beach. I knew what it was, it was Sam Redvers stealing gravel, and it gave me new heart for Sam was a rebel on account of his livelihood being taken away by the Custers' withdrawal of village foreshore rights. I thought the coast must be clear up above or Sam wouldn't be digging into the shingle by daylight.

Nick was still sleeping and a bit of colour had come back into his cheeks. His wound had congealed and I wondered if the ball was still lodged there or had passed clean through his arm without breaking a bone. I had it in my mind to take a closer look and find out but I thought better of it and decided to let him lie and snake down to have a word with Sam Redvers.

I kept to the gorse and poked my head out not two yards from where Sam was digging. His cart was backed down the track on the Exmouth side of the landslip.

I whistled and he jumped like a cat. The moment he saw who it was, however, he had the sense to go on shovelling, and gradually edge his way towards the bushes where we could talk.

'I got Mr Allardyce in Jake's cave half-way up the gully,' I told him.

He looked mighty surprised. 'We all reckoned he was dead by this time,' he said, 'keepers are saying he must have bled like a stuck pig after they back-tracked you to the old fort. How in the name of God did 'ee get down the gully?'

I wasn't going to waste the little daylight that was left by giving Sam a long account of our adventures.

'What's happened in the village?' I asked him.

'Squire Custer has offered one hundred guineas reward for the pair of 'ee dead or alive,' he told me.

He didn't need to say more. That much money meant that most everybody west of Dorchester would be eager to lay us by the heels, and it didn't increase our chances of getting clear, even if we kept out of sight for weeks.

I took Sam's loyalty for granted. I knew that anybody who had suffered under the Custers would help us all they could, even with a bag of golden guineas held under their nose, so I told Sam exactly what to do.

'First thing,' I said, 'you got to get us clean bandages, warm clothes, a blanket or two, and some food. Then you got to get word to Miss Dulcie – and not let on to anyone, not even to 'er,

27

where we're laying up.'

I reckoned Miss Dulcie would have walked barefoot a hundred mile to help Nick, no matter what dangers she had to face to do it, and as it turned out I was right. It was Miss Dulcie who did more than anyone else to get us out of the awful trouble we were in.

'I'll come down 'ere soon as it's dark,' said Sam, 'but I won't come near the cave in case I'm followed. I'll leave the stuff in my mole-skin bag under that rock.' He pointed to a large boulder well beyond the high-tide mark. 'Well,' said Sam, throwing his shovel on to his cart, 'there's one thing, Ben, one of 'ee settled scores with they Custers, and me for one won't ever forget it, not if it means standing beside 'ee at the Assizes!'

It did me good to hear Sam Redvers say that and gave me the first bit of hope I'd had since I saw Basil Custer lying on his face in the glade.

As we were talking the sun had dipped over the hills and it was almost dark. I scrambled back up the gully and into the cave where I found Nick sitting up, and groping round in the half-light for the brandy flask. I found it for him and gave him a swig, telling him what I'd asked of Sam, and if I'd done right in passing the news on to his sister.

He said something but I couldn't make sense of it. I suppose the fever that was coming had already taken a hold of him. Soon after that he went to sleep again, and I sat crosslegged at the cave-mouth on the watch. The sun went down, all rosy and smokey, and a cool night breeze set the pines talking. I was that empty and wet that it made my teeth chatter.

I must have dozed off, because I started up quickly on hearing a step on the shingle. I didn't dare go down right away but presently I heard a night-jar screech three times, with a longish break between the second and third calls. That was one of our old poaching signals so I knew it was safe to go down.

It was Sam all right, with a moleskin bag of victuals, and alongside him none other than Miss Dulcie herself.

'I'm coming up with you, Ben,' was all she said.

There was no point in arguing with her. She wouldn't have listened anyway, and it was dangerous to stay talking down there on the open beach.

'You wait, Sam,' she told the carter, 'and stay out of sight. Ben will bring me down again.'

I took her by the hand and led her up the gully. It was stiff going, in wet clay, and over great slabs of soft sandstone, but she never faltered, or paused to rest for a spell; in fifteen minutes we were at the cave.

Inside, of course, it was pitch dark. We could hear Nick's breathing and there was a nasty, gasping wheeze to it. In the bag Sam had had the sense to stow a masked lantern and I lit it. Nick was lying on his back, his face running with sweat and red as a turkey cock. Miss Dulcie looked hard at him and then told me to get busy with the victuals, while she began to uncover the wound.

I fetched her running water from the brook and she started on him then and there, every so often diving into a reticule she had with her, and sometimes asking me to hold the light directly over him.

She worked maybe an hour and then, just as I was stowing away the remains of the food on a ledge, and had my back to her, I heard a sharp click and a long, deep groan out of Nick. When I turned round she was smiling.

'I found it,' she said, and held up a pair of forceps about the length of a man's forefinger. Fast in the prongs was Basil's ball and I saw that Nick was bleeding a little from a fresh cut, just below the collar-bone.

The shot, fired from the hip, must have travelled upward, and all but come out on the lower shoulder.

She packed both wounds with some sort of salve she carried in an alabaster pot, and then set about rebandaging, lacing him good and tight.

'You can't make a fire in here,' she told me, 'so I'll send down blankets, and plenty of warm clothes. Keep him well covered, and don't let him use his arm, not even to hold a bowl on his knees. Here, Ben, you'll be glad of this.'

She put her hand in that bag of hers and brought out a plug of tobacco, and a short clay pipe. She was that sort of woman was Miss Dulcie; there wasn't anything she overlooked.

'I'll be here the same time tomorrow night,' was her final word after I'd taken her down to the beach, where we found Sam fidgeting under his rock.

She had never so much as mentioned the shooting, or how we came to be in such a situation.

CHAPTER THREE THE PARSON'S SON

(With a brief commentary by J. Hawkins)

WHEN Ben first told me of the escapade that began his adventures it seemed to me that he was omitting the most important part of the narrative.

What I wished to learn from him was his own thoughts regarding the situation in which he now found himself, a hunted outcast, with a price on his head, and for no other crime than that of loyalty to a recklessly irresponsible employer.

His feelings regarding this matter, however, were difficult to discover and when, by judicious questioning, I finally probed them they helped me to forge a key to his entire character.

Ben was a man whose excessively simple wits could never grapple with more than a single issue at one time. To a person with more intelligence, and perhaps to a wholly witless man, the immediate dangers of Ben's position at that time would have been resolved by immediate desertion of the wounded man and prompt surrender to the authorities. Ben was quite innocent of raising his arm against the Custers. He had done nothing but make a praiseworthy effort to succour his injured patron and, when he realised how things stood, there was nothing to prevent him from extricating himself from his difficulties by making a clean breast of his part of the sorry business. The Custers would have gladly spared Ben to put a rope round Nick's neck.

Such a course, however, did not so much as occur to him. His loyalty to Nick Allardyce was the loyalty of a dog towards a stricken master. He stood by, frightened and puzzled, but eager to render any assistance he could and, when I discussed this attitude of mind with him he scratched his grey head, fixed me with his wonderfully steady blue eyes, and burrowed back over the long interval of years in a pitiable effort to examine the possibilities of any alternative course of conduct.

He found none and I think I loved him for it. In a world rich with ingratitude and petty treachery his simplicity and devotion shone out like a rare jewel. He went on:

We were lying up in that cave nineteen days and twenty nights, and not one night passed but what Miss Dulcie didn't show up, sometimes with Sam, sometimes alone, but always with something to make us more comfortable.

By the end of our stay down there the cave was as snug as a farm kitchen in winter. We had sheepskin rugs, a square of carpet, as much food as we could eat, rolls of bandages, tin plates and knives, a silver ewer for bathing the wound daytimes, fresh clothes and even a pistol apiece.

There was nothing Miss Dulcie or Sam didn't lug over that cliff top, and all the time Custers and Custer agents were combing the villages, and manning day and night patrols between cliff edge and valley. They knew we were somewhere close by but they never came near to laying hands on us, although I thought at the time that if they had the sense they were born with they would set a patrol to watch Miss Dulcie, and follow her to the head of the beach track. Maybe they did, and maybe she was too spry for them. Anyway, the long and the short of it was that we were undiscovered, and Nick's wound healed up wonderfully fast. He was clear of the fever that followed it within three days of his sister's first visit.

When he could sit up and talk they sent me out of the cave and it was after one of these spells that Nick gave me an inkling of what they'd been hatching up while I was out of earshot, or was down on the beach pumping Sam for news of the hunt.

You ask me why I didn't cut and run, seeing as I'd had no hand in the killing. Well, the truth is I hadn't the inclination to, and maybe it was because I felt kind of safe so long as I was with Nick.

You've seen those regular hurdle-jumpers in the races over at Clysthayes Easter week? They go for a fence, take it slantwise, and almost roll off over their mount's neck when they land the far side of the brook, and the horse gathers itself for a new spring on the level ground. Then they sort of hang for a minute, in mid-air as it were, and slowly inch themselves back into the saddle, while the horse pounds along for the next jump. I reckon I was like one of those hurdlers, Jim, most out of the saddle, and flat in the mud, but still hanging on, and hoping to wriggle back as soon as I'd caught my breath.

Because of everything that had happened I belonged body and soul to Nick Allardyce and without him I was lost. You might say I was lost with him, and so I was in a manner of speaking, but the thought of us parting, and me having to fend for myself sent cold shivers down my back, and I knew then that I was his man, come fair weather or squall, for as long as I lived.

And that's the way it turned out, Jim, with him coming between me and Almighty God, as you might say, and if you ask me at this distance would I do any different if I had a second chance I should be telling a lie if I said as I would. I was young then, and I'm a deal nearer the grave now, but when you ask me why I didn't slip out of that cave and take my chance with the Custers by turning King's evidence I can only tell you I'd rather have died there and then by my own hand.

Truth to tell, when Nick and Miss Dulcie had their plans set he did give me the chance to go. He said as how his mother had sent enough money to get us clean out of the country, but if I preferred to stay nearer home I could leave him and head east for the cities, once we were free of the district. If I did this, he said, I was welcome to a half share of the guineas. I told him that wherever he was heading for was good enough for me and, as like as not, that I'd be picked up the minute I parted from him, and that would put Sheriff and Custers on his track within hours.

He smiled his quiet, sleepy smile when I said this and all he replied was, 'Well, Ben lad, I got you into this and it's up to me to get you free of it! You've been a good friend to me, and I won't ever forget it in times ahead of us.'

Maybe if I'd known just what did lie ahead I would have struck out on my own once we were clear of that cliff, but that's fool's talk. Any man's course would be different from the one he sets himself if the Almighty gave him the power to see round corners.

Nick didn't deign to discuss our escape plans with me, and it was not until long after that I found out how it had all been arranged between Miss Dulcie, her mother and a cousin of Mrs Allardyce, who happened to be a retired naval man, and was now snug in a shore job at Plymouth. It was made possible by Nick being half a doctor, as you might say, and I've a notion that Mrs Allardyce travelled all the way to Plymouth to arrange the details, and that it cost her more good money into the bargain.

However that may be, one night Nick told me to pack our things into a portmanteau that Miss Dulcie had brought, and be ready to move out by midnight, as soon as Sam gave us the signal. We were leaving by boat, he said, which was the only safe route, and our first step would be Falmouth, far down in Cornwall, where we were to be picked up by some sort of naval vessel that would take us on to Kingston, Port o' Spain, or some other jumping off place for the Main.

'We'll be working our passage,' said Nick, as he sat smoking, his arm still in a splint, 'me as master surgeon, and you as my servant. Have you ever had a taste for the sea, Ben?'

I told him no. As a boy I had tried mackerel fishing and proved a bad sailor. Add to that I didn't like the notion of boarding a naval vessel and if I'd thought much about it I'd as soon have chanced my luck with the Assize judge as ship aboard one of the floating hells that flew the King's colours. I knew local men who had served a term in the Navy and all of them were ready to do murder rather than go back for a second. Nick must have guessed my doubts for he went on:

'Don't fret yourself, Ben, it would be a poor return for your loyalty to winkle you out of this for the forecastle of a man-o'war. It's just our passages we'll be taking, and then, hurrah for the plantations, and a fortune for each of us out of reach of the King's warrant!'

I wanted to ask him how it came about that we couldn't take an ordinary passage in a merchantman but just then Sam's call came from the beach, and we struggled up and began picking our way down the gully where, in the darkness, I could hear the faint creak of rowlocks and the grating of a keel on the shingle at the water's edge.

Miss Dulcie was there and she and Nick stood apart, whispering while Sam motioned me down to a scow that was lying in shallow water just off the beach. There was one man in it whom I didn't recognise and he told me to stow the luggage in the sternsheets and get in. I wanted to say good-bye to Miss Dulcie, and ask her to take care of Jake's whippet, but as I turned back for the beach, the man in the boat cursed in a foreign lingo and then said in English that the sooner he was offshore the better he'd like it, and that we had a stiff row ahead of us and not a minute of tideway to waste.

Just then Nick came splashing through the shallows and climbed aboard. In the faint glimmer of starlight I caught a last glimpse of the tumble of rock that marked the end of our gully, and that was my last sight of England for many a long year.

I was so ignorant of sea lore at that time that I judged we were going to voyage all the way to Falmouth in the scow, and the way she dipped and plunged as soon as we were clear of the bar didn't do much to strengthen my hopes of getting there.

Nick was no comforter that night, he sat silent in the stern, seemingly wrapped in his own gloomy thoughts, and my heart leapt into my mouth when suddenly, out of the blackness, a big hull that was immediately ahead answered from the darkness above. We were soon alongside some sort of deep sea-going craft but what it was, a brig or a four-master, I couldn't see, because she was showing no riding lights and had been hove to a mile or so outside the bar.

We had to climb aboard by a rope ladder and Nick, with one arm in a sling, found the ascent a ticklish business but he managed it and the man who had taken us off eased the scow astern and climbed up by some other means, leaving the boat to be towed.

Immediately we set foot on the deck there was a bustle amidships, and somebody shouted orders into the wind. The vessel, whatever it was, bore off into the tideway, and we were taken below and shown a small cabin where we could sleep on locker bunks. I was tired by then, not having had an unbroken night's rest for long enough, and the strangeness of my surroundings didn't keep me awake. I turned in and slept the clock round.

*

When I woke up Nick was sitting at the cabin table making a hearty meal of shoulder of mutton and white bread. He must have brought his own victuals aboard, for the brig – that was all it was – was no place for a man inclined to be fancy with his food.

We were aboard her two days and three nights and all I ever saw served out to the crew of seven was a greasy yellowish pork and biscuits plumb full of weavils. I got used to hard tack later on, but at that time, and with my stomach turning queasy from the pitch and roll of the little craft, I gave more than one thought to the big iron stewpot that always hung from its spit over our kitchen fire at home.

Adventuring is well enough, Jim, for those that want it, but looking back I see now that I was born for a quiet steady life, and no hardships. That was one of the things I soon learned to admire about Nick. He had been brought up dainty, and had never lacked for anything money could buy, yet he took to a rough seafaring life as a fledgeling takes to flight. From the moment he came aboard, until the day we sailed our final sea-mile together, I never heard Nick complain of salt pork or hard usage. He was a strange creature, taken all round, and maybe the strangest thing about him was the way he could mix with the roughest company afloat and act as though he wasn't, and never had been, a gentleman born and bred, and a man who had been taught reading, writing and catechism at his mother's knee.

I don't recall overmuch about that first voyage. The brig was called *Grace of God* and was out of The Hague, a Dutch-owned smuggler with an open cargo of flower-bulbs (Dutch gardens were mighty popular with the gentry just then) and a row of casks below, ready to be dropped off at convenient points along the coast. It was a safe way of travelling and Mrs Allardyce, or her seafaring cousin had arranged it to everyone's satisfaction. Nick and me were treated handsome, as paying passengers have a right to expect, and we had the run of the ship throughout the voyage. All the crew were foreign, so I couldn't ask questions. That first day out I wasn't inclined to, but by and by my stomach gave over trying to part company, and I got my sea-legs a deal quicker than I thought I would. Soon I was liking it enough to stand on the forecastle hatch, and listen to the wind's song in the rigging, and watch the green rollers sliding by towards the distant coast. I soon forgot what I was doing there, and how it had come about that a man like me, who should have been digging graves alongside his father in a Devon churchyard, was cresting the swell off Start Point in a Dutch brig, heading for God knows where and exiled, as like as not for ever, from country, home and family.

A man in his thirties and forties thinks of these things, Jim, and maybe broods on them as I did through many a long night as a castaway, but at that time I wanted but two months to my nineteenth birthday, and I was ready to paint the future all colours of the rainbow.

We put into Falmouth without incident, but Nick said we

were to wait aboard until the Captain brought him word of a barge sailing to join the ship that was taking us overseas. When that happened, he said, the scow would transfer us, and our voyage out would really begin.

Word came two days later.

From where we were lying, close in, I saw a group of men march down to the quay between two files of red-coated marines. I borrowed a spyglass from the mate of the brig and trained it on the party as they began to embark in a flat-bottomed tender. It didn't take me long to decide that the passengers were felons, chained four by four, and that they were being shipped out to a vessel that hung low on the skyline, five maybe seven miles out.

They were hustled aboard by a red-faced marine sergeant, who sped their movements with a long goad, the sort I'd seen farmers use on bullocks in cattle enclosures. I was still squinting at them, and wondering about them, when Nick touched my elbow. He had the portmanteaux and was wrapped in a new boat-cloak.

'Look alive, Ben,' he said, 'there's our transport.'

Sure enough it was, and the scow took us aboard when the barge eased off in mid-channel. The sergeant who sat in the stern greeted Nick politely, and gave me a curt nod. He was a bad-tempered looking man, with a red roll of neck blubber spilling over his tight, gold-laced collar. I remember feeling thankful I wasn't linked to one of those foursomes, and within reach of that goad.

The voyage over the bar occupied the better part of the morning and wedged in the bows, between felons and rowers, I had plenty of time to study my future messmates. They were a pitiable lot, half-starved and in the filthiest rags. All of them had a drawn hopeless look, all that is, except one, a shortish, broadshouldered wretch, who sat nearest me.

There were close on two score transportees in that barge and he was the only one who wasn't bowed down with the misery of his situation. The other men were taking their final look at home, but this one had a pair of sharp green eyes fixed on the horizon, and there was something in his expression that made me think he was leaving England without regrets.

Every now and again, when the sergeant's attention was occupied with Nick, he shot the marine a look of cold hatred that would have frightened me notwithstanding the ankle chain and wrist-fetters that hung about him. His face was pinched but not from hunger and ill-usage, it was made that way, with cheek-bones prominent as a Chinese mandarin's, no lips to speak of, and a mouth like a rat-trap. One way and another that man looked to be the only felon in the boat who needed chains.

About noon we were near enough to the transport to read her name, painted under the stern. She looked like a low-rated frigate and yet not like one, being uncommonly cluttered about the deck, both fore and aft. I also saw nine-tenths of the gun-ports were blocked in and this puzzled me. She wasn't an ordinary prison ship, for the transported felons always travelled in a specially-built merchantman called *Fury* that cleared Plymouth Sound once every spring. I knew that because two or three of my neighbours had made the trip, and had never been heard of since. Their families had travelled on foot to Plymouth to see them off, and brought the news back to the village. Yet our ship, *Walrus*, couldn't be a warship, witness the manifold deckhouses and the built-in gun-ports.

As we neared her an officer with a trumpet bellowed at us from the poop, and told us to scull round to the port side and make fast. I wished I was close enough to Nick to ask questions. All the chirpiness I'd found aboard the brig had oozed out of me. There was something about that frigate-merchantman-gaolship that looked evil and I climbed aboard her with mis-givings I couldn't have put a name to. I had a queer sort of feeling that to set foot on her cluttered deck was death and that all aboard her, captain, crew, marines and felons alike, were bound for the port of no return. Maybe Nick, too, had the same sort of warning, for as he swung himself over the bulwarks, and I reached out to take his portmanteau, I touched his hand and found it cold and clammy. Then he seemed to shiver a little and his eyes, looking straight into mine, seemed to say: 'Well, Ben, this is it – this is where it really begins!' Then the Captain came forward, a calm, elderly man, in neat blue uniform with-out epaulettes, and addressed Nick in a matter-of-fact tone.

'Mr Allardyce, I presume?' and when Nick smiled, and nodded, 'You and your servant'll berth amidships with the Marines. It's hardly a cabin but, as you see, we've a largish complement. I shall require the Falmouth passengers to parade for your inspection at six bells before they go below. You can leave the others until tomorrow. We've already lost two, Mr Allardyce. I have hopes that now you've joined us you'll show us a clean bill of health all the way to Port Royal.'

'That,' said Nick civilly, 'depends on how I find them, sir. If this batch are a fair sample I take leave to doubt it.'

The Captain gave him a swift sidelong glance, but made no further comment. We picked our way amidships, led by a seaman who had been hovering at the Captain's elbow. Ten minutes later, when I was trying to find space to stow our gear in the cubbyhole of a deckhouse that was to serve for our cabin aft of the mainmast, I felt the *Walrus* heel over and sheer off. Glancing through the open door I saw white sails shaking out, and men darting about the spars and rigging like monkeys. Nick said:

'This was a forty-eight-gun frigate, Ben. She was built to berth a hundred and ten officers and ratings. Can you guess how many she carries today?'

I told him I hadn't a notion and couldn't imagine that he had, seeing he had only just come aboard.

'It's good for a man to know a little about what goes on around him,' he said, rubbing his long chin with slow sweeps of his hand – a habit he had when he was serious-minded – 'I had a talk with our friend Sergeant Hoxton of the Marines. We've a crew of sixty, and short handed at that; then there's a score of marines and two officers to keep them at their duty. Below decks, where the guns used to grin, are two hundred and forty-one chained men, Ben, too many I've a notion, to permit deck exercise, even in split watches!'

That was all he had to say on that occasion. The next moment he had lit one of his quick-burning cheroots and strolled out on deck, leaving me to ponder his words as I crawled to and fro, trying to shake down the beds without knocking the skin from my knees and elbows.

CHAPTER FOUR   THE PARSON'S SON

SEEING how big a part the *Walrus* played in events that lay
ahead I'd best tell you the sort of craft she was, and how the
cut of her struck me (a lubberly landsman at that time, mark
you), the day after me and Nick boarded her off Falmouth,
along with the Cornish convicts.

She was a vessel of no more than three hundred tons, a
frigate, designed for speed, and easy enough to handle. Stripped
back to her original lines she could have outsailed most craft
of her rig, but her conversion from warship to transport had
made her top-heavy and she was inclined to wallow in a choppy
sea, and lose way in a headwind, maybe on account of her
conglomeration of ramshackle superstructure above decks.

She was old, of course, having been laid down in Chatham
a quarter-century ago, but she had seen plenty of active service
in the Spanish war, and would never have been withdrawn from
commission if the war hadn't ended suddenly, and the Navy
yards hadn't been chock full of vessels.

Apart from that she was smaller than the type they were
laying down just then, and less than half the size of a newly-
built frigate that leaves the yards nowadays.

I got to know her and her ways pretty smartly, Jim. As I
said, I took to the sea like a man bred to it, maybe because I
was strong and active, though wanting in inches, and maybe
because I'd been born and reared within sight of the Channel.

I came to love her lines and her rakish masts, and the way

39

she answered to the helm in a sudden squall, and because I loved her I felt sorry for her, doomed to plug to and fro once a year with a load of misery between decks, and no chance to do the work she'd been built to do, chase the French and Spanish off the seas and into their ports to plug the shot-holes she'd blasted in them.

If you see what I mean, it was kind of sad, Jim, like a prize-fighter, with his eye still bright and his muscles a-rippling, being set to a stool in a lawyer's office, until he was too old and too fat to do more than brandish his knuckles.

She was a two-decker and it was the lower, or gun-deck, that had been fitted out as a pen for the felons. The upper, or orlop, was used partly for messing, and partly for storage, for with that number of men aboard we needed a deal of extra storage space for water.

All along the open deck, wherever there was space to drive a nail, a line of deck-houses had been built for the escort, and some of the crew. The deck-houses were flimsy and looked like a row of hen-coops. In a hard sea they were always coming adrift and in hot weather they were as close as Dutch ovens.

Captain Ayrton, the skipper, was a good seaman who had taken the berth offered by the Prison Commissioners because he was too poor to live on his half-pay. He wasn't a specially harsh man, like most of the naval officers afloat then and now, but an iceberg who kept very much to himself, and seemed weighed down by his responsibilities. He was about fifty, tall, spare and battle-scarred, especially about the face and hands.

His mate was a lieutenant, a mere youngster called Awkright, and there was a Bo'sun aboard who lacked an arm but was a better seaman than the mate would ever be, and watched over him like a wary old grandmother. The marines were officered by two fops, wrong men for the job and on their way to West Indian stations. Their duties were carried out very largely by Sergeant Hoxton, the thick-necked bully who took us aboard, and he was soon the best-hated soul aboard, not only among the convicts, whom he treated barbarously, but among the crew and escort.

The use of a laid-by frigate as a prison transport was due to the lively amount of crime that year in the West-country seaports. Bad harvests had followed the Peace and outbreaks of violence followed the bad harvests. During the Spring Assizes at Winchester, Dorchester, Exeter and Taunton, no fewer than six hundred and forty men, women and boys had been sentenced to transportation and the regular ship, *Fury*, had already un-loaded those who survived the voyage and shared them among the planters of Jamaica, Georgia and the Carolinas, there to work out their terms as plantation slaves among the niggers the regular slavers were shipping over from the Guinea Coast.

Few of them, even the short-termers, ever saw home again. The war had caused a great shortage of Negro slaves and once on a plantation the whites were worked main hard by the pitiless half-breeds the planters employed as overseers. Taken all in all, it was a cold mercy to save a man from the gallows for this sort of future. He died just the same, but it took him a lot longer.

Even so, the Commissioners back home had wrinkled their noses over the last manifests of the *Fury* – nearly a hundred of the felons having given up the struggle in transit, and thirty more dying within a few days of being set ashore. A dead slave, or, come to that, an ailing one, is no use to a planter, and there had been complaints out of Port Royal that led to the Commis-sioners deciding to ship a surgeon along with the next batch. Good surgeons, however, didn't hang around seaports waiting for a berth of this sort and they had been glad to connive at Nick's passage through the agency of his mother's cousin.

I didn't learn all this, of course, until much later, when I lived cheek by jowl with fugitive felons and bondsmen from the Indies. Bondsmen were common enough in the Indies at that time, boys and men who had nothing to sell but themselves, and undertook to work for a certain period on a plantation in exchange for a fixed sum and bed and board. The money they got in exchange for their freedom was generally dissipated in a week at the rum-jar, and after that they were no better off than a transported man and could write finish to hopes of ease and plenty.

The buccaneers of the Caribbean recruited almost all their numbers from escaped felons, runaway bondsmen and pressed seamen. The latter were men who, having been boarded by pirates in warm latitudes, chose to join their captors and exchange salt junk and the rope's end for high living and the shadow of the gallows. Seeing the way most of these men were treated by the shipowners and their officers it was always a puzzle to me there weren't more of them. If you treat a man like a stupid, dangerous beast, Jim, he's liable to become one, and set his teeth in you the minute you are off guard. I dis-covered this aboard the *Walrus* that first week out, and had

41

the lesson rubbed in when I went below deck with Nick on his surgeon's rounds.

I don't know how I can make you see what it was like down there on the gun-deck among men who were to become the terror of the coast under that arch-devil Flint.

The stink was the first thing that clawed at you – nearly two hundred and fifty men, chained four by four, and packed into a space where one might have slung half a hundred hammocks at most. The gun-ports, as I said, had been blocked up, and the only air that circulated came in by two gratings, one fore and one aft, or when the hatches were unbolted twice a day for the issuing of rations.

Long before coming aboard these men had lain half-starved in gaols up and down the country, and what we had aboard were the toughest survivors of the epidemics of gaol-fever that swept through the prisons like the Angel of Death between every Assize.

There were men down there who deserved little better than a mere escape from hanging, wharf-rats and footpads from Plymouth and Falmouth, highwaymen's pimps who passed the word to their Tobyman when a wealthy traveller put in at a tavern, forgers and coin-clippers out of the cities, and trained batsmen from smuggling syndicates who would have brained a Crown Officer for a noggin of French brandy.

There were others, however, who deserved mercy, men like my Uncle Jake who were nothing but petty poachers, or rustics who had stolen to feed their children during a hard winter. There were runaway soldiers and sailors who had enlisted when their heads were deep in the cider-jug, and who had slunk off as soon as they sobered up, only to be knocked on the head by the recruiting squad or press-gang, and for one reason or another sent overseas as chained felons instead of being sent to their units and ships. All manner of men were down there, youths fresh from the country, and middle-aged destitutes with grey hair falling over their eyes; strapping great rogues with hands like hams, and whining cripples who had fallen foul of the vagrancy laws, all with one thing only in common, a measure of desperation that made it unsafe for a free man to go within reach of them, unless he was flanked by a marine squad carrying fixed bayonets and ball cartridge.

That was how Nick and me made their acquaintance, moving gingerly along the rows, with me holding a lantern, and Nick singling out men who were detailed for a spell of fresh air above decks, and maybe a dose of physic before being herded back down the iron ladder that was hooked to the hatch-cover, and removed whenever hatches were closed.

This was about the best Nick could do for the sick and right from the start it made him mad, the way he had been angered by the Custers' ways back home. The day three men died, and were sewn up for Christian sea-burial at sunset, he tried to get the Captain to agree to letting the felons come up in large batches for regular periods of exercise, and a good sousing with buckets of seawater. He said if they could gulp down a few daily mouthfuls of sea-air, and keep themselves reasonably clean, he could fight the danger of an epidemic that bid fair to carry away two-thirds of them in a week, but that under present conditions he couldn't be answerable for handing over more than the toughest of them by the time we fetched Port Royal or Charleston. The Captain, however, wouldn't hear of mass exercise. He had the safety of the ship to consider, he said, and to let healthy felons above decks would be taking chances that were not covered in his instructions. He was short-handed and could not spare a watch to supplement the Marine escort, a mere twenty-two men to guard two hundred and forty hardbitten scoundrels. Their physical plight didn't touch him – he had sailed in the King's ships since he was a boy and said a man had no business to look for a feather-bed afloat.

Nick turned sulky after this exchange of views. He certified more and more of his charges as being in dire need of sick rations, and the prescribed hour a day on the hatch-covers, and this didn't make him very popular with the Marines, who were called upon to stand guard hour after hour when they should have been resting between watches. The officers in particular hated him. Their eternal game of picquet was constantly being interrupted and Sergeant Hoxton declared that he had never seen a shipload of Satan's scourings more pampered and cossetted.

One night, after our sunset rounds, when hatches had been battened down and we had dipped down into the Trades, he spoke his mind to me as he leaned on the rail, watching the last rays of the sun turn the water to a bowl of red gold.

'Ben,' he said, 'I'm more with them than against them! If they were to storm up and butcher every King's man aboard I should stand by and wave my hat at them and there's the truth!'

It made my flesh crawl to hear him talk like that, him, a

man who was well brought up, and an officer himself while aboard. Maybe he was thinking that without luck and money he himself might have been stifling between decks, with a chain on his ankle. It was something I'd thought oftentimes to myself but never put into words. He ran on:

'There's a man down there capable of doing it, a man they can't bully and starve into swimming with the tide. That man won't stay a slave, Ben. He's been one before, and fought his way free, and unless I'm mistaken, he'll do it again, and good luck to him!'

Suddenly he braced himself and spat into the sea. 'God's curse on the powers that can ship whites off as cattle for profit,' he blurted out. 'It's the Custers and their like that cause men to run foul of the laws in the first place, and once down they can never walk upright again! Don't you see what that does to a man, Ben? It makes his heart a cauldron of hate like that man Pew – not just hate against the King, and the Judges who put him down there, but against every mother's son in creation and that's wrong, Ben, it's wrong and bad and stupid! That's the worst part of it, it's stupid!'

I wished he'd keep his voice low. I knew he was in bad enough odour with the ship's officers as it was, and this sort of talk was encouragement for someone aboard to start probing our past and hatching up fresh trouble. I knew the man he was referring to, Pew, and you'd have known him too, Jim, although he was all of twenty years younger when I first ran across him. He was the man I'd noticed in the tender, the broad-shouldered felon with green eyes, and I'd taken special note of him and his chain cronies during our rounds.

He was fettered to the master-chain that ran the entire length of the gun-deck close under the forehatch, and he had for companions three other men as rough and as resolute as himself. One was a powerful fellow in his early twenties, with a forearm like a weaver's beam, and wild eyes that glared out from a tangle of matted brown hair and whiskers. His name was Anderson and he even in those days was as fierce and untamed as a bear.

Alongside Anderson was Black Dog, a small-boned pock-marked youth, who had been a locksmith's apprentice and had taken to picking locks other than those on his master's workshop bench. It was his lank black hair, hanging each side of his pasty face, that earned him his nickname, for it gave him a look like a water spaniel. Right from the start he was Pew's creature, and remained so all the years I knew him.

The fourth man on the chain, the man nearest the bulkhead, was another old acquaintance of yours – none other than Israel Hands. At that time he had never run across the other three, all of whom had come to us from the same gaol. Surly by nature, Israel had kept himself to himself as far as he was able, and during the voyage had been closely occupied fashioning a piece of carving from a shinbone that he rubbed tirelessly against his fetter staple. I thought at the time that he was making a model ship, to sell perhaps for a few pence when he disembarked. It turned out that he had been able to manufacture a short, murderous knife from this unlikely material. I mention this because Hands' occupation down there in the dark proved an important link in the fate of every man aboard.

Perhaps now is the time to tell you a little about that precious quartet who were the bone and sinew of the devil's company I sailed in along the years ahead.

Pew, the acknowledged leader of the party before John Silver showed up, began life as a warehouse urchin in Deptford, and I've heard him say he never set eyes on father or mother. Maybe this was just as well, they were hanged as likely as not. Pew went to sea as a boy, and served as a privateersman in the early part of the Spanish War. Like most privateersmen he soon went on the account – which means he forsook privateering for open piracy, and plundered every vessel he sighted, notwithstanding the flag it flew.

He had served under Davis on the Main, and had made a voyage or two across to the Guinea Coast, and round as far as Madagascar, where he joined up with Captain England's crew of cut-throats, and plundered the wealthy Indian vessels that were carrying pilgrims across the Gulf to Mecca. It was England's habit to lie in wait for these rich prizes at the entrance of the Red Sea, and right fine pickings he made of it until his crew mutinied and marooned him in the Mauritius. Unlike Silver, Pew never concerned himself with the slave trade, but kept to freebooting until the warships cleared the Gulf, after which he drifted back home and exchanged piracy for smuggling, joining up with a powerful group that operated along the Cornish coast.

In those days there were two types of smugglers, known as batsmen and carriers. The carriers were, for the most part, harmless country folk, willing to transport goods inland on their shoulders or ponies for a handful of silver whenever a cargo was landed near their homes. The batsmen, however, were nothing more or less than hired bullies, armed to the teeth, and stationed at various vantage points to protect the landing parties from revenue interference. They were the sort of men who shot and stabbed without asking questions, and in one such encounter, on a moonlit beach near Fowey, Pew was wounded in the leg, and left behind when the others ran off into the dark.

He would have been hanged at Bodmin Assizes had it not been for his comparative youth and obvious physical strength. Hale and hearty slaves were worth their weight in sugar cane in the Islands after the war, and Mr Pew was worth more to the Government as a slave than he was likely to earn on the gibbet of a Cornish crossroads.

Job Anderson was a slow-witted longshoreman, captured in the same encounter. He was a Bristol man by birth, and had been engaged in the smuggling trade since he was a boy. Like most of these men, his main failing was drink; he was a lion when he'd been at the bottle but without drink inside him he was ready to do anyone's bidding. Israel Hands, then round about thirty years of age, was already steeped in villainy. He had served under the most notorious pirate of them all, none other than the famous Edward Teach, beter known as Blackbeard, whose bloody career had been cut short some time back by a spry Lieutenant from the Colonies, a young fellow called Maynard, who swore to bring Teach to book and did by surprising him whilst he was careening in shallow waters off Charleston.

Blackbeard, who usually fought with slow matches burning in his hair in order to terrify his opponents, went down with fifty-seven wounds and Maynard sailed home with his ugly head hanging from the bowsprit.

Israel Hands, who had been Blackbeard's gunner, owed his life on this occasion to the fact that he was ashore at the time recovering from the results of one of his Captain's pranks. It was Blackbeard's habit, whilst carousing in his cabin with his boon companions, to enliven proceedings by quietly taking a pistol in each hand, crossing them under the table, and discharging them at random.

Two or three days before Maynard's attack Israel Hands, sitting opposite his Captain at one of these parties, had received a ball in the knee in this manner and thereafter always walked with a slight limp.

After the death of his chief Israel made his escape to New Providence, the pirates' Island Republic, and saw service with

47

several captains, including England, Davis and Stede-Bonnet, the wealthy planter who threw up a life of luxury in Jamaica and went on the account for sheer lust of adventure.

Israel must have been born under a lucky star. England was marooned, and Stede-Bonnet was caught and hanged, but somehow the gunner escaped these disasters and came back to Bristol in the hope of enjoying the proceeds of his accumulated loot.

Rum did for him, however, as it did for most all of them, and in six months he was fored to take to petty thieving in order to keep alive.

He was concerned in a Customs warehouse raid at Watchet that summer, and thus found himself chained alongside his future sailing master Pew, and bound once more for the scene of his principal misdeeds.

Well, Jim, that's about the long and short of it and it's my view that those four were mighty lucky to last as long as they did, for there wasn't one of 'em that wouldn't have looked better dangling from the gibbet by the time they were twenty years old. Howsoever, that's the way of the world, men who take to crime because there's no help for it are most always the first to pay scores and go below, while men like Pew and Hands seem to drag out their wicked lives year after year, and put off settlement until they're as grey as badgers and their bill with the Almighty is as long as a ship's cable.

And now to tell you how we ran across the wickedest of them all during that unlucky voyage.

As I said, me and Nick were talking things over on the forehatch that windless night, when suddenly there was a blaze of light, low down on the port bow. The lookout saw it, and set up a holler, and there was a running to and fro as the Captain came out on deck and strained his eyes in the direction of the light.

At first we thought it was a vessel on fire, but after a minute or two the blaze died down to a pinprick of red and then disappeared altogether. We guessed then it was some sort of signal from castaways of one sort or another, and Captain Ayrton immediately ordered the helmsman to bear off in the direction of the flare.

I remember thinking how odd it was that the skipper should concern himself over the matter. Here was a man ready to keep two hundred-and-forty fellow creatures penned below decks for weeks on end, and was seemingly indifferent to how many died for lack of fresh air and good victuals, yet this same man was willing on the instant to alter course and go to the aid of sailor-men that he didn't even know, and to do it as if it was the most natural thing in the world.

I asked Nick about it at the time and he said he thought it was superstition and as good as a law for all men who followed the sea to go to the assistance of one another in distress.

As it turned out it would have paid the skipper more hand-somely to practise humanity below his own decks.

We kept a good lookout of course for another flare, but none came and Nick judged that the castaways, whoever they were, had nothing left to burn, and had set fire to their sail the moment they glimpsed our riding lights, in a last desperate attempt to be picked up before we bore off in the darkness.

It was dawn before we came up with them, and in the rosy glow of first light we looked out over the flat seas to see a ship's longboat becalmed and with only two men in her.

Nick borrowed a glass and, after a squint, passed it to me. I remember I was excited at the idea of those two men being down there alone on that great flat ocean, and how certain their doom would have been if we hadn't seen their one and only distress signal. By this time we were well down into the Trades, and more than a thousand miles from the nearest land. Their chances of another vessel sighting them in daylight were maybe ten thousand to one.

The glass showed me a tall, powerfully-built man about Nick's age, steadying himself against the bare pole. He was wearing a suit of good broadcloth, and had a laced hat pushed back on his broad shining brow. He was beaming, as well he might, but the other man, a short, stocky seaman, with a face burned almost black by the sun, looked to be in the last stages of exhaustion, and was sprawled flat on his back in the thwarts.

I thought maybe they were both too weak from hunger and exposure to warp round to our port ladder, but I'd misjudged the big man, for he skipped nimbly into the stern, shot out a single oar, skilfully edged the heavy boat alongside, and made fast to a painter the Bo'sun threw down to him.

Almost everyone above deck was now crowding the bulwarks, and wearing that gleeful expression that sits on a man when he's done someone a good turn, and is feeling pleased with himself.

'Can you come aboard or shall I send somebody down?' shouted Captain Ayrton.

The man in the hat gave him a smart sea salute and sang out:

'I'll be with you in a trice, sir, but Tom, he'll be needing the Bo'sun's chair I'm thinking, the poor devil's about done!'

There was nothing in the boat save the ordinary gear, a bundle or two, and a cutlass. I wondered how long the poor wretches had been adrift in that empty ocean, and how many of them had been in that boat to begin with. I was soon to learn, for the big fellow swarmed up the ladder, and climbed on deck before the Captain, whose rescue he acknowledged with another salute, and a grin that split his broad face from ear to ear and set his mild blue eyes dancing like a schoolboy's.

'Captain Silver reporting, sir,' he said in a pleasant and civil tone, 'late of the barque, *Rosalie*, a slaver, part-owned by me and six days out of Guinea Royal! God bless you, sir, for an honest seaman and I won't be forgetting you saved our lives – leastways, I reckon you saved mine, for it's my view my carpenter is beyond human aid.' Ayrton asked him how long he had been adrift.

'Twenty-three days,' said the castaway, 'and four of us was all that was left of the ship's company when fire broke out amidships, a week after we sailed!'

'What happened to the other two?' asked the captain.

'Gone aloft, sir, as seamen who stood by their Captain to the last gasp,' replied Silver promptly, 'Dick, he took to drinking sea water, and jumped overboard raving mad. A shark got him afore we could fish him out and truss him up. The other was a nigger who gave up after the first day. And, now, sir, begging your pardon, I'm your servant for life, seeing as you'll give me a long drink of cold water and it's water for me, sir, from now on for you'll see me dead afore I takes anything with it again!'

Captain Ayrton laughed shortly.

'Ah, they all say that my man. You'll be back to the bottle I've no doubt, as soon as the salt's washed out of your windpipe.'

While they were talking two seamen had slid down into the boat and laced the unconscious carpenter into a cradle in which he was hauled aloft, and carried below. The boat, which was waterlogged and low in the water, was thought not worth the saving, and was cut adrift as we turned back on course. I watched it until it became a black speck on the horizon.

That was all I saw of the castaways for the day and the night that followed. They were kindly treated and I heard from Nick, who had been called in to examine the carpenter, that he would be up and about in a day or two, but that Silver, the Captain,

50

was seemingly none the worse for his twenty-three days adrift.

'If ever a man was lucky, it's that slaver,' said Nick, 'he must have the constitution and temperament of an ox.'

CHAPTER FIVE   THE PARSON'S SON

Now seems as good a time as any to tell you the little I learned about John Silver in all the years I sailed along with him. Nobody, mind you, really knew John, seeing he was all things to all men at all times, as your party had cause enough to discover after the Squire signed him aboard the *Hispaniola*, but I reckon I knew him as well as anyone, and because of that had most cause to fear him, as I never feared a man before or since.

There's good, bad and middling men as sail in ships, Jim, and in twenty years afloat I ran across all three, but never another like Barbecue, and for why? – because his double don't exist this side of the grave, or if it does I never crossed it, nor sought to.

You see, John was neither black, white, or piebald, and no-one, not even a man like Flint, ever found a way to come safely alongside him. Sometimes you'd reckon he was rank bad, through and through, from stem to stern, crow's nest to keel, but no sooner had you made up your mind to this than he'd clap you on the shoulder and set you wondering if you was sadly misjudging the best shipmate you'd ever run across.

You could never trust him, of course; sooner or later, the minute it suited him, he'd always leave you in shoal water, but no matter how many times this happened you could never profit by it, for inside the hour he would have talked you into believing he'd done you a good service. He could do that after leading you slap up to the gallows-foot, and have you blessing him with your dying breath so to speak.

Men like Flint, and Billy Bones, and Hands, were led children beside him. They were all cut-throats, or as dangerous as wounded bulls, and always sure to run true to form, but Silver, he wasn't a man at all but rather a cross between a devil, a savage, a good messmate and a lady's maid. No one, least of all me, ever knew which way to come at him at one particular time.

He wasn't gutter-bred, like Pew or Black Dog, having had a measure of learning hammered into him as a boy, before he ran off and took to the sea. His father, I heard, was host at the 'Sloop Inn', in Topsham, Devon, and about the turn of the century had made enough money to educate his son as a gentleman. He didn't get very far with the process. Young John was too much of a handful for any schoolmaster who handled chalk and after giving one of them a thrashing he was on the point of getting for himself, he ran off and signed articles aboard a brig engaged in a coastal trade.

After a short spell of that he became a blue-water man, and made a number of voyages to the Levant. Up to this time he was wild and reckless but as honest as most sailormen, who can't afford to be as honest as the Almighty or their mothers would wish them to be.

One voyage looked like ending his career. He was captured, along with his ship's company, by Algerine pirates but Barbecue was too slippery for the heathen to hold, and after winning the confidence of the rover captain, and getting on the poop-deck by night, he took and threw him overboard, after which he knocked the watch's head together, freed the whites and sailed the galley into Genoa with a rich cargo aboard.

With money in his pocket he bought a share in an Orient venture and might have become a prosperous owner-master given time but his ship, the *Maid of Kent*, was boarded and plundered by freebooters off the Cape, and Silver, seeing little profit in the promise of being set safe ashore in his shirt, became one with the pirates, and drifted into Captain England's camp down in Madagascar.

At that time Madagascar was the buccaneers' paradise. The native kings were always at one another's throats, and a white man who could use firearms was always sure of making a fortune in gold simply by hiring himself out to one or other of the war parties.

John soon became a sort of Commander-in-Chief in the northern half of that bloody island, and lived there with a houseful of wives and servants between the voyages he made to the Red Sea, to get the fever out of his bones as he always said.

It was up here, under Captain England, that he met Pew, and when the ship's company quarrelled, and mutineers set England ashore in the Mauritius, Silver sided with the Captain and joined him in a slaving venture that took them back to England's old hunting grounds in the Caribbean.

Here John and his skipper parted company. John had had enough of the tribal wars, and a houseful of chattering women, so he loaded up with slaves and turned his attention to ferrying for the planters.

He made good sale in Cuba and Haiti and went back for more slaves. It was on his third trip that he ran into the worst of all sea-disasters – an outbreak of fire aboard.

He got clear of course, you could always lay to that, and he had told our captain the truth when he said there were only three other survivors apart from himself. These four escaped in the only boat that was launched when the ship was abandoned.

What he didn't tell the Captain was what I afterwards learned from Tom Morgan, the Welsh carpenter who was hauled aboard the *Walrus* more dead than alive that morning. Morgan told me as it was John Silver who had made short work of the other two as soon as the water started giving out, and that Morgan, with his own eyes, had seen him knife the white and toss the black overboard. Morgan was always dead scared of Silver, and had a right to be. He reckoned that he would have been the next to go overboard if they hadn't been picked up when they were. He was uncommonly good at guesswork, was Tom Morgan.

CHAPTER SIX   THE PARSON'S SON

THEY do say if you fish a man out of the water when he's on
the point of drowning, you're obliged to abide him for the rest
of your life, Jim. Well, that's how it came to look with Silver
and the *Walrus*' company. Within hours he had the run of
our vessel. The young mate, Awkright, found him a berth in
his own cabin, and he took to messing with the skipper himself,
and the two Marine officers.

The long voyage was tedious and I daresay they found him
good company, for, although he didn't talk like a gentleman
born, he was a wonderful yarn-spinner and he knew well enough
how to behave in the company of a gentleman. His great neigh-
ing laugh was often heard to issue from the Captain's cabin
where he was taking wine, and talking of ventures lost and
won, from Cathay to the Bay of a Thousand Wrecks. When
John was affable he could always be sure of a good audience.

Most of the lower deck soon got to know him as 'Barbecue',
his seaname, and what with his taking ways, and the distribution
of silver bounty he made among the men from the jingling
canvas bag he brought aboard from the ship, he was welcome
anytime he cared to show himself.

Strangely enough, the only man he failed at that time to
impress was Nick.

One night, when we were not more than a few days' sail
out of Port Royal, our second port of call (we had watered in

the Azores), Nick happened to say to me:

'There's a deal that puzzles me about that man Silver, Ben. Whenever I meet a man as glib with his tongue as yon I look to my priming, as the saying is! Now how does it fall out that a slaver is on such familiar terms with the Almighty? I'm not a religious man myself, Ben, but I'm the son of a parson and parsons are particular about the company they keep!'

All this was true enough. Taken below to inspect the felons, Silver had minced his way along the centreboard and kept up a flow of pious talk that would have done credit to a dissenting preacher. He blew through his nose, clicked his tongue and rolled his eyes over, as he put it, 'over so much sin and wickedness ironed together in one ship,' and piped his eye over the fact that so many promising men could be the victims of drink, greed and idleness.

'There's another thing,' Nick went on, 'when we were below, and Silver was on my heels, I heard one of the convicts greet him by that nickname of his. Now how comes it that men battened below already know him as "Barbecue"?'

'Maybe they heard the tars addressing him that way when the sick were sitting out on the hatch-covers,' I suggested.

'That won't add up,' said Nick, 'the shout came from the men under the foredeck, and they haven't been up for air since we left Plymouth Sound!'

That night, we learned part of the answer. Soon after sunset Silver pops his head into our deckhouse and salutes:

Beggin' your pardon, Mr Surgeon,' he said, respectful as ever, 'but Captain Ayrton's been so considerate as to grant me permission to go below and distribute a ration o' baccy to them unfortunates!'

I was mighty surprised at this but if Nick was he didn't let on that he was.

'Without escort?' he drawled. 'Why, Mr Silver, aren't you afraid to trust yourself among such company?'

'No, sir, I'm not,' replied Silver, very levelly, 'and for why? Because it's my reckoning that the Pilot-on-High, Who saw fit to guide that longboat o' mine into the track o' this here vessel, didn't do it for the purpose of having me torn apart by a pack o' villains in irons! I'm minded as He's saving me for worthier things, sir!'

Nick laughed outright. Being a parson's son, and bred to it as you might say, this sort of talk didn't go very far with him. More than once he told me that pious words were as often as not a cloak for impious intentions, and I reckon he was right at that.

'Well, Mr Silver,' he said very affably, 'I've been below twice, and I'm not spoiling to go a third time. Here's the key of the hatch-cover. I don't need to tell you there's little to see, and overmuch to smell on that gun-deck.'

'No, sir, you don't,' replied Silver, with a knowing wink, 'but I've lived between decks with Turks and Blackamoors, and this big nose o' mine isn't as particular as some.'

He took the key and we went forward, with the duty marines to stand at the head of the ladder and watch out for squalls. They looked surprised at us going below unescorted, but Silver didn't hesitate a second and was down in the gloom with me at his heels the minute the scuttle was removed.

As soon as we were alone he addressed me in a confidential tone.

'Ben, boy,' he says, 'I reckon I can tell you the truth and trust you with it. The fact is, it goes to my heart to see white men treated like cattle, and apart from the baccy I've brought from the quartermaster, I've laid by a bucket o' scraps from the mate's table as I mean to give to the most deserving among those poor devils. Now just you slip up the ladder, and ɛlong to the deckhouse. It's empty, the mate being on watch. You'll find the bucket behind the door.'

I did as I was bid and gave him the lantern to pick his way along the centreboard alone. It seemed a natural enough act for a man of his disposition, and if I thought about it at all at the time I reckon I put his kindness down to a thank offering on his part, like a man putting silver in the plate at church the first time he takes the sacrament after an illness.

I found the bucket, it was full of bread and broken meats, and I knew it would be welcome enough below. It must have taken me five or ten minutes to fetch it, and return below, but when I'd reached the foot of the ladder, and began to pick my way from it past the rows of sleeping convicts towards Silver's lantern a hand reached out of the dark and grabbed me, pulling me behind a bulkhead. Then Nick's voice hissed in my ear telling me to stay where I was. He must have followed us to the forehatch, and waited until I went aft before slipping down the ladder to spy on Silver from the bulkhead shadow.

In the bobbing rays of the lantern I could see Silver standing talking to Master Pew, and there was just enough light to see Hands, crouching as close to the pair as the length of his chain

would permit. Nick and I both strained our ears to listen to what was being said but they were conversing in whispers, and the only two words we heard were 'Flint' and 'Port Royal'. These didn't signify much at the time, although they fitted snugly enough into the pattern of future events.

Presently Silver straightened himself, and bawled 'Ben! Are you there, Ben?' which was Nick's cue to snake back along the gangway, and out of the forehatch. All he said by way of parting instructions was: 'Bring him to me the minute you come up!'

I went along to Silver, and handed him the bucket which he passed on to Pew. I expected to see the felons wolf the scraps as soon as they laid hands on them, but they didn't. Pew just put it between his knees and exchanged glances with the other three, while Silver said in a loud voice:

'Now see it's shared among the batches this end, and there'll be more tomorrow for such as deserve it.'

'God bless you, Mr Silver,' said Black Dog, 'we won't none of us forget this kindness, will we, mates?'

There was a mutter of agreement from the others, but I had an uncommonly strong belief that the thanks were expressed for my benefit, and not as being due to Silver.

'Come, Ben,' said Silver, 'I've a notion to go aloft for a breath of sea air!' and he led the way back to the ladder.

As soon as we had secured the hatch, and moved away from the marines, I told him that Nick wanted a word with him. He came readily enough, and when we got into our deckhouse Nick was sitting on his locker, puffing away at one of his cheroots, and making the atmosphere of the cubbyhole foul enough to choke a man.

'Silver,' he said bluntly, as soon as I'd closed the sliding door, 'are you going to tell me what you're up to, or do I have to ask the skipper?'

Silver's face was a picture. Half a dozen expressions chased their way across his broad features before the final one, a mixture of sorrow and pained surprise, settled in his eyes and round the corners of his mouth.

'Well, Mr Surgeon,' he said finally, 'I reckon you've rumbled me! I ought to have knowed better than to try and hoodwink an educated gentleman like you!'

'Never mind about that,' said Nick, and there was laughter behind his voice, 'What's the cause of this sudden sympathy for the fallen? It does you credit, but it sets me wondering. You see, Silver, I've met slavers and they don't spend their profits on government charges. How many men down there have you earmarked for your own?'

Silver sat down. By now he had completely recovered his composure.

'Seeing as you've boarded me you'd best have the truth. All I can add to it is that there's profit in it for you if you'll go along with me, Mr Allardyce,' he said. Nick said nothing so he ran on: 'It's not just a matter o' business, there's a deal more to it than that and you can lay to it. Two o' the men rotting in irons down there is old messmates o' mine, and I'm not the man to turn my back on a messmate fast on a lee shore, and that's about the whole of it, Mr Surgeon!'

'Which two?' asked Nick, raising his eyebrows at this blunt admission.

'Gabriel Pew and Israel Hands,' said Silver readily. 'I've sailed alongside both of 'em, the one in the Gulf, when we was berthed aboard the *Royal Fortune*, and the other after they settled scores with Ned Teach, and Hands sailed penniless into New Providence more than two years agone!'

'*Royal Fortune* – "New Providence", you've been free and easy with your shipmates have you not, Captain Silver?' said Nick with a chuckle. 'The *Royal Fortune* was a pirate vessel the last I heard of her, and New Providence was the buccaneers' free market, where cargoes changed hands without questions being asked!'

Silver didn't blink an eyelid, but looked Nick straight in the face.

'That's true enough,' he said, 'and it's a keen eye and a long memory you've got, but maybe you never heard of the King's Amnesty or that I took advantage of it, along with most all the Brethren of the Coast. We're free to sail where we will now, Mr Allardyce, just so long as we've a "Woodes-Rogers" pardon in our pockets!' and he dived into the pocket of his coat and threw a grubby piece of parchment on the table.

It was a scroll with a lot of lawyer's writing on it and below it was a big red seal, cracked and broken at the edges, but bearing the Royal Arms.

Nick examined the paper with interest, and since I'm telling you all I know of the heyday of freebooting in the Caribbean, perhaps this is the time to tell you what a 'Woodes-Rogers' pardon was.

Captain Woodes-Rogers was a private citizen who came as

Governor to some of the islands forty years before the time I'm speaking of and wiped out the pirates' haven at New Providence, for a spell at least, with a stroke of the pen. All he did was to get the King of England to issue a general pardon to all who would sail in and populate his new colony and become honest planters and traders, and the success of his offer lay in the fact that the pirates were allowed to keep all they had got at the time of surrender – ships, gold, plate, goods, everything.

Most of the Brethren at that time came in and for a longish spell piracy vanished from that part of the world, Woodes-Rogers being a man not to be trifled with, and hanging a back-slider every time he judged it necessary to keep his unruly subjects in line. When he died, of course, it soon started up again, and other pardons were issued from time to time. They were issued by different Governors of Jamaica and other settlements but were always known after the name of the man who first thought of them in those parts.

'I'd heard about these but never looked to set eyes on one!' he said, 'however, if the Amnesty is open to everyone how comes it that your messmates below are still in irons?'

'There's some,' said Silver solemnly, 'as don't have the wits to take advantage of the new start His Majesty offers we outlaws. Pew and Israel, their heads was never of much account, and when they heard of the Pardon, and a new Governor sails in to take over New Providence for King George once again, putting hatches over the past, as you might say, they sailed on freebooting until the king's men laid 'em by the heels, as we all knowed they would, sooner or later. As for me, I give up, and took to honest trade as you can see by 'he bit o' paper.'

'Would Captain Ayrton know all this?' asked Nick.

'No, sir, for I've seen as he didn't,' said Silver promptly. 'There's a true saying about giving a dog a bad name and not touching pitch without soiling the hands, so let's stow the talk and sign articles, here and now. There's two good men down there as I could use when I get myself another slaver in Port Royal, and if I can't get 'em one way I'll get 'em another!'

'You could buy them, I've no doubt,' said Nick who seemed much taken with Silver's cool admission.

'No, sir, I can't that,' said Silver, 'for the skipper tells me that every felon aboard this here ship is earmarked for one or other of the planters, on account of the terrible shortage of blacks in the Islands. Every man jack of 'em is for the Carolinas, and the price they'll fetch in Charleston will make an honest slaver's hair turn white!'

'Then what do you propose to do?' asked Nick.

'Slip their cable when we're provisioning in Port Royal,' said Silver bluntly. 'I need 'em, I mean to have 'em, and it's the least I could do for shipmates!'

'You're taking a lot on trust, telling me all this,' drawled Nick.

'No, sir, I'm not that,' said Silver with a slow grin. 'Beggin' your pardon, you look to me like a man who is open to business and me, I'm ready to pay twenty guineas for a blind eye!'

Nick roared with laughter.

'Then what would you say if I promised a blind eye and agreed to forgo the bribe?' he demanded.

Silver's eyes narrowed.

'I'd say one of two things, Master Allardyce. Either you was an uncommonly open-hearted gentleman, or you'd been in bad trouble yourself, and was man enough to remember it! I don't like being under an obligation to a man, particularly a man wearing the King's coat, but then, neither do I like throwing twenty Jimmy-o'-Goblins overboard when there's no particular need for it. You're a gentleman, as I said at the first, and your hand's good enough for me, sir. Would you come handsome and shake on it?'

'Just those two?' said Nick.

'Those two, and here's my affydavy!' said Silver.

Well, that was the start of it, Nick Allardyce, son of a parson, and John Silver, pirate and slaver, striking a bargain in my presence and taking one to the other like mating birds as you might say.

I don't mind telling you, Jim, it made my scalp rise to hear Nick agreeing to connive at the escape of convicted felons, as though it was the most natural thing in the world, and all because of that streak in him which seemed to take pleasure in sailing close to the wind, and throwing dust in the eyes of the Law.

After that night he and Silver were inseparables and many's the time I watched them on the foredeck, with Silver doing most of the talking, and spreading his hands in that preacher's way of his when he wanted to drive a point home, and Nick, hunched on a hatch-cover, hugging his knees, and every now and again throwing back his head to let out a laugh at something in John's talk that had tickled his ribs.

Then came the long-awaited screech of 'Land-ho!' from the lookout, as we fetched the first of the Islands that lie scattered about that big blue sea like emeralds in a bowl, and soon enough the long coastline and dazzling white waterfront of Port Royal shows up and the great anchor is splashing to her moorings between ships of all sizes, and half the nations of the world. For a spell I forgot Silver in the excitement and wonder of it all, seeing as I'd never so much as set eyes on so much as a picture of foreign parts up to that time, and was still not much more than a village-reared boy.

Ah, Jim, you don't need to tell me you felt the same as I did when first you took ship half-way across the world. You was like me, I reckon, struck dumb with the colour and the noise and differentness of it all – flat-bottomed bumboats nosing alongside, crewed by coal-black niggers, or copper-faced half-breeds, and each boat piled high with melons, and oranges, and pomegranates, as made your mouth water when you stared down at 'em from the bulwarks. Great ships flying the British, French, Dutch and Spanish flags, with sails close-reefed as they rode at anchor in the big crescent of the bay. Schooners, luggers, snows, barques, brigs, yawls, all manner of ships, skimming over the shining water, or lying snug against the mole, with their men coming and going aboard 'em, and crying out to one another in a dozen different tongues. And the colour, Jim! The wonderful splashes of colour, each every way you cared to look, bright red of the marines' jackets, gold of the sand beyond the breaker-line, white – so white, it hurt your eyeballs to look – of the government buildings on the quays, and twinkling points of silver from the polished arms of the sentries on the fort ramparts, and the buttons of the well-dressed men in the boats. Add to that the flaming red and yellow of the mulatto women's skirts, as they emptied their straw baskets into the bumboats, colour and noise everywhere, rising out of the bay like showers of sparks from a bonfire, and taking your brain by storm as it were. And in the piled up town behind, where the houses seemed to be jostling one another to get down to the cool beach, a devil's riot of gaming and wenching and drunkenness and greed as would make the angels in heaven weep for the pity of it, seeing what men were making of a Garden of Eden God had seen fit to set down in that spot.

That was Port Royal when I first set eyes on it, and that was Port Royal, or any other berth of the Main, all the time I knowed it and plied from it, and the men living there, men like Flint and Bones and Silver, they were the cause of it being what it was, and I can only liken 'em to the slugs you find nestling in the petals of an English rose.

If I'd have knowed this much at the time, Jim, well, maybe it would have spoiled the beauty of it, but I didn't, I only come by its true nature gradual-like, and that first morning we dropped anchor was maybe the happiest hour of my whole sinful life, and one as I've looked back on with joy many a year since.

It was Silver who first took me ashore, later in the day to show me the sights of the port, and for an hour, or maybe two, he was his old, companionable self, pointing out this and that with, as you can imagine, hardly a word out of me, until suddenly up comes a big nigger, with a scrap of paper which he hands to Silver, and stands waiting, as though expecting an answer.

Silver read the note and blinked once or twice before clapping me on the shoulder and telling me to wait for him on the breakwater where our skiff was moored, while he attended to a matter of business.

'Pressing business it is, Ben,' he hastened to tell me, 'a matter o' buying myself a new ship as I can get cheaper now than be hanging in stays.'

I watched him cross the quays and disappear into a grog-shop, not a cable's length from where the nigger had run him down. I don't reckon I'd have given the matter another thought if I hadn't happened to notice the way he stopped under the grog-shop awning, and looked first this way and then that, like a whippet on the edge of a burrow, all tense-like and quivering.

That set me thinking. I said to myself, 'That message has more to do with a pair of cheat-gallows, lying in the gun-deck of the *Walrus*, than with Master Silver's future vessel, otherwise, what makes him careful to note nobody from our company sees him go for to buy it?' I don't reckon he counted me, then or afterwards, as anything more than Nick's hanger-on and boot-polisher and, come to think of it, he had no reason to, having blown his gaff as they say in my presence the night I took him and his shipmates the bucket.

I tell you though, I was uneasy from the start and this made me more so. I reckoned I owed it to Nick to see if I could learn part of what Mr Silver was hatching up, and if possible, to steer Nick clear of a man who smelled of trouble, for all his shoulder-slapping and hearty words.

One way and another, Jim, I pride myself that I was less took in by Long John than you or any of your ship's company as sailed out with him from Bristol years later, but perhaps that's because a man who is himself out of law is liable to entertain suspicions worthy and unworthy of most everyone he runs across.

Well, as I say, I decided to snake up on him and as it happened the grog-shop he'd entered was well situated for the purpose, being nothing but a deepish, three-sided, one-storey shack, with slatted cane curtains hanging on the open side to keep out flies which buzzed in their millions over the open refuse dumps along that steaming waterfront.

I let a minute or two go by and then edged away to approach the place from the Fort Causeway that ran up from the dirt road on the west side. I couldn't approach it direct because the big nigger, having taken Silver inside, immediately showed up again, and stood with his arms folded and back to the curtain-split that served for a door.

I got to windward of him, however, and stood close against the baking wooden frame of the cabin, which was made of rough-hewn timber and had chinks in it big enough to put a rat through in places. There wasn't much activity round this side, so I was able to lounge here comfortably enough, and take a peep inside. I knew I wouldn't arouse anyone's suspicions by doing that – there must have been two-score such loungers for every furlong of the waterfront.

I can't say as I saw or heard much on that occasion to justify my suspicions.

Silver was sitting at a table on the far side with two other men, sea-going by the look of them, and as hard-faced a pair as I'd ever clapped eyes on. From what I already knew of Silver's past it didn't take me long to make up my mind they were freebooters, and freebooting captains at that, to judge by the gaudiness of the clothes one of them was arrayed in.

It was this one as caught my attention from the first. He was big built but long with it, his broad shoulders and narrow waist giving him the appearance of a man who could hit hard and move fast enough to dodge the return buffet. He had on a faded red skirt-coat like that commonly seen in a cavalry barracks, a pair of worn but good leather sea-boots, open at the knee, and fitting snug to the calf, a silk sash with long tassels, and over it a broad, buckled belt with four pistol clips and the barkers they was made to carry. His blue cambric shirt was sweat-soiled, and open at the neck and, to top this faded finery, he wore an ordinary seaman's woollen cap that fitted flush to his skull and made me think he was bald underneath and ordinarily wore a periwig.

It wasn't his clothes, however, that took me, but his face, which was as long and cruel as a vixen's, with a complexion that reminded me, somehow, of my mother's bilberry jam, it was that mottled and clouded.

You've heard tell, Jim, as Flint's face was blue and that he was ugly? Well, plain blue won't describe it somehow, it was more muddy and blotched, with eyes that burned in it like two coals jabbed into a grey pudding, and under a thin pair of moustaches was a mouth like a slit, that hardly moved when he talked and turned his voice into a sort of hiss.

He wasn't born with a visage like this – nobody could have been and stayed inside range of God's mercy; rumour had it that he was disfigured by a powder explosion that all but blew the face off him, and left him peppered with grains from forehead to throat.

I always reckoned the worst thing about Flint was not his face, nor yet his voice, nor his cold-bloodedness, but his laugh. Whenever Flint laughed it was time to run over your catechism and look back on your shortcomings, for he didn't laugh often and when he did somebody close at hand was for the next world, but not in too much of a hurry. He laughed *inside* as it were, no sound coming out, and no movement showing on his face, just a silent shaking of his shoulders, like a man set on springs. I'd as soon jump for an uncrippled man-o'-war with the boarding nets out, as sit in a room alone with Flint and have him laugh at me.

The other man was a good deal less remarkable, although he was outstanding in a way of his own, being respectably dressed in good sea cloth, with clean linen, and a cocked hat set well forward on his plain broad face. It was no good guessing at Flint's age, but this man was nearer forty than fifty and might have been the master of a small ocean-going craft, or pearling schooner. He had a brown, seamed skin, and a big curving nose, but, generally speaking, looked out of place in the company of the freebooter, or even the more genial-looking Silver.

All three were conversing in low tones, and looked mighty earnest about it, I thought. I caught a word here and there – 'frigate' and 'bullion' and 'below-decks' but no scrap that made sense. Then the curtains behind them parted, and another man came out, carrying a punch-bowl, and a brace of copper cups that hooked on to the lip of the bowl by little, crooked handles.

Silver greeted the punch-server with a great gusto, clapping him on the back and calling him 'Darby'. He was as unlike any of the others as it's possible to imagine, being short, bow-legged and humped-backed, a pitiful enough creature, with a vacant look in his eye that put you in mind of an idiot.

He smiled faintly at Silver's greeting but didn't say anything, just making clucking noises like a hen. I found out later that he was dumb, having fallen in with Spanish buccaneers of Tortuga years before, and provided them with an evening's entertainment before he escaped, leaving the better part of his tongue behind.

This was Darby McGraw, as I summoned up that last day of the fighting on the shoulder of Spyglass, and he was Flint's man, body and soul. Flint hated Spaniards and I reckon he and Darby had that much in common, and it was sufficient to hold them together, come fair weather and foul, until rum and a broadside put an end to the partnership. Darby was never a real pirate, just a body-servant to Flint, filling the same post, then and later, as I filled for Nick Allardyce, and getting more cuffs than riches into the bargain.

Flint's other companion, the man in broadcloth, you will have guessed and guessed rightly, to be Billy Bones, the same old sea-captain who brought you and yours so much trouble, and as much good fortune, but the man I first glimpsed through the chink of that grog-shop was only half-way to perdition. In some ways he was the best man among them and in those days he still had some distance to travel to the Devil's chimney-corner.

The Negro outside on guard was Billy's creature – a runagate slave from the Florida plantations, known around Port Royal as Big Prosper. He was a strange creature and as handy a man at a prize-taking as ever I saw. He used a peculiar weapon, a heavy, iron-tipped, long-handled mallet, that he swung as lightly as a toothpick, sometimes laying down three at a sweep, and more if there was room to circle. Big Prosper was the vanguard of every boarding party, and Bones always reckoned he was worth his weight in doubloons. He was devoted to Bones, who had picked him up in the Delta when the hounds were close on his trail, and ever since then the Negro had followed him like a shadow, and would have killed Flint for him if Billy had so much as nodded his head.

Well, as I say, I didn't get much chance to eavesdrop that time because no sooner was the punch drunk than all three got up and followed Darby into an inner room behind the curtains. No doubt they wanted a more private place to talk over their business, and the inner room had no wall to the street and was backed by a big kitchen, so I made off towards the break-water and hung about until some of the tars picked me up and took me back aboard.

Silver didn't leave shore that night. If I'd have stayed by the quay, like he said, I should have had a tediously long wait.

I told Nick all that had happened, of course, but he only pulled my ears, and said any business of Silver's was bound to be the wrong side of the law, but no more so than murder (meaning us), so what right had I to be spying on him?

I turned into my hammock and tried to think over what I'd seen and heard, and find some meaning to it, but the effect of tramping that waterfront after close on three months on shipboard must have tired me more than I knew, for the next thing I remember was Nick shaking me, and telling me to show a leg and help with the distribution of fresh fruit to the felons.

I turned out after him to see broad daylight over the anchorage, and half a dozen hogsheads, as high as a man's chest, being swung up by winch from a loading barge and lowered into the after-hold, which was the only part of the gun-deck not made over into a cage.

It was a main sunny morning, with a fresh, cooling sea-breeze. I rubbed the sleep out of my eyes and looked over the bay. There was nothing to tell me it was the last dawn I was to witness as a man who could live alongside his conscience, Jim.

PART TWO

THE RELUCTANT BUCCANEER

NICK and I spent most of that day ashore, together.

He hired a one-horse curricle, and a Negro to drive it, and we went up into the cooling hills, and put in the time lazing and talking.

I'll always remember how quiet and sweet-smelling and restful it was up there, away from the stink and squalor of the ship, and with our past well behind us, so to speak. Nick was mighty pleasant to me that day, and talked to me like a brother, saying again as I'd have no cause to regret the trouble he'd got me into, and how I'd look back on our flight as a new start that would open out the sort of life for me I should never have been able to live in England.

Towards noon I put him a question that had been bothering me a week or more, and especially since I'd seen Silver meet his friends in the grog-shops. I asked him outright how he reckoned Long John would free his two messmates, Hands and Pew. He answered me frankly enough, saying that Silver had put files in that bucket of scraps as I'd taken below decks, and that by this time both men would have freed themselves of their leg-irons, and be ready to jump ship the minute the chance offered. As for getting them above hatches, Silver must have arranged that also, for he seemed to be a taking a deal of interest in the loading of the water-casks into the after-hold; Nick had heard John acting as go-between in a conversation with the quartermaster and a ship's victualler, who was bringing rum and pork aboard, and that was partly the reason why he had decided to come ashore and be out of the way if anything went wrong, and Silver was caught cutting through from the after-hold into the cage.

I didn't give the matter further thought after that. It seemed to me that whatever happened now was Silver's business, and that we were both well out of it.

We went back on board at sundown, and heard we were revictualled and due to sail with the morning tide the day after tomorrow. It still made me uneasy to reflect that Hands and Pew were yet aboard – there would have been a turmoil if any felon had been missing – but I judged Silver would naturally wait until dark before he smuggled them out of the after-hold, and over the side. I turned in that night without so much as seeing him.

I woke up with a fearful screech ringing through my head. It was so sudden, and so awful, that I thought it was part of a dream. It was still dark and must have wanted some two hours to sunrise. I soon realised the scream I'd heard was real enough, for it was followed by a hideous uproar right out on deck, not fifty feet from where I was sleeping.

There was no moon at all and I couldn't so much as see Nick's bunk, and tell if he was there or not. The whole ship was in tumult, shouts and running feet, with the clash of steel, and an odd isolated shot or two cutting through the uproar.

At first I didn't connect it with Silver, or even the felons chained below decks. I didn't imagine I thought of what caused it at all, I was too dazed and, when my head cleared a bit, too much occupied thinking of my own skin.

After a short spell I pulled myself together enough to strike a flint that I always kept handy on the bulkhead shelf. In the first flash I saw Nick, fully-dressed, and sitting, white-faced, on the bolted cask near the door of the deckhouse. The mere glimpse of his face scared me more than what was going on out on deck.

'Stay in your hammock, Ben,' he snapped, 'it's death to show your face outside!'

'What's happened?' I managed to croak out. My teeth were chattering so I could hardly speak.

'They've taken the ship!' he said shortly.

'The felons?'

'Silver's party!'

I didn't see how that was possible. The ship was moored above a quarter-mile from the shore, and under the guns of the fort. I knew the Captain and the Marine officers were ashore, they had been entertained at Government House ever since we dropped anchor, but there was always a watch of ten to fifteen men, not counting the duty squad of marines, doubled at sunset while we were off-shore. That meant at least a score of armed men, wide awake, and all issued with firearms. Even supposing Silver's messmates had freed half the felons what could a hundred half-starved, and unarmed wretches do against a dozen firelocks aimed down the hatchways?

By this time the noise on deck was dying down a little but there was still a lot of running to and fro, bare feet slapping on deck, and every now and again, an outburst of shouting and a big splash alongside.

I was just thinking of taking a peep out of the ventilator slat when a group of men ran aft and started belabouring our door. Nick had fastened it with a bar but it was flimsy wood and would have gone down under a few determined blows from outside. We were still in darkness but I felt Nick go taut and I heard him mutter:

'Look to your knife, Ben, we haven't so much as a cutlass between us!'

At that minute however, I heard Silver's voice, and it was a tone I'd never heard from him before but was to hear often enough in future. In the heat of action John had a roar like a charging bull's.

'Belay there, Tom, the Sawbones is part o' the prize! Get the boys aft to the poop, and rout out the last of the lobsters!'

The men outside our deckhouse scrambled aft without a word and I heard Nick give a dry chuckle. Silver often called Nick 'Sawbones', a general enough term for a surgeon afloat, and it looked then as if we were to be spared from the general slaughter that was going on unabated outside. By 'lobsters' Silver meant the marines, who were called such on account of their red jackets. A moment later I heard a renewed uproar from the poop deck where, it appeared, they were making their final stand.

It didn't last any more than a minute or so. There were one or two shots, a volley of oaths, and then a series of heavy splashes. I reckoned the lucky ones were those as could swim.

A few minutes later Silver himself rapped on the door.

'You'd best open up, Mr Allardyce,' he said, 'we're getting sail on her and the lads'll have this deckhouse open in a trice!'

'Well,' said Nick, with something like his old drawl, 'the first two over the threshold won't live to boast of it, Barbecue! We're both armed and we can't miss at that range!'

I thought this was a cool enough lie but Silver only guffawed.

'Come now Mr Allardyce,' he called, 'there's none here as'll harm you so long as I'm above board. That's why I paid ye a call, and took the liberty of borrying your barkers! Open up and we'll parley!'

'We'll parley with the door between us, so it please you, John,' said Nick grimly.

'Suit yourself,' said Silver, 'I mean you no harm and I've said so. Any man who lays a hand on you will have me to answer to, you can lay to that. We've men here needing a surgeon and unless you go below there's none as'll tend 'em, unless I'm much mistook. Your trade is your ransom, as you might say. How does that strike you, Mr Allardyce?'

'Well enough,' said Nick, 'but that has to go for Ben as well as for me!'

'That goes for Ben!' promised Silver, and Nick promptly pulled out the bar and flung open the door.

Silver was there, a bloodied cutlass in hand and behind him the carpenter Tom Morgan, holding aloft a masked lantern.

Beyond Morgan I could see a small group of men, Prosper, Bones' Negro, among them, and just inside the circle of light Israel Hands, naked to the waist, and bleeding from a flesh wound on the shoulder.

As soon as they saw Nick's uniform coat a low growl ran round the group but Silver silenced them with a lively gesture.

'Get aloft, every man jack of you,' he barked, 'we'll have the fort guns on us the minute the first o' those lobsters touches shore!'

It was sound enough sense and even I, muddled and shuddering as I was, could follow his reasoning. The fort sentries must have heard the uproar and guessed something of what was taking place on board, but had so far withheld their fire for fear of scattering grape among felons and crew alike. The moment they received news from the first dripping survivor they would train every gun at their disposal on deck and would have been sorry gunners to avoid crippling the vessel with roundshot, quite apart from doing terrible execution with their swivels.

Even now a mob of men, whether Flint's storming-party or freed felons I was unable to see, were at the capstan bars, raising the anchor, and others were springing aloft and unreefing sail. They were lucky with their wind that night, there was an offshore breeze strong enough to warp the *Walrus* out of the harbour with the minimum of sail. It was just a question of who moved fast enough, Flint's foretopmen or the survivors and the fort gunners.

'We'd best go below, Sawbones,' said Silver, after the men behind him had dispersed. 'Show us the way, Tom.'

We filed aft and down the main companion to the captain's cabin. The ship was a shambles, that much I could see in the beam of Morgan's lantern. Three or four dead seamen, members of the watch no doubt, were huddled against the after deckhouses, at the foot of the companion-way, their firelocks still clutched in their hands.

The door of the captain's cabin was splintered and inside were two more marines, dead where they had made a final stand beyond the chart table, one of them wearing a faint look of surprise even in death.

My brain was reeling. I could hardly believe what had happened, much less get round to reasoning that, in a sense, it was all due to Nick and to me, and that a word from us in the right direction might have saved many good lives now sacrificed to duty. I was a longish time coming round to that, Jim. For the time being my brain shied away from it, and small wonder.

Silver poured himself a dram from the captain's decanter and, having done so, rooted about in a locker until he found a couple of pannikins and poured out a tot for Nick and me. I drank mine down quickly enough, as you can imagine. I needed that tot like a drowning man needs a spar.

'Well,' said Nick, after draining his glass, 'you've got the ship, and you've made up your mind to run out under the guns of the fort. What have you in mind for us, seeing as we seem to be the only king's men alive?'

'Ah, there's work enough for you,' said Silver, wiping his cutlass on the captain's table linen, and slamming it back in its sheath. 'The watch and the lobsters had more fight in 'em than I reckoned on, and more's the pity, seeing as I could have talked 'em round given the chance, but there's no help for it when Flint's once smelled blood and we'll be shorthanded from here to Tortuga. Billy's got himself an ugly slash as'll seam his leathery chops from now to Doomsday and four of the others have a ball or two in 'em that comes o' too much impetuosity, and not enough crab-rushes as puts the best o' men off a true aim with small-arms!'

'Am I expected to patch up these scoundrels in exchange for my life?' said Nick coolly.

'Aye,' says Silver, 'that's about it, Sawbones, and lucky you are as Billy's among 'em for he's the only man here as can set a course, and if he bleeds to death it's guesswork from then on.'

'I took you for a master mariner yourself, Silver,' says Nick, with a kind of sneer.

'You was over complimentary,' replied Silver, with a grin, 'for navigation was never my dooty, neither in these waters, nor the far side o' the Cape. I'm a quartermaster, and my work is to keep hands civil and prompt to obey orders. Come now, poor Billy's a-losing rich blood. What's it to be, the surgeon's healing touch, or slit throats and a double splash alongside?'

'What about afterwards?' argued Nick, and I began to sweat afresh, lest he should try Silver's patience too far. It was already plain enough that we should have been butchered with the rest of the men aboard had not Silver value Nick's services above the worth of our carcasses.

'Afterwards?' said Silver, raising his eyebrows, 'A gentleman o' fortune such as you are from now on, like it or not, lives out his life hour by hour, as you might say, and leaves the future to Merciful Providence. Now maybe we'll give you the chance o' joining us, with articles signed and all shipshape for a share and a quarter, you being a qualified man so to speak, and useful to have along of us. Other than that I can't say, not liking to make promises as I should find it outside my power to abide by. If that's not good enugh for you I'll wager Flint'll let Billy bleed, and take his chance in shoal water from now 'till he finds himself a new navigator!'

Well, that was how it was, Jim. Nick agreed to patch up the wounded in exchange for his life and mine, and glad enough I was that he came round to it, for Silver would have thought no more of cutting my throat and tossing me overboard than he would have hesitated to swat a blue-tailed fly that was bothering him.

We went below to the cage where, to my surprise, I found the greater part of the felons still in chains, but there was no time to ask questions and we were led forward to where a section of the cage – that formerly occupied by Pew and his cronies – had been given over to a sick bay.

There were five men laid out there, two of them past Nick's skill or anyone else's, for they died before we cleared the bay. The others, including Billy, were painfully but not dangerously wounded. Silver told Nick shortly to pass over the others and concentrate on Billy, who had a monstrously big slash that had laid open the whole of his left cheek. He got it, I heard, from Sergeant Hoxton, who had fought like a lion when they cornered him in the bows.

Billy was a game old scoundrel and never so much as groaned when Nick sewed up his cheek in the light of Morgan's lantern. You mind the livid scar Billy carried to his grave? Well, that was how he came by it and lucky he was it was a glancing blow or half his head would have gone with it. It was a bad light down there and Nick did his best with the needle. If it wasn't a neat job of surgery it wasn't Nick's fault, for once sewed and bandaged Billy struggled up and went to the tiller. The ship already had way on her as she nosed out to sea and the first shot, too high by a mile, had come soughing out of the fort and kept every man on deck below bulwarks.

Of the other two wounded, they were men I'd never seen before. One had a ball in the upper part of his arm and the other had one lodged in his wrist, breaking the bone. They howled when Nick probed them but both recovered shortly afterwards, though the man with the wrist wound, Dirk, could never swing a cutlass with his right arm again, and always went into action with pistols.

When all three had been attended to, Silver came down again with some spirits and bread and cheese. I could see by his expression we had won clear, and that the subsequent shots I heard had gone wide. The gunners in that fort deserved to be strung up for not scoring at least one hit that might have crippled the vessel, and thus given the folk ashore a chance to come at us, with some of the light cutters or sloops as abounded in the harbour.

Nick and I weren't allowed up on deck that day but there was so much happening below that we hardly noticed the fact.

First, about six bells, down comes Israel Hands to be patched up. His shoulder wound was little more than a scratch – a bayonet graze received at the foot of the companionway from one of the dead marines I had seen. He looked us over sourly enough, but didn't say much. Nick put a smarting salve into

the cut and enjoyed doing it, for Israel was a surly, dangerous man at best of times, and neither of us took to him. He was brave enough, with or without rum, and the best knife-thrower I ever saw, but not a man as you might choose for a companion on a moonless night, especially if you had valuables under your belt.

Later on down came two other survivors, young seamen who had been knocked senseless in the attack and had been lucky enough to be brought to by Silver and sea water. Silver never took life if he could avoid it, but if he ran into opposition he was deadlier than any of them. These two, one an armourer and the other a sailmaker, readily agreed to join the buccaneers, having had more than enough of Ayrton's discipline and his bo'sun's rope's end.

It was from these men, both of whom had split pates, that we learned how the ship had been taken, and a pretty story it was, a tale of Flint's cunning, and rank bad watch-keeping.

Nick's guess about the freeing of Hands and Pew had been accurate enough – they had filed off their irons four days out of Port Royal, and had lain doggo, biding their time to strike. What Nick didn't know, but what we might have guessed, was that Hands had also freed Anderson and the young locksmith Black Dog, and this was an important part of their plan, for Anderson's brute strength and Black dog's familiarity with locks had stood the buccaneers in good stead. Between them these two had picked out a dozen or so more resolute spirits among the felons, and had the irons off them in time enough to take part in the battle when they used their fetters as flails. There was no time, of course, to file the fetters but Israel had not wasted his time fashioning the bone knife. Black Dog picked two master-locks with it and freed eight felons, while Anderson, with room to get a full purchase, tore the staple out of a third bilbo with his bare hands and freed four more, although this group had to fight with manacles on. The buccaneers were careful to free only those few they had sounded, and felt they could trust. The remainder, some two hundred and twenty-five in all, were still in irons when we came below, and remained so until that evening.

Now came the clever part of the ambush. You recall how Silver had fixed up a victualling deal with the captain, and that some large hogsheads of salt junk had been shipped into the after-hold the day we arrived? Well, those hogsheads carried short measure, for two of them contained no pork at all, but

Flint and Bones' big nigger, Prosper.

These two lay quiet until sundown – the barrels had been holed for air – and then slipped out and set to work on the false bulkhead that divided the cage from the after-hold.

Flint reckoned the convicts would need good leadership and reinforcement, and by the time the night watch came on Prosper had sawn through the bulkhead, and joined up with Hands and Pew. The four ringleaders waited in the after-hold but the dozen freed men were left to deal with the rush down the ladder which was sure to follow any disturbance below.

All was now ready for the signal, a sea-shanty from a supposed bumboat, nosing across the dark anchorage. In the bumboat were Bones, Darby, and half a dozen other cut-throats Flint had dug out of the waterfront grog-shops, all men who had served with the Brethren of the Coast before the latest Woodes-Rogers' amnesty and King's Pardon.

As soon as the shanty was heard Flint, Pew, Hands and Anderson slipped out of the afterhold, which hadn't been battened down on account of more supplies going in the next day, and fell on the marine squad that was card-playing over the fore-hatch. That's what comes of senior officers neglecting their duty to wine and dine on shore with Governors and their ladies.

The buccaneers had it all their own way, or nearly all, for as you've seen their losses were slight considering the magnitude of the enterprise – to take a frigate by storm with less than twenty half-armed men.

While they were disposing of the squad Bones' boat slipped alongside and his party stormed the poop-deck, chasing such as survived right into the bows, and fighting it out with Sergeant Hoxton, and one or two others. It was here that Bones got his sabre cut, but he settled with Hoxton on the spot, and the sergeant went overboard with a dozen death wounds. I didn't regret him, he was a brute and a bully and deserved no less.

Meantime Flint and his companions had opened up hatches, and out poured the freed felons, with Big Prosper at their head. They were whooping mad for blood and routed out the survivors and disposed of them in a matter of minutes. It was neatly done but could never have happened if the chief officers had been aboard. As it was, only a lieutenant and two midshipmen were present, and all three jumped overboard at the first alarm.

Flint shot the lieutenant in the water, but the middies, being boys, dived deep and came up out of pistol range. It was these two who swam ashore and alarmed the fort, but too late, as you've seen.

That's about all I can remember of the taking of the *Walrus*. Why Flint required a vessel of that size for freebooting in the Main I didn't find out until much later. The buccaneers in those parts usually preferred much smaller ships of shallower draught, for there was shoal water everywhere, but he had deeply-laid plans of his own, and to execute them needed a powerful ship that he could adapt for his own purposes. The refitting of the *Walrus* commenced that very day, and below decks we could hear hammering and sawing going on as we stood north-east before a brisk wind.

Before we had a chance to look over the alterations, however, down comes Silver again to address the felons. Situated as we were, in the staved-in afterhold, we heard every word he said to them. Whenever there was any talking to be done it was always Silver that did it. Flint was no talker, nor Bones either. Only Long John had the gift of the gab, and no pirate crew needed more than he had at his command.

The felons, you can imagine, were greatly excited over all that had happened, for Silver had already promised them freedom and riches, so that they lay back to enjoy the fresh air that was sweetening the gun-deck from the open hatches, fore and aft, and they gave their new masters little or no trouble from the outset.

Silver had also issued a rum ration, the first they had tasted since their arrest in England, so the gun-deck was a lively enough place that afternoon when we were bowling along under crowded canvas and rapidly forging ahead of any possible pursuit.

Shortly before sundown Silver made a rousing speech to the felons from the fore companion.

'Mates,' he said, 'I reckon you was born under lucky stars, each and every one of you. Here you was, chained like bears at a fair, and all set to work out your lives in the sugar and 'baccy plantations of Virginny, and make some rich swab richer and greedier. There's no fear o' that from now on, lads, seein' as your dear capting fished me out o' the locker, and give me the chance o' recruiting the likeliest looking lot o' gentlemen o' fortune as I ever clapped eyes on, and me a tried hand at such things, having drained tots with the best of 'em both in these waters and further south! "Who is he?" says you, and rightly, for it don't pay to take seamen on trust. Well, I'll speak out, fair and honest, and tell you my name's John Silver, and I'm quartermaster of this here ship, taking orders from no one from now on, saving only Cap'n Flint, and him only when a prize is sighted. "What's to become of us?" you ask, and rightly again, and my answer to that is that it rests with you, soon as those irons is knocked off, and you come up on deck to breathe the pure air as is nature's gift to all men, notwithstanding any little differences they might have with King George or his lickspittles!'

This part of the speech was greeted with prolonged cheers and the rattle of fetters. When the uproar had subsided Silver went on:

'Now here's your choice, mates, and you can make it of your own freewill. No one's a-pressing of you, not me, nor Flint, nor even King George, who's slap out o' touch with his ship as you might say! You can sign articles with us, and share alike with the prizes we take, but if freebooting's not to your choice, and don't rest easy in your mind o' nights, why then, I'll see to it that every man jack of you is returned to His Majesty, irons and all, the minute we touch the first island flying the Union Jack! Fairer I couldn't say, but I'd be wantin' in dooty if I didn't warn those as is ready to sign with us, that if you serves under me, Jolly Roger or no, so to speak, I'm a man as likes to give orders and see 'em obeyed, promptly and cheerfully, and if that's not to your liking, and any man among you sees fit to question me, then let him up and say so right out, and we'll prove who's best man right off with cutlasses, hand-spikes or any weapon of challenger's choosing! And more I'll say to that, seeing as we're started on it, if any such man exists down there, and is able to best me, then seeing as I come out of it alive that man's my master from time forward, and I'll pipe down and touch forelock to him with the best of 'em! That's about all I got to say, for the articles'll be explained in detail above decks, as soon as they're cleared, and now, lads, here come the ship's armourers to knock off them irons and make gentleman o' fortune of such as is willing to feather his nest along o' me, Cap'n Flint, and as sailorly a crew as ever squeezed ransom from a Spanish settlement!'

You can well imagine how this speech was received by the poor wretches below, men who had abandoned hope and thus had their freedom miraculously restored to them. They set up a racket as could have been heard back in Port Royal, and all that night the two armourers, one of them a member of the *Walrus'* original crew, hammered away at their irons, and sent them aloft to sign articles under Bones on the quarterdeck.

Only one man steadfastly refused to exchange his chains for his soul, so to speak, and of him, Jabez Patmore, you'll hear more as time goes on, for in some ways he was the strangest character of all that mixed-up bunch, and everybody but me and Nick soon came to regard him as more than a little mad.

He was an oldish felon, with sparse grey locks falling into his eyes, and how he came to be transported I never found out for he'd been a Methody preacher in his time, and had tramped from one end of England to the other, spouting brimstone and damnation to people at fairs and markets. He had most of the Good Book by heart and was fond of quoting it, though a less likely congregation was never assembled. He told the armourers to leave his irons be, as they was put there by God, and could only be struck off by the Almighty. Even Silver could find no answer to this and let him stay below, with a dog-eared testament he had managed to bring aboard.

He'd have starved no doubt had not Nick seen to it that he got regular food and water, and, later on, when Silver offered to set him ashore, he said he preferred to stay, so they kept him as a sort of ship's mascot. When we did manage to persuade him to cut free of his irons, he could be seen o' nights crouched in the anchor chains, singing psalms into the wind, and prophesying the end of the world every full moon.

He was still with us years later and you'll hear, in good time, the part he played in my story, and how, in a sense it was old Jabez Patmore, long rest his leathery soul, as positioned me for a slender chance o' salvation.

CHAPTER TWO   THE RELUCTANT BUCCANEER

No doubt you'll be wondering how Nick and me came to sign
articles and join up with the buccaneers the way we did.

That's easy enough answered as to the first week or two
after the taking of the *Walrus*, but maybe it's not so clear in the
time that followed.

You'll allow we was kidnapped to begin with, and had no
choice in the matter. It was sail along of them or go overboard,
particularly in the days that followed, when Bill's slash healed
up, and he was able to stand the sun above decks and give his
sailing orders.

You see, the route we followed through the Windward Channel, and along the coast of Haiti to Tortuga or Turtle Island,
which was the new rendezvous of the Brethren, called for tricky
navigation, and although there were plenty of seamen aboard
as could obey orders, and knew the coast pretty well, there was
no one except Billy who had ever held a command or, for that
matter, had a tenth of his experience in those waters.

By rights he should have been below, particularly during the
hottest part of the day, but everyone felt easier if he was above
decks, and I'm bound to say the old rascal stuck it out gamely
enough and sometimes stood watch the better part of twelve
hours at a stretch.

Our position then was a dangerous one, and we had to watch
points mighty carefully. Silver was friendly enough, and Flint
kept to his cabin most of the time, but men like Hands and Pew

still looked upon Nick and me as King's men, and if it had been left to them we should have been food for the sharks long before we rounded Cape Dame Marie.

Quite apart from this Nick had got it into his head that we were more than half pirates already, having been responsible for Silver taking the ship in the first place, and, what with our own trouble in the background, and the questions liable to be asked if we ever got before a Magistrate, it might be difficult to explain how we came to be spared when every other hand, save only the two youngsters I mentioned, had been slaughtered or thrown overboard.

Nick and I talked all this over during the first days out and he decided our best course was to let things slide, at all events until we got within reach of an established settlement. Then, he said, we could lie a course that seemed the most likely to win us clear of our present situation, and strike out for the plantations on the Main, our original point of disembarkation.

He had plenty of money, which was something, but we kept mighty quiet about that, seeing the company we were in. If it had once got about that Nick wore a belt lined with English guineas neither one of us would have seen another sunrise. The pirates took us for what we seemed to be, a ship's surgeon and his valet, and we didn't do or say anything to set them thinking otherwise.

The long and the short of it was we went up to the quarter-deck that second day and signed articles, Nick adding his signature to the big round robin attached to the screed that Silver had drawn out the first night, and me adding my mark and thumbprint.

The pirates always signed on a round-robin, so as no particular man could ever be marked down as ringleader if the articles came to be used in evidence before judge and jury. Not one in four of the men aboard could write his name and there were some queer, outlandish marks decorating that circle.

Maybe the time has come, Jim, to set you and others right about the nature and customs of the Coast Brethren forty odd years back.

Since I settled down ashore I've heard some odd stories and been asked some odd questions about them. Most of the people who have written about pirates seem to me to have relied more on their imaginations than facts come by first hand, and what I tell you now is gospel truth, for I'm long past the time for covering up and, as I said to begin with, I trust you not to squawk about my part of it until I'm out of reach of all but the Big Judge. Him I'm willing to take my chance with, for I'm persuaded by now as He knows all, not just part of it, and will give judgement according.

In the first place pirates never sailed under a pirate chief in the sense that a fleet or a man-o'-war sails under an admiral. It was a good deal more free and easy than that and no man, not even a Flint or a Davis, could have controlled a crew like ours, except during the actual time o' prize-taking and boarding.

The captain was a freely-elected officer, chosen for his reputation as a fighter and maybe a thinker-up of prize-getting, and he could be deposed by popular vote the same way as he was elected, and sometimes was if things didn't turn out to his crew's liking.

Often enough he was no seaman at all – Flint wasn't – and relied on a real skipper, like Billy, to carry him where he wanted to go, either athwart the trade routes in the Florida Channel and the Bahama Banks, or across to a small-garrisoned settlement for a town-sacking, or to a collecting point of the Spanish plate fleet that set out twice a year from the Isthmus after it was made up of richly-laden smaller vessels from the Spanish settlements up and down the Main.

This last, the Spanish Plate, was the heart's desire of every buccaneer, and a swoop on any one of these approaching vessels, which hugged the coast and often sailed without escort, would set any pirate up for a year or so, and would have meant riches for life to a thriftier man.

The real power on board in the spells between forays was the Quartermaster, who was a sort of cross between treasurer and ship's bo'sun. He was usually an educated or half-educated man like Silver, and his duties called for a strong arm and a sharp tongue, particularly during the division of spoil. Generally speaking it was the quartermaster who had charge of the crew, and was responsible for the maintenance of discipline.

Yet it wouldn't be quite true to say there was no such thing as a quarterdeck on a pirate ship. There was the same distinctions as you run across anywhere, on land or afloat. The skilled men hung together, and lorded it over the lower decks, and the two groups on a freebooter were always known as 'The Lords' and 'The Commons'.

The Lords consisted of Captain, sailing-master, quarter-master, chief gunner, boatswain, coxswain, carpenter and armourers. They formed a sort of committee, and it was impossible to run contrary to them.

The Commons were the ordinary deckhands and foretopmen, and drew but one share to one and a half allocated to the Lords; Nick, being surgeon belonged to the Lords, but I, having no sea trade, was always berthed forward with the Commons.

There was discipline aboard, of a kind.

The articles set out what was right and what was wrong, what could be overlooked and what had to be punished, how disputes could be settled, and how quarrels could be avoided – all shipshape and down in writing, like the Articles o' War aboard a naval ship.

There were some queer regulations as I remember.

No one was to bring a woman aboard on pain of death. No duels were to be fought on shipboard, arguments of this sort being settled ashore with seconds attending. The best pair of pistols aboard a prize were awarded to the man who first sighted her. Extra shares were to be handed over to men who lost a limb or an eye or even a finger, in the fighting, and so on, close on five score of 'em, down to the rule laying down that any carousing after midnight had to be done above deck, and the law against card-playing for money during a cruise. If Hands and that Irisher O'Brien had minded this particular rule you would never have been able to take the *Hispaniola* away from them for you recall as it was this card flare-up that finished them when you cut their cable in Kidd's Anchorage.

I haven't told you anything about the past of two of the chief men aboard – Flint and Bones.

Flint had been an outlaw since he was a ship's boy, having sailed under England, Davis, Blackbeard and even Stede-Bonnet, before he became a captain in his own right.

When I learned to lip-read I found out a little about him from Darby McGraw, his dumb shadow. It seems he was the son of a convict, transported to Barbados towards the end of the last century after taking part in a rebellion against King James down in our part of the world. I heard that close on a thousand West-countrymen were shipped overseas under hatches after that particular outbreak.

Flint's father was only a lad when he came out and later on, when some sort of pardon came over after Dutch William took the place of King James, he worked his own plot on the island, and married a quadroon – that, is a three-quarter white – and started raising a family.

According to Darby he was of a religious turn of mind, and a terrible hater of Popery on account of what he had suffered from it. Most all his friends died on the plantations before the pardon arrived, and Flint senior must have had a tough hide to survive four or five years of a slave's life in that climate.

Our Flint was the old felon's third son, and might have grown into a respectable planter, or ship's chandler, if it hadn't been for the Spaniards, who were always waging war on English, French and Dutch in these parts on account of the King of Spain claiming the whole Indies and Main as part of his realm.

A privateer put into the settlement one night and burned it to a cinder, hanging old Flint and his two eldest sons from their own awning poles. Young Flint escaped to the brush, and later joined up with the French buccaneers off St Domingo. Alongside these he harried the Spaniards year after year, and came close to driving them right off the seas.

As he grew up the native blood began to show in Flint's nature. He began to practise cruelty for cruelty's sake, and didn't confine himself to harrying Spaniards, but anyone whose vessel could show a profit in the free market the buccaneers had established in New Providence.

He took the King's Pardon like Silver, but only to get a breathing-space and the chance of a larger vessel. He was tired of rifling sloops, and small schooners, and had made up his mind to go after the gold fleet, or take a look at some of the larger settlements on the Main. The actual capture of the *Walrus* was Silver's plan, but Flint fell in with it readily enough, and they hatched up the main details the day I saw them in the grog-shop at Port Royal.

Bones' background was very different. For years he had been an orderly Yankee skipper, with a trade between Boston and Cuba, but when his brig was sacked by a privateer off Havana, and he lost everything he possessed, he turned sour and determined to get his goods back the way they'd been lifted off him. He never mixed much with the others and his solitariness was much respected, for he was a terrible man in a fight, and a notable hand with cutlass or marlinspike. Even Flint and Silver were wary of him, particularly when he was deep in rum, which he most always was, except when handling ship.

He was a fine seaman was Billy and could read, write and reckon. If he hadn't lost that brig he would have doubtless ended his days as a member of Boston City Council, with half a dozen ships at sea, and maybe fine sons a-manning them.

That's all I can tell you about Flint and Bones; now you know as much about them as any man alive.

The strange thing to me during that first voyage was the discovery that all that had taken place hadn't stopped Nick hobnobbing with Silver. In a day or two they were as close as they'd been aboard the *Walrus*, on the voyage out, and Nick freely admitted that he was as taken as ever with the man.

At first I thought Nick was cultivating him, so to speak, in order to keep us both safe from the other pirates, and maybe chart a course for the pair of us to jump ship as soon as we put into a port where we could get an honest berth for Charleston. Soon enough, however, it was plain there was much more to it than that, and it began to be clear to me that a link had been forged between the easygoing scapegrace of a parson's son, and the smooth-tongued ruffian of a pirate and that, between them, they were attracting several of the long-headed men aboard, notably half a dozen of the better sort of felons.

I think Silver's idea even then was to strike out and form a crew of his own, as soon as the opportunity offered. His liking for Nick was genuine enough but it didn't run to so much as contemplating a change in his way of life, although Nick told me more than once that Silver would be a master-hand at managing a plantation ashore.

He told me this, I suppose, by way of explaining his tolerance of the man, and I got to thinking that he was ashamed of the ease with which he was slipping into their ways, and needed to excuse himself, even to such as me.

That's how it was the day we dropped anchor off Tortuga, and most of the crew went ashore. Nick called me to one side and said he wanted a private talk with me, so I followed him below to that section of the gun-deck as had been set aside for sleeping quarters.

I ought to say now that the *Walrus* had been completely transformed during the voyage. All the housing above decks had been cleared away, and the bulwarks heightened by above a foot-and-a-half all the way round.

A pirate always likes high bulwarks and a clear deck, the bulwarks giving his boarders protection against grape and musketry when he's closing in for the kill, and the space above decks offering a smaller target to the roundshot of such who defend themselves.

Add to this the fact that a pirate usually carries a very large crew, and every inch of space aboard is required for accommodation and storage. To this end the cages below had been cleared away, and the gun-deck restored to more or less what it had been before the vessel was equipped as a prison-ship.

When we got below Nick took off his belt and counted out fifty guineas which he poured into a little bag and handed over to me.

'What's this for?' I asked, 'there's nowhere ashore to spend it as I can see.'

'It's yours to keep Ben,' he said, 'and it'll help you to go wherever you've a mind to.'

I was a bit taken aback at this. He saw as much and went on quickly, though avoiding looking me in the eye.

'Ben,' he said, 'I'm joining for good, leastways, until Silver and I have enough between us to set up ashore in a big way. As for you, I don't reckon I've a right to pilot you any further, and Silver'll get you a berth for the Main as soon as you're minded to go. There's a power of boats sail out of Tortuga as soon as they've stowed all the goods that can be bought from the prizes. Well, what do you say, Ben?'

For a spell I couldn't say anything, I was that staggered. After a spell I managed to voice the thought that was uppermost in my mind. I said:

'Won't you need me no more then, Mr Nick? Is this the finish of it?'

That troubled him, I saw that at once.

'It's you I'm acting for, Ben, and it's to your advantage we break. I took you along this far because, as I say, I reckon I owed it to you, for looking after me the way you did when many a man would have thought only of his skin. Contrariwise it was you as looked to me to get you clear o' the Sheriff's warrant, back in Devon, but you're safe enough here, and it wouldn't be acting right for me to run your neck into another noose when there's means to hand of dodging it.'

'How about your neck?' I asked him.

'Ben,' he said, patient-like, as he always talked when he was trying to explain something to me, 'I want you to try and use that thick skull o' yours, and follow what I'm about to say. I daresay it seems strange to you to see me openly offering to join up with desperadoes like those aboard this ship, but that's only because you don't see me as one of 'em.'

'No,' I told him, 'I don't by the Powers!'

'But I am for all that,' he went on, 'and I can't ever change the fact. Further to that, I've had my eyes opened about a variety of things since that night in the covert, when I settled with young Custer, and one of the things I'm main clear on is that Silver's right when he says God only helps those who help themselves!'

'By robbing and killing people?' I asked him.

He laughed at that. 'You still see things as black and white, Ben,' he said. 'One man works slaves in the tropical sun, until he's sold enough sugar, or 'baccy, to buy himself a seat in Parliament, and become a Custer, and that's called "commerce"! Another, like Silver, is more open with it. He stakes his neck on making money the quicker way on the high seas, and they call that "piracy"! What's the difference?'

This was too deep for me. If I knowed the Good Book then as well as I know it now, Jim, I could have reminded him of that bit about giving to Caesar that which was Caesar's, and to God that which was God's, but all the times I could have got that sort of talk by heart I was sleeping through the sermon in Church, or playing chuck-farthing on the gravestones behind the vestry. The Bible don't mean much to a man, Jim, until, like me, he's had a chance to chew it over in solitariness. Maybe if I'd had that spell alone on the island the day I was old enough to shift for myself, I'd have been a bigger credit to the mother as bore me.

'I don't want to sit here and talk you into acting ag'in your conscience,' he went on, when he saw his remarks had struck home, somewhat, 'but just you think o' those men as we shipped out here, chained between decks. Why, hardly, a one of 'em had done more than help himself to some trifle when he was hungry, the same as your Uncle Jake did, and was man-trapped for his pains. You don't have to look that far either! What about your own family, living in that damp vault of a cottage under the church wall, and bowing and scraping to the Custers for enough crusts and vegetables to stay strong enough to keep working for them? Is that God-given justice? Does a man have to crawl on his belly for the right to feed his children?'

'But you've got money,' I argued, though it seemed to me there was a deal of sense in what he was saying, 'you've got enough to start up above board, without stretching your neck on a gibbet.'

'I haven't enough, Ben,' he told me, 'I found that out talking to Silver. With slaves the price they are out here I couldn't work no more than a plot at that! No, Ben, I made up my mind. From now on I stop running, and fight back for just as much time as it takes me to set up on a big scale, big enough maybe to go back and fight the Custers in the open.'

Maybe that was it. Maybe all this talk about getting enough money to start planting in earnest was so much dust in my eyes, or dust in his own. Maybe it was the Custers who were still gnawing at him, and making his pride smart, so that the only thing that really mattered to him was to make himself rich enough, and powerful enough, to go back and have it out with them on his native heath. I don't know, not even now, if that was the true answer. I only know that it meant more to be a freebooter alongside Nick than an honest man with Nick the far edge of the horizon and I told him so, as simply and directly as I knew how.

He heard me out and then rubbed his chin thoughtfully.

'Well, Ben,' he says finally, 'this is how I see it. If you was to take ship for Charleston, with the fifty guineas I've given you, it wouldn't be long before you were penniless and driven to the same shift as any outcast in this part o' the world, namely, to indenture yourself to buccaneers, same as you've got at this moment. Now seeing as that's your choice maybe I'm still responsible for you, and that being so you'd best stay alongside and make the best of a bad job. If you're berthed where I can keep an eye on you at worst we can go on sharing our luck, the way we have so far. So get yourself a cutlass, and a brace of pistols from the armoury, and come ashore with me now and we'll drink to it!'

I had no qualms after that. I ought to have, seeing as I was once and for all turning my back on honest men, and pledging myself to a life of sin and shame without so much as the excuse of doing it to save my skin, but all I felt was a wave of relief that I wasn't being cast off by Nick, and left to flounder in a strange land without him to look out and think for me.

We went ashore that same afternoon, in the company of Silver, Morgan, Pew and the others, and by sunset the whole company of us were rip-roaring drunk in the free port of Tortuga. Not that this was in any way singular on our part – everybody was drunk in Tortuga by sundown, everybody that is except the pimps, and the Jews, who sailed over in the schooners every so often to buy pirated goods from us at about a tenth of their market value, and lade them back to Cuba, and the ports of the Main, where they sold them to the folk they were shipped out for in the first place.

There were some shameful places in the islands thirty years

back, Jim, but you could have gathered a thick crust of barnacles and weed under your keel while you was looking for a place as wicked as Tortuga. Sodom and Gomorrah, those towns in the Bible, I don't reckon they could have come near it for all-out deviltry.

CHAPTER THREE   THE RELUCTANT BUCCANEER

I'M not going to tell you all that happened in the years I was sailing in Flint's *Walrus*, Jim. I couldn't recall the half of it in any case, for a man likes to draw a veil over the deeds he's downright ashamed of, and there were many such deeds as could be entered on my page of the Book during the time I'm talking about.

I don't say as I was as cruel as Pew, or as murderous as Hands, or as drink-sodden as Billy, or as callous as some of the hangers-on, like Morgan, Anderson, or Black Dog, but taken all round I was pretty thoroughgoing in the trade I'd apprenticed myself to, and if I don't recall a coldblooded killing on my part, I looked on while others did it, and soon grew a thick enough hide to take little account of it, no more than when a rabbit back home is bowled over by a terrier, and knocked on the head by its master.

What I will do is tell you the main course of events after we refitted, and sailed out of Tortuga for the south-west, and how we came to gather such a harvest of treasure and sink it below ground on Treasure Island, for you and Squire to come looking for it years later.

I remember the first prize we boarded, a Dutch barque called *Hans Vooght* out of the Hook, bound for Cartagena.

Our practice in those days was to run up the Jolly Roger and fire a shot across the bows of our victim in the expectation that she would heave to, and wait for us to come up and board.

It was this way with the Dutchman, and we boarded her without another shot being fired. She had a cargo of Rhenish wines, calico and, what was even more welcome, good quality powder of which we were short at that time.

Pew and Silver went through her like Bristol pick-pockets. I reckon even the cockroaches went hungry after those two had had the sacking of a vessel, and afterwards a tally was made out on the *Walrus* poop-deck, so as shares could be allocated at the end of the cruise. Billy always presided over the share-out, and was mighty fair and just about it; he knew the market price of most everything, and carried it all in his head. Plundered clothing, as came from men's backs, didn't count in the share out, and the best thing I got off that prize was a pair of leather breeches that lasted me for years.

All the time his ship was being plundered the Dutch captain sat on the hatch-cover and smoked a huge pipe, with a bowl carved like a nigger's head. He never let out a word from first to last. Either he was well used to it, or he was the most philosophical seaman I ever struck. When his ship was riding light Flint told him he could go, and he shook out sail and moved away, with his crew reduced to a round half a dozen, the remainder having joined up with us.

Those first months were quiet enough for everybody.

We never went out looking for a fight and would avoid one whenever we could, relying on the terror of the flag to make the master, or the more chicken-hearted of the people sailing along with him, shorten sail, and wait to be plucked. Cleared of superstructure the *Walrus* was a fast sailer, and there was never much chance of a prize showing us a clean pair of heels, unless, of course, she slipped away under cover of night-fall.

We carried the flags of all nations aboard and used them to deceive the vessel we had marked down. If it looked like an English vessel up went the Union Jack. Then, when we were close in, up to the peak went our true colours, and a roundshot plumped into the water just ahead of the quarry.

Our best hunting ground was the Gulf Channel, between the tip of Florida and the Bahamas, but we often cruised along the north coast of Cuba, looking for smaller fry, and sometimes south-west, as far as the Leeward and Windward Islands, touching in at places like Martinique and Grenada, where we were always welcome if we had spoil to dispose of, and were far too well armed to care whether there was a garrison or not.

Many of the English and French Government officials on such islands as had been torn from Spain worked hand in glove with us, and feathered their own nests in the process. There's many a family owning its mansion and acres in England and France to-day as was founded on profit derived from the stolen goods Flint and other buccaneers dumped on the Governor's doorstep. In that way, Nick and Silver were right in one sense – God did seem to help those who helped themselves, and I've sometimes wondered who was the more sinning, the buccaneers, who at least risked their lives pilfering the stuff, or the resident governors who stayed safe ashore, bought it from them and lined their pockets reselling at a big profit.

These last had their excuses, of course. The Home Government neither protected nor supplied them, and many of the settlements were far from the usual track of ships, harried by the Spanish, and short of everything necessary to life except fruit, sugar and maize. They were only too glad to pick over the mixed cargoes we brought them, and were never particular as to how we had come by them in the first place.

With a ship and crew like the *Walrus*, Flint could outsail and outgun almost everything afloat in the Main. Nine out of ten ships we challenged ran up the white flag after the first gun-shot. The tenth, as opposed the storming-party under Silver and Pew, had its company, as like as not, put to the sword before the hatches were opened.

In cases where the crew made no resistance there was rarely any bloodshed. The crew either joined up with us, or were put ashore on the first land we sighted after the capture.

Sometimes Flint put a prize crew aboard and sailed the prize into a harbour where he disposed of her cheaply.

More often he rifled her and let her go, hoping she would load up again and bring him fresh plunder the following season. We once plundered the same ship three times three years in succession.

Where a master had shown fight, and his ship was badly damaged, she was set on fire and left to sink, with him for company.

Sometimes, though not often, we caught a tartar. Once we tried to board an American lugger that must have had expert gunners aboard, for we were holed in a dozen places, lost a mizzenmast and had to sheer off after dark and limp into a harbour in the Grenadines to refit and lick our wounds. When this happened Flint was in a dangerous mood for a week or more, and everyone left him alone with his rum and dumb servant.

One piece of nonsense I ought to set you clear about right off. In all the years I sailed as gentleman o' fortune I never saw, nor heard of, a prisoner being made to walk the plank. I don't know who dreamed up this way of killing prisoners, but neither Flint nor any buccaneer of the Main as I knew ever practised it. There were far quicker ways to hand of killing a man than making him walk the plank blindfold and, as I say, we never shed blood if we could avoid it. Most times there was no necessity to, the merchant vessels being like sheep cornered by wolves, and their companies glad enough to escape with whole skins.

Twice a year, when the ship's bottom was foul enough to cut down on our speed, we put in for careening. In these warm waters a ship needs to be careened as often as possible, and when we were scraping her we were at the mercy of any Spaniard or frigate patrol as had wind of us.

To careen a vessel as big as the *Walrus* was a sizeable job. We had to run for some secluded haven, strip her of guns and tackle, beach her on sand, heel her over by windlass, and then set to work removing the crust of barnacles and weed that had accumulated during the voyage.

Treasure Island, or Kidd's Island, as I knew it at that time, was one of our favourite places for careening, and that was how I first came to the place. I first went there about a year after I'd signed articles.

The place had been a buccaneers' haven for close on a century and it was Kidd who built the blockhouse which he manned like a fort while his ship was helpless on the sand.

Most buccaneers are powerfully lazy fellows, Jim, and although we called at the place several times few of the crew ever strayed beyond the immediate locality of the south anchorage, or the fringe of trees round North Inlet. Nick and me did, we were always glad of a chance to stretch our legs, and that first time Silver took us up on the slopes of Spyglass to shoot goats. It was Silver who taught me how to salt the meat, and lay up a store for future cruises.

It was strange, in view of everything that happened after, that I should spend so many pleasant hours with Silver and Nick on that island.

When we were out hunting in the Spyglass ravines we were like boys on holiday, and the rocks rang with the shouts and laughter of Nick and Long John when they made a kill. In the years I was alone there I sometimes fancied I could still hear them skylarking above the pines. A man gets strange fancies when he's marooned, Jim, and I used to call back, again and again, but never got no more answer than an echo.

Flint never used the blockhouse when he was ashore. He used to mount a battery on Skeleton Island and keep a keen lookout for strange ships in the channel. We never saw one but once, and that was a French pirate as subsequently became our consort.

It was the third time we had careened at the island and Flint must have been planning bigger business, like the sacking of a settlement, for a long time, for he warned Israel not to loose off at the Frenchman as soon as his bowsprit showed round the bend, and ran up the Jolly Roger to a jury-mast we had rigged on the sandspit.

It turned out that the Frenchman wasn't looking for trouble either and answered the signal from his own peak. She was a biggish boat, bigger than ours and she looked like an old fourth-rater out of Rochelle, or maybe the French settlement on the St Lawrence river. She was called *La Paone*, which was the French, they told me, for peahen, and she had a fat peacock, or peahen, as a figurehead, and drew overmuch water for a pirate. You've seen her, Jim, or the shell of her. She was beached, and left to rot in North Inlet after the fearful raking she got from the three-decker, but I'm ahead of myself, that was two years or so from the time I'm telling of.

Well, the French captain comes ashore and him and Flint have a long pow-wow and carouse together, up under the trees, above the anchorage. It was just about the spot where the *Hispaniola* mutineers pitched their camp.

The Frenchman was called Pierre Le Bon, which means, I'm told, 'the good', but he wasn't a whit better than any of the Brethren except, maybe, that much better dressed, for he was a dandy from ostrich feather to suede boots, and looked like his own figurehead when he was tricked out in his best.

Le Bon favoured bright colours. His coat was sky-blue, sewed all over with gilt buttons and silver frogs, his shirt white as a gull's breast, and he wore a frothy lace cravat nine inches broad. He always went about fully armed, with a rapier swinging from a jewelled swordbelt, and a bandolier stuffed with Moorish pistols, long, thin-barrelled, and all mounted in silver. Altogether he was the most colourful pirate you hear tell about, much gaudier than the tatterdemalion ruffians aboard the *Walrus*.

His crew weren't only Frenchmen, of course, they were a more mixed-up bunch than ours, French, Dutch, Spanish, American, full-blooded Negroes, and plenty of half-breeds. We didn't see much of them that time, as they only put in for water, but Flint made a rendezvous with Le Bon, and later on we formed squadron with him, and had good pickings out of it.

Together, we were more than a match for a warship, British, French or Spanish, and cruised in consort at least twice a year.

We had a spell of good luck after that meeting.

Cruising along off Haiti a month or so later, we fell in with one of the Spanish Viceroy's private vessels, stuffed with silks, satins and all manner of costly furnishing for his new palace in Cuzco. It was the richest prize we ever took barring one, and the passengers were a gaudy lot, with pearl earrings, gold chains, and stacks of jolly dollars. Every man aboard drew something like seventy to eighty pounds on that prize and the Lords half as much again.

We didn't get it without a fight, of course. She was well armed and carried soldiers, but Flint sneaked up on her from a headland at sunrise, and the sun shone full in the Spanish gunners' eyes, so that we got off with a broken mizzentop and a single broadside that holed us above the waterline, and carried off seven of the crew.

Flint abominated Spaniards, and everyone was fighting mad when we came alongside, particularly as they still seemed set on resisting.

That was the first time I had ever been in a real fight, or seen why Flint was respected the way he was, even though he was no seaman. He was the first over the side and, close behind him, went Billy's Negro, Big Prosper, swinging his hammer like a demon out of the pit.

After these two came Hands, black with powder, Pew, Bones, Silver and Anderson, pistols blazing and cutlasses swinging, as they hacked their way through the boarding nets, and jumped screaming on to the Spaniard's after-deck.

The Spanish were gathered in a knot round the mainmast, with musketeers popping off from the fighting tops, and dropping our men in twos and threes before we could come to grips.

I went over alongside Black Dog, and I saw him get the swordcut that carried away two of his fingers, and sent him

howling to the deck. He would have been run through the body if I hadn't shot the Spaniard who slashed him. Saving his worthless life, I reckon, is just another black mark against me, along with all the others.

The leading buccaneers went straight for the group of soldiers gathered round the captain, a tall, pale man in half-armour, with a spade beard and flashing eyes. Flint singled him out and they went at it hammer and tongs, for the better part of a minute, but the Spaniard was long ways behind the times, and fought with a rapier, which Flint beat down after a cut or two and laid him full-length on the deck with a downstroke that glanced off his helmet and bit deep into his shoulder.

By this time Prosper had cleared a ring round him and Silver and the others had chased the survivors right along decks and boxed them up in the bows. After a minute of cut and thrust they threw down their arms and cried out for quarter.

Maybe Silver would have given it, but Flint, running forward after disposing of the Captain, shouted: 'Kill! Kill!' in that terrible voice of his, and all the Spaniards that were able jumped overboard, the wounded following as soon as Pew and Hands had time to rifle them and tip them over the side. In five minutes from the moment of boarding there wasn't a living Spaniard above deck.

Nick joined me at the mainmast and I hardly recognised him. He was bleeding from cuts on the arm and ear and his mouth and eyes looked as set and savage as the worst of the others.

He flashed me a sort of tight grin and said: 'This is the life, Ben, this is the life!'

I reckon the sight and sound of him turned my stomach more than the sight of that deck, with the dead men lying everywhere between the tumbled heaps of rigging shot down by Israel's gunnery. I suddenly thought of his sister, Miss Dulcie, and what she would do if she saw him now, all bloody and wild-looking, and cruel as the sea itself.

We lost seventeen men in that encounter but everyone judged the booty aboard was worth double the casualties. There were a half-dozen women aboard and they were stripped of pretty nigh everything except clothing, before being set adrift with such of the seamen who survived. We weren't more than a league or two from land, so I reckon they landed safely enough. It was fortunate for them we had a strict rule about berthing female passengers.

It was from this boat that Silver got his parrot, the bird you know as 'Captain Flint' but which he called at that time by the name of 'Pedro'. You recall that Silver claimed this same bird had been present at the raising of the plate ships off the Isthmus, and had learned there the saying 'Pieces of Eight' on account of the number they raised? Whether this was so or not I can't say, as the bird's owner, one of the women passengers, left the parrot behind her in her scramble for the boats and didn't tarry long enough to give us the bird's history.

Silver set great store by that parrot and trained it to go about on his shoulder from the outset. He was as persuasive with pets – birds, monkeys and the like – as he was with men when he was minded to be, and we used to watch him clap a piece of sugar cane behind his ear and call on the parrot to peck it out which he did, sure enough, with a powerful lot of squawking.

Long John had several pets as I recall. At Martinique, one time, he came aboard with a white-faced baboon as he named 'The Bishop', on account of the way the ape would hang in the shrouds and gibber away like a parson at prayers. This creature was a bigger thief than his master and would dart on to the poop deck when the helmsman was off his guard, and tear away the man's earrings, diving out of reach before the owner could clap a hand to his face. He stayed with us some time, and was a general favourite, until one night he got among Israel's slow-matches and most set the ship afire, after which John got Tom Morgan to make him a wicker cage in which he would have pined away if John hadn't turned him loose on one of the Grenadines.

There was a leopard cub, too, as Silver made a great pet of, and kept in his quarters for long enough, until he began to grow full-size and tolerably fierce, sinking his teeth into Pew's shoulder and getting a ball between his eyes for his pains, as it were. Animals never took kindly to Pew, and showed sound sense at that, but it was unlucky for this one as Pew happened to be armed at the time and the incident would have ended in a shore duel between Gabby Pew and Silver if Flint and Bones hadn't stepped in, and smoothed things over, Silver giving the sailing master ten doubloons and a new boat-cloak by way of reparation for the clawing he got.

It took us the better part of two days to plunder that vessel and then Flint set her alight. All that night, as we bore off to the south-west, we could see her hull flaming like a beacon. I tried to console myself for my part in it by recalling all Silver had told me about the pitiless cruelty of the Spaniards in these

CHAPTER FOUR — THE RELUCTANT BUCCANEER

I'LL pass over the next two years or so, Jim. It gives me no pleasure to reflect on them and, in any case, a pirate's life soon gets to be as dull as a shopkeeper's once you get used to it.

We divided the time cruising, plundering, and carousing in one of the havens, and during that spell we must have careened half a dozen times, twice in the Grenadines, and four or five times on Treasure Island.

Nick I saw less of than you'd imagine, seeing we were shipmates, for he could speak French like a Frenchman, and when we were in consort with Le Bon he was aboard *La Paonne* most of the time as Flint's interpreter.

He never lost touch with us however, and found time to quarrel with both Flint and Pew, the one over the rule of carousing above deck after midnight, and the other on account of Pew's cruelty to prisoners before they were set ashore.

Silver took Nick's part in both quarrels, which was a good thing for Nick. He was a stickler for the rules was Long John, and even went so far as to tell Flint he'd tip him the black spot if he didn't stand down and do his drinking where it didn't rob men of their sleep.

From then on Flint hated Nick, though how he could have managed without him it's hard to say, for the Frenchman was a wily bird, and would have got off with the lion's share of the plunder if Nick hadn't been there to do the talking for us.

Bones always liked Nick, and was kind to me too in his

103

gruff growling way. He taught me all I knew of navigation and I make so bold as to say I was a quick and rewarding pupil.

I didn't do a great deal of fighting but helped Darby in the galley when we were cruising, and this gave me an entry into the Lords' quarters aft. I kept my ears open and generally knew what was being planned for the future. This was how I knew Flint was pondering a masterstroke, as seemed likely to make us the richest buccaneers since England's taking of the *Viceroy*.

In the meantime, life ran on pretty much as usual and there were pleasant times as well as squalls.

The happiest occasions, as I remember, were the concerts we had on deck from time to time, mostly by moonlight during a spell of flat calm. Then the Lords and Commons would gather in the waist and foredeck, and the poop-deck would be turned into a sort of stage for the fiddlers and dancers. I can hear them at it now, and see them too in my mind's eye, the fiddles scraping away at a dozen outlandish tunes, and bare feet slapping on the scoured deck while the men, some of them in fine voice, sang songs and ditties they had come by as children, and which reminded them no doubt, of home and long ago.

They were bad men, Jim, most all of them, but few were bad all through, like Pew and Flint, and there were plenty of them, particularly among the felons and outcasts, who had known days of peace and family hearthstones. When they were singing out there by moonlight you wouldn't have known them from cottagers down in our village street, and tho' I don't expect you to believe me, I've seen them weeping after one of their number had stood up by the poop-rail and sang them a shanty as brought back memories they thought well buried under a pile of misdeeds.

So I come to the time when Flint and Le Bon agreed on a joint attack of Santalena, a small but important settlement on the Main, where part of the plate fleet collected.

Up to this time the plate fleet attacks had been made on single ships coasting up to the rendezvous, but this venture was the biggest we ever attempted and was in the style of Captain Morgan's land march against Panama years before.

Although not much more than a village, Santalena was at that time a principal collecting point. From then on the plate fleet sailed under heavy escort, and was safe from anything short of an enemy fleet. But a month or so before sailing you could always reckon on four to ten of the plate transports being berthed under the guns, and there was certain to be bullion in the storehouse ashore, as well as mixed plunder in the holds of the vessels.

One thing might interest you. We used to put in sometimes to an islet of the Leewards for fresh water when we were down that way, and the island we called at was little more than a long, high rock, shaped like a coffin. This was known as 'Dead Man's Chest' and the pirate song you heard so much of on the voyage of the *Hispaniola* was made up about this place, and about a party of fifteen buccaneers who had been ship-wrecked there years before. Silver told me these castaways salvaged scores of hogsheads of rum washed ashore, but could find no proper food for weeks on end, and were all raving drunk when they were taken off by one of Davis's ships.

In past years the plate ships had all made straight for Panama, where their freights had been added to the gold, silver and stones brought over the Isthmus by mule-train, but not long before the time I'm speaking of the Spaniards had tried to shorten the odds against losing stragglers in the long haul north, by setting up a string of small, fortified posts at various stages along the coast.

The newest and smallest of these posts was Santalena, three or four days sail south of Cartagena, and Flint picked on it because he reckoned it was likely to have half a dozen vessels in the bay, providing he judged his time correctly. His time, of course, was the latest date he could manage, before the convoy moved on up the coast to the fleet assembly point ready to begin the home run for Spain.

He had picked up this information from a ship's boy, the sole survivor of a party marooned on a cay off Barbados that spring. These men, six of them, had been left behind by a Yankee buccaneer, who had been having trouble with his crew, and got rid of the ringleaders by a scurvy trick. They had been sent ashore for turtles and then abandoned to almost certain death, the skipper having bribed one of the shore party to bring off the boat.

I told you I was marooned, Jim, that first day we met, but although, in a strict sense this was so, for I was set on shore against my will and abandoned, I was never a maroon within the buccaneers' meaning of the term, for I had a biggish island to myself, and enough powder to keep myself in goats' flesh for years. This being so I was more of a castaway, like that seaman Crusoe, whose adventures you read aloud to me last winter.

No, a maroon was different inasmuch as he was as good as pork from the minute his ship dipped over the horizon. He was usually set down on a cay where there was no shade and no water, and his executioneers always left him a pistol with a single charge, to use if he was so minded.

This bunch had firearms and for a few days lived on the birds they shot and ate raw, but after a spell two of them killed one another, and the other three died raving, so that the only one alive when we happened along was the boy, a lad about fifteen or so, who had been spry enough to build a tent out of his dead mates' clothing, and dig around for turtle eggs which had somehow kept him going until we saw his signal.

That boy was George Merry, the same George, Jim, as would have had your liver and lights on Spyglass that day if old Ben Gunn hadn't drawn a true bead on him from the nutmeg bushes. It was no hardship on my part to settle accounts with George. He was always a treacherous, quarrelsome sort, and when he was younger Silver once gave him a drubbing for selling common property to the half-breeds. You could never leave a fathom of old rope on deck when George was around. He'd find it, coil it, and dispose of it before you could turn round.

The only thing I came to admire about George was his cleverness at keeping alive and I wasn't that much surprised to see him turn up with your lot in the schooner. He came through everything without so much as bruising his knuckles and, as you saw, he was the last one of the mutineers to settle up accounts on the island.

Well, he repaid Flint well enough for stopping to pick him off the cay that time. He had been galley-boy on a trader, with a special licence to supply the Spaniards, and had seen the building of Santalena a year or so back, when his ship sailed there with a cargo of planed timber for the fort.

George was a bright lad and given to collecting information, as well as other folks' property, and he knew how many and how powerful the fort guns were, how to approach the town from the land side, what garrison we could expect to defend the place, and whether it was made up of Colonials or trained soldiers from Europe. All this and lot more, that Flint and Le Bon found mighty interesting, and it wasn't long before a master plan was worked out for reducing the place and taking off the biggest haul any two ships had made since England and his consorts had plundered the Mecca-bound pilgrim ships in the Persian Gulf.

The plan was a good one. I thought so at the time and I think so still. After all, it succeeded, for we got off with a fortune, or two fortunes, and if no one but me lived to enjoy it (and I had to wait years for my small pickings) that can't be laid to Flint's door, whose luck took a turn for the worse the very day we sailed out of Santalena Bay with a king's ransom in the hold.

Flint's plan was to divide forces and get the Frenchman to make a show slap outside the harbour at sundown, while we others left the *Walrus* a dozen leagues north, and landed by the boats at the far side of the swamp that protected the settlement from the north.

Until he got our signal Le Bon wasn't to do more than cruise inshore, just out of range of the fort guns, and keep at it until we were in position for a night march up-river to a point where George Merry said the stream could be crossed on a creeper bridge. Then we were to sneak seaward again, and rush the fort from the land side. If we were held up the Frenchman was to weigh in from the sea with all guns blazing.

It meant us laying up in the brush for two days, and either making scaling-ladders, or carrying them with us to get over the fort ramparts when we arrived, but Nick said he could puzzle a way round that and he did, thinking up a ruse that enabled us to dispose of the garrison at a blow.

Darby and I heard most of the plans while we were serving the food and liquor in Flint's cabin during consultations, and when everything possible had been arranged in advance we headed for the Main, and parted company a day's sail off Santalena, the Frenchman turning south-west, and us due north, till we fetched up in a snug, deep-water creek Billy knew midway between Cartagena and the settlement we had marked down.

We sighted several possible prizes on the way but Flint issued strict orders to leave them be and we flew the Spanish ensign all the way.

That night Silver marshalled the men aft and explained what we were after – a prize as would make every man present rich enough to leave the sea for ever if he was so minded, and set up on shore as a gentleman of means, with a fine house, a coach, and as many wives and slaves as King Dick down in Madagasky.

Then he numbered us off, a bare score to stay with the ship, and a hundred and thirty-one of us to pull south in the boats, and do it by night in case we were spotted from the shore.

The danger of this was slight, for the jungle here grew right down to the water's edge, and the Caribs in these parts would never have paid the Spaniards the compliment of passing a warning to them, but there was always the chance of us being seen and remarked on by a white hunter, and Silver judged it best to leave nothing to chance. There was too much at stake, the lives of every one of us and a fortune in precious metals.

Everything went according to plan. There were six boatloads of us, and of the people you know about only one, Bones, was left behind. We could ill afford to lose him but Flint judged, and judged rightly, that the whole success of the enterprise depended on having the *Walrus* to go back to, and nobody else could have been trusted to sail her down the coast and arrive neither before nor after the exact hour of the storming. Even as it was it would be ticklish work, with only a score of men to man the yards.

Flint and Big Prosper were in the first boat, with Silver, Pew, Hands, Anderson and Nick in command of the other. I was in Nick's boat, at the tail of the procession.

George Merry, as the guide, was sailing with Flint, and after two long nights' haul, entailing work that did nothing to improve tempers all round, we fetched up in the swamp bordering the little delta of the river that guarded the approaches to Santalena.

Here we put in under cover, and Flint ordered the boats to be stove in and sunk.

There was a lot of grumbling at this. The men were in dangerous country – it was always death in the mines for a foreigner to be caught on the Spanish Mainland – and they didn't take kindly to seeing their sole means of escape destroyed. One man, a big poacher who had been one of the original felons out of Plymouth, went so far as to voice his displeasure. Flint heard him out and then shot him dead on the spot. After that no more contrary views on the matter were expressed.

We lay up all that day, and the insects and flies served us cruelly in the marsh underbrush. Two or three men went down with heatstroke, and one was bitten by a snake and died inside the hour. We were glad enough to move inland after dusk, and follow the river bank for maybe ten or twelve miles, before we came to the creeper bridge George had told us about.

It was unguarded and we made a perilous crossing in single

file. Crossing that river was like carrying coals over a Cornish tin mine on a tightrope, and the men with the small brass swivel Israel had insisted on bringing looked, at one time, like having the gunner to thank for death among the tiger-fish and alligators underneath.

We got over all right, however, and about one in the morning started our cautious approach towards the town.

The attack was timed to open at sunrise, or as near sunrise as we could make it, and what with the soft ground, and the pains we'd been put to since leaving the ship, it looked as though we should arrive too exhausted to strike a blow. Silver, however, proved a wonderful leader on the journey. He covered near twice as much ground as everybody else, splashing up and down the line of march, praising and bullying, promising the men satchels full of gold and a life of ease if only they would keep up, and move a bit faster. Nick said afterwards that if Long John had chosen to live honestly he could have been an admiral or a general who would have left his mark on history, and I reckon Nick was about right; there was no one as could get more out of unlikely material than John, just so long as there was booty on the end of it.

About half-way down to the coast Nick gave me his musket to shoulder. He was lugging along a heavy bundle made up of sailcloth and wouldn't be parted from it. I couldn't guess what was in it that made it so heavy, but Black Dog said he reckoned it was spare ammunition for the swivel-gun.

Well, just as the sky was beginning to pale over the bay, we finally won clear of the swamp, and came on the first signs of the settlement, a sort of guardhouse on stilts set close by the stream, and a coloured woman under it washing clothes on the riverbank.

One of the men in the leading file snaked forward through the rushes and grabbed her. She let out a squawk but nobody inside could have heard, for everything around was as silent as the grave, and nothing moved in the delta but the seafowl fishing for breakfast.

The woman told Flint everything he wanted to know. She didn't need threatening, one look at his plum-coloured face was enough to convince her that the Devil had come out of the mangroves during the night, and she told us there was only two men in the guardhouse the others having been withdrawn to strengthen the fort garrison on account of pirates being seen beyond the bar.

This was good news and meant that our plan was working.

Flint wanted to know how many ships were in the bay, and how many able-bodied men were ashore in the settlement. She told him there were five ships at anchor, four of the plate fleet, and one lugger as had recently put in for repairs, and that the regular garrison consisted of a half-company of regular infantry, the hidalgo's town guard of about twenty men, and such of the ship's crews as were not sleeping aboard their vessels.

This was something of a set-back. It meant that there were at least a hundred defenders, half of them trained soldiers, and if the ships' crews showed fight we might find Santalena a nut to break our teeth on. Israel and Black Dog sneaked up the ladder of the guard-house and cut the sentries' throats in a matter of minutes. The woman we trussed up and laid inside to keep the dead men company. She had sense enough to set up no outcry. Then we filed down through the rushes to the head of the single street of wooden houses that was Santalena.

The signal to those offshore was to be the hoisting of the Jolly Roger from the fort flag-post, so we could expect no help from the Frenchman until the fort was in our hands. Even then, he could only fire into the town on friend and foe alike, and Nick told me he was going to use his judgement whether to land a storming party from the sea.

The first person we struck in the street was a fat half-breed, who slouched out yawning to take down the shutters of the store. We were on top of him before he had time to do more than gape, and a few seconds later the street was choked with shouting, mud-splashed pirates, pouring like flood-water down to the waterside where the road branched, running east to Government House, and west to the fort, the latter having been built about half-way along the northerly hook, or cay, that enclosed the anchorage on both sides.

I never saw the buccaneers act with better discipline. They obeyed Flint's orders to the letter, a score of them, under Silver, forking east to the Government building, and the others, under Flint, scudding over the sand towards the fort gate, and getting right under it before the rampart sentries had time to loose off their firelocks and raise the alarm.

The fort, I might say, was a ramshackle affair, built of imported timber, and surrounded by a half-finished ditch with no water in it, it being low tide.

There was a plank drawbridge over the stone causeway that approached the gate but it was down, a plain piece of foolishness seeing as there were pirates offshore. We found out afterwards that the commandant was on the point of coming out to inspect harbour defences at the very moment we attacked.

I was in Flint's party and not over pushing, though I was excited like everyone else, and as eager as the foremost to warm my hands in all that gold.

I ran forward as hard as I could pelt and I remember wondering as I ran what was expected of us when we got under the fort walls, for they were all of fifteen feet high, and more where the ditch had been dug. So far as I could see we hadn't a ladder between us.

I might have known Flint would think of that, however, and next minute I was thrown on my back with a tremendous explosion that shook the earth under me, and filled the air, for the space of a long half-minute, with a fountain of sand and splinters.

Nick had touched off a mine right under the fort gate, blowing one half of it sky high and the other back on its massive hinges. Inside that mysterious sack he had been humping was a home-made infernal machine the size of a twelve-pounder ball. It must have taxed him somewhat to carry that all the way up and down the river banks for he hadn't let go of it since we left the boats.

Howsoever, it was worth all the trouble Israel took making it, and Nick transporting it. The gap it tore in the fort gate was large enough to let us in three at a time, and with big Prosper in the van, and Flint roaring and slashing at his side, the first half-dazed soldiers we met were bowled over like ninepins. In less time than it takes to tell every man jack of us was fanning out along the ramparts, and whooping through the rooms of the central building after the fugitives. Hardly a one of them ever recovered his wits after that first big bang.

The Commandant and two officers tried to make a stand in one of the upper rooms, but Israel trained the swivel gun on the barricaded door and when we broke in all three of them were dead or dying, and the fort was ours.

Flint despatched me and Anderson to run up the signal and not fifteen minutes from the first moment of assault the Jolly Roger was flying from the standard post.

You'd hardly believe it but we lost only one man killed and two lightly wounded in that attack, such is the value of surprise and careful forethought.

Meantime Silver had been hardly less successful at Government House. The hidalgo and his lady were abed, which is where you'd expect them to be at four in the morning, but three or four of the more venturesome among the buccaneers had been pistolled by the night watch that was coming off duty after the harbour patrol.

By the time we got there, however, Long John had the hidalgo and his staff trussed up in the cords of their own bed-curtains, and was demanding to know where the plate was stored, and how much there was of it.

As I went back along the waterfront I saw *La Paonne* cruising slowly into the litle harbour, right past the silent guns of the biggish vessels moored there. Their captains must have seen the Jolly Roger fluttering from the fort and judged there was no sense in further resistance, as indeed there wasn't, for the town was now at our mercy.

Flint was too good a general to fool himself into thinking this state of affairs could last, however, and meantime he had to work fast if he was to squeeze the last ounce of gold and last seed pearl or second-grade diamond out of that settlement.

The first thing he did was signal Le Bon to come ashore with half his crew, leaving the others to keep their matches burning and watch the ships. The moment the Frenchman's ruffians touched shore they were sent to occupy the fort, where we collected all surviving members of the garrison. Having made certain of these the French posted squads of musketeers along the length of the street, in case the settlers tried a rally to free the Governor.

You have to remember that, allowing fifty men apiece for the vessels, there were still some two hundred odd Spaniards with arms in their hands, and we coudn't be sure that at least one of hidalgo's men hadn't slipped off, and ridden hell for leather to Cartagena or some other settlement for help.

Meantime the thing to do was to get the storehouse keys and off-load the gold. Until Billy showed up in the *Walrus* we dare not so much as send a party aboard the ships.

Flint reckoned that about half the available plunder would be in the storehouse, and the other half aboard the vessels. He decided to make a start on the storehouse, and keep the ships quiet by letting them know that the first one to slip cable would be raked fore and aft by the fort guns, as well as those of the *La Paonne* in the bay.

The moment Billy appeared the crews must have abandoned all hopes of trying to slip out to sea, for he was soon seen cruising right outside the bar, and how were they to know he had less than twenty men aboard?

With everything shipshape for at least a day Flint then turned his attention to the hidalgo, who was still trussed up in his own building, along with his wife and servants.

The Spaniard proved obstinate. He was a man of about sixty-five, brave as a lion, and proud as Lucifer. He might have been willing to treat with a foreign naval captain, and maybe buy himself and the settlement off, but he wouldn't have the least truck with common pirates, and Silver hadn't been able to get a word out of him.

What we were after was the keys of the storehouse, the only building in the town built of stone, and with a door and lock to it like the gates of a city. It was too solid to blast open and we hadn't the means at hand to try.

Le Bon and Pew were for putting a slow match between the old man's toes but Nick persuaded Flint to let him try reason before they resorted to torture, pointing out that the old Spaniard would probably die before he voluntarily handed over his king's property to a mob of sea-thieves.

Flint knew enough about Spanish pride to give Nick a bare half-hour to try his persuasiveness, but not a minute more he told him. If the old man didn't give up then it was slow matches for all of them.

Nick went to work on the womenfolk. There were three whites, the hidalgo's wife, his old sister, and the wife of his secretary, who had been killed when Silver's party stormed the building. Nick took all three aside, and talked to them politely but bluntly. He said he was about the only member of either crew who was able to prevent the pirates burning the town, and putting every man and child in it to the sword. The women, he said, white and coloured, would be carted off as slaves unless he had those storehouse keys, and the thing to do, for people in their position, was to give the buccaneers something else to think about, namely, gold and silver bars, and such precious articles as were ashore.

He made no headway with the hidalgo's wife. She was as brave and proud as her husband, and only swore at him in Spanish. She could swear passing well for a woman and spit too, which came as a surprise to me, her looking a lady born.

The old sister, however, who had a bloated face, and so many ornaments about her that she clanked every time she breathed, was more open to reason. When Nick told her Flint was getting ready to string up her brother by the heels, and turn him over a fire like a roasting hog, she burst out a-blubbering, and said the keys of the storehouse were kept in a special cavity let in to the floor under the old man's bed, and that if we were to spare their lives we could have, in addition to the plate, a ruby necklace of hers that she wore when she had appeared before the King of Spain in Madrid. To prove she was in earnest she started pulling off her geegaws as fast as her fat, trembling fingers would allow, and threw them down at Nick's feet in a heap. I shall never forget the look of scorn the hidalgo's wife shot the old dame when she broke down and told Nick about the storehouse keys.

Nick gave her a bow and smiled his crooked smile. All the time he had been making a show of court gallantry, as if the whole affair was nothing more to him than a piece of play acting, but I think he was as relieved as me that we were going to get the plunder without torturing anybody, and Flint, who had an eye cocked at the tide, was glad for a different reason. All he wanted was to be up and out of it without wasting a second. At any minute, for all he knew, a Spanish warship would come sailing into the bay to escort the berthed vessels up to the general rendezvous.

Well, the long and the short of it was that we got the gold, a hundred and ten bars of it, and fifty-three bags of minted coin, more money than the whole of us had ever seen in one place, and more than most of those scarecrows ever reckoned existed in the New World.

In addition, there were four hundred and eleven bars of silver, a big fortune in itself, and more than a basketful of rubies, topazes, emeralds and diamonds made up into brooches, watches, bangles and suchlike. There were also ten stand of finely worked arms, pistols and rapiers mostly, some of them studded all over with precious metals.

It was carted out, and piled into the boats the French had brought ashore, and it made our men whoop like schoolboys to see the sun sparkling on all that loot, as the bars and jewels were lifted from storehouse to quay by the niggers we told off to do the carrying.

Flint wouldn't let one of the men put his weapon out of hand while the loading was going on, and all the time he stood by the landing stage, a pistol in each hand, and not so much as a smile on his face to match the whoops and cries of his followers.

When all was about loaded, and the sun was dipping behind

114

the mangrove swamp back of the town, down comes Israel from the fort, to stand licking his lips over the last of the silver, and whistling a shanty to signify how happy it made him.

Flint went over to him and snapped out: 'You spiked those fort guns, Hands?'

Israel looked at him a bit surprised.

'Why no, cap'n, not yet I haven't, there's time enough before Billy drops anchor, ain't there?'

Flint exploded like a Chinese cracker.

'Time enough, you boneheaded lubber!' he screamed, 'I aim to be at work on the ships before dark and catch the morning tide for Tortuga. Do you want us blown to kingdom come while we're a-doing of it? Get back and spike 'em, you moon-faced son of a yaller-girl, and join me on this here quay inside o' the hour or I'll blow a hole in your back!'

I tell you Israel skipped up the sandspit smartly enough, and his men with him. He was back again in less than an hour, having put every gun on the fort out of action, and soused the powder magazine with fire buckets.

There were sufficient boats lying about for all of us, and after the last of the bullion had been loaded aboard the consort we started to work on the ships. These had been abandoned by their crews for the most part, the men having jumped overboard, and swum ashore into the woods the moment Billy's sails showed outside the bar, and they saw there was no escape by sea. I didn't know this as I was inside Government House when it happened, and nobody told me on account of none of them having words for anything else but the loot.

All night long we were kept at it, combing the transports, fifty or more of us to each vessel, and ferrying over to the *Walrus* in the small craft we found in the harbour. This was our third night without sleep, and most of us were about fit to drop, but Flint stood by with his pistols, and Silver beside him, so there was no question of lying down, or swallowing more than a mouthful of rum to keep us at it.

Silver shot a man he caught trying to pocket a gold snuffbox from one of the cabins, and Flint gave another as he caught asleep a thrashing with his scabbard as he was like to remember to his dying day. They weren't men to play at freebooting were Flint or Silver, and at peep of dawn, just twenty-fours hours after we came out of the swamp, we had everything of value in that settlement below hatches and were ready to sail on the tide.

All this time we had no manner of trouble from the people

ashore and I reckon they owed their lives, and the saving of the town generally, to the fact that they left us strictly alone. Even as it was Flint would probably have set light to the place out of plain cussedness if he hadn't been in such a hurry to make for open water.

La Paonne sailed shortly before us, and I never understood how we lost touch so soon, for we cleared on the same tide and were both heading for Tortuga and the shareout, but a light sea-fog came down on us that evening and when it cleared, shortly before midnight, the Frenchman's riding-lights were nowhere to be seen, and the word went round that she was trying to give us the slip, and make off with her share which was larger than ours, her having taken most all the bullion aboard.

I didn't share in this alarm, because I was in my hammock below, and sleeping the clock round, I was that worn out with pulling, floundering in the bog, and all the fetching and carrying we'd been put to getting the stuff aboard. Looking back on it I don't reckon Le Bon was trying to shake us off. We could sail four knots to his three if we had a mind to, and there was plenty in those two holds for all of us. It wouldn't have paid him to make that much of an enemy of a man like Flint, and I think it was a plain case of us missing one another in overcast weather; it can happen to anyone in those waters.

However, intended or not, the separation had serious results for the Frenchman, and for all of us aboard the *Walrus* too, in a manner of speaking, for the French wouldn't have run into the scrape they did if we'd been sailing together, and the whole story might have turned out differently if we had made Tortuga as we intended.

About noon, on the third day out of Santalena, with the weather calm but a good enough sailing breeze coming out of the west, we heard gunfire over the horizon, and Flint immediately ordered the helmsman to ease off a point in the direction from which the sound was coming.

We bore off and cleared decks as we were going, the men looking to their weapons, and determined, as you can imagine, to fight to the last for the plunder they had below hatches, and maybe pick up some more if there was a chance of it, for there's no limit to men's greed, Jim, once they've turned their back on honest toil.

Well, as it happened, there was no loot, but a precious narrow squeak for the lot of us.

116

Soon enough we saw a pall of smoke on the skyline and not long after it, with the glass to his eye, Silver roars out:

'It's the Frenchy by thunder, and a Spanish man-o'-war apounding her!'

So it was, and Le Bron getting much the worst of it by the looks of things. When we got in close enough to her we saw she had lost mainmast and mizzen and was afire amidships, a great pall of black smoke hanging over her in the lazy air, and the Spaniard laying off about two cables' length, and pounding her for all she was worth.

Flint made up his mind what to do in a second.

'Run up the red and gold!' he barks out, and 'Gunners below to sail close in alongside. Hold your fire, Hands, until I give the word. Silver . . . ' as Hands and the gunners scrambled down the companions, 'issue up the men above deck with morions and we'll give this Don some assistance he don't seem to need.'

Silver saw what he was at in an instant. We had enough Spanish steel-caps and jerkins aboard to make some sort of a show on the poop. We seldom used armour, but the morions were kept in the armoury for just such a stratagem as this, and we'd used Spanish uniforms once before when we called at an island settlement for supplies.

With the red and gold ensign at the peak, the Spanish Captain, providing he was fool enough, would jump at the notion that we were sailing up to help finish off *La Paonne* and he wouldn't discover his mistake until he was holed in twenty places by our first broadside. After that we could sheer away, finish him off and go to the aid of the French ship.

There wasn't one of us aboard the *Walrus* who cared the dregs of a pannikin whether the French crew sank or swam, but neither was there a man aboard who wasn't thinking of the bullion below hatches. To see *La Paonne* burn down to the water's edge before our eyes, or heel over and sink carrying the bullion with her, was more than any of us could bear to watch.

Silver and Bones issued out the caps and jerkins and told us to line the bulwarks, shouting and waving, while Bones set our course right between the two vessels, and held on through the smoke that was now shutting out the sun over the whole area of the fight.

Flint came down from the poop and stood by the forehatch, where he could bellow to Hands to loose off the minute we drew level with the Spaniard.

I think the man-o'-war's captain must have guessed what was

happening when he saw the course we took, but if he did he was too late to do anything about it, and as we passed broadside on we gave him round shot and cannister at point-blank range, and the tall vessel heeled through forty-five degrees with the awful weight of that discharge.

When we had sailed clear, and were turning on the starboard tack to go about, and give her the other broadside, she too was afire, and her foretop was shot away, covering the foredeck in wreckage and carrying away her bowsprit as it fell.

She drifted round and positioned herself nicely for the second discharge. It wasn't necessary but she got it just the same and it about finished her.

In ten minutes her sails were a mass of flame and men were jumping overboard in dozens. As we turned again, and brought up within hail of the smoking Frenchman, the Spaniard blew up with a roar that sounded like the crack of doom.

Before all the splinters had come down she was heeling over to port, and her decks were awash. Another few minutes and she was gone, leaving the whole sea around dotted with spars and debris, and every here and there a poor devil clinging to some of it, and trying to wave in our direction.

Every man aboard now turned his attention to saving *La Paonne*. It would have been folly to close in, and board, for in no time at all we should have been afire ourselves, so we hove to and lowered the boats as fast as we could, and mighty lucky it was for us that Billy had insisted on replacing our own with a few of the lighter craft we picked up at Santalena.

I was one of the first aboard the Frenchman and, hardened as I was, I turned sick at the sight of her decks. She must have been raked through and through before we came up with her and well over half the crew was dead or dying, including Le Bon himself, his sailing-master and chief gunner. Those of the crew as survived were amidships, trying to fight the fire with chains of buckets, and we set to and helped them, without a word being exchanged. Fortunately the *Paonne*'s magazine was aft, and with more than a hundred of us to put new heart into the firefighters the blaze was soon under control, with the ship still afloat, though listing badly to port and a whole section of her planking torn open above and below the waterline.

I won't ever forget the two days that followed.

If the ship had been less damaged we could have unshipped the plunder at our leisure and left her a derelict, or if she had one or two seams open she would have gone down under us before we could transfer a bar of gold to the *Walrus*. As it was she was in between, bad enough to remain in hourly danger of sinking, yet kept afloat by the efforts of every man who could be spared from the *Walrus* to work the pumps, clear away debris, and caulk below decks.

We tried to get some of the gold into the boats, but the weather worsened and every man jack of us was needed to keep the pumps going full blast. The minute we eased off she began to settle, and list further to port, so that before night came we had to jettison the guns and everything above deck and stand by in teams of eight to keep up the back-breaking work on the pump-handles.

There was no question, of course, of making Tortuga. If another Spaniard had shown up, and caught us at our work, we couldn't have fired a shot in our defence, but the choppy sea remained empty and presently we got a towline aboard, and dipped off to the south-east, heading for the nearest island we knew where we might take a breather and strip the wreck before leaving her to sink or rot.

It so happened that our nearest haven was Kidd's Island, some two day's sail under a fair wind, and thither we made off, close hauled, and one behind the other, like a couple of lamed geese.

Billy needed at least half of us aboard the *Walrus* for the weather looked like thickening. The rest of us, some seventy in all, stayed aboard the wreck, pumping for dear life in half-hour shifts, and snatching for food or rest whenever we had the opportunity. The only thing that kept us going, I reckon, was the thought of losing all that gold.

There was a cheerful side to it, as Silver, who was aboard with us, was quick to point out. In the fight with the Spaniard, Le Bon's ship had lost seventy-eight men, and their shares now belonged to us. Eight more died of their wounds before we sighted Spyglass peak and that, with our losses ashore, reduced shareholders in the last enterprise to a few over two hundred men. There was as good as a fortune for each and every one of us.

Kidd's, or Treasure Island, is curiously placed.

At this point in the Caribbean, the Leeward and Windward Islands curve south and south-east, from Porto Rico all the way to Trinidad, strung in a sort of broad bow or, you might say, like a huge reef. There are a few outlying islands, both sides of the main group, but most of them are little more than rocks, like Dead Man's Chest, and only one, Kidd's Island, is of any size.

Its position, south-south-west of Tobago, is well out of the track of ships. There was never a settlement there and nothing to tempt a visit except for such as us, who liked our own company when our ships were in need of a refit and we were open to attack.

We hadn't careened for close on six months, and were overdue for it in any case. Flint figured that if we could reach the Anchorage, or better still North Inlet, we could beach *La Paonne*, strip everything off her, careen the *Walrus*, and then head out for Tortuga, for we had a power of stuff to put on the market apart from the bullion.

A Council of War agreed on this, the Frenchman now being commanded by a Levantine, called Gaspard, a big, stupid oaf, who had only got himself elected captain on account of his brute strength, which was equal to that of Big Prosper, the negro.

The Lords aboard the *Walrus*, that is Flint, Bones, Silver, Pew, Hands and Nick, all agreed that this was the best all-round plan, and so did the men before the mast when it was explained to them. What we didn't know, I reckon, was the private plan Flint and Silver were hatching up between them – to diddle the French out of their share as they reckoned Le Bon had been trying to diddle them when he was overhauled by the Spaniard. I'll swear Bones and Nick weren't a party to this – it didn't carry their mark somehow – and as for Hands and Pew, the one was too stupid, and the other too disliked by Silver, to have been trusted with such a secret.

All this, of course, I only found out as time went on, and much of it I didn't know until I talked with John Silver during the first part of the homeward voyage of the *Hispaniola*, just before I got shot of him on the Main. He held nothing back then, he was too low in spirits, I reckon, and it was all too long ago to matter anyway, seeing how few of Flint's crew still breathed.

We were dead lucky again. The weather cleared unexpectedly and we nosed into North Inlet without sighting another ship. I tell you, Jim, but we were all glad to see those rocky hills breaking the skyline. I don't think I could have pumped another hour, and we were the more anxious because we knew that by this time word of our attack on Santalena would have reached Panama, and every Spanish warship in the Main would be searching for us.

Billy came aboard the French ship and beached her where you last saw her, right up under the trees at full tide, and left her to heel over on the ebb. We had cut adrift from her in slack water and the men went ashore to mount the usual guard battery, and get the *Walrus* ready for careening.

There was no goat-hunting for me and Nick on this occasion. Nick was kept busy with the sick and wounded, and all hands not engaged on refitting the *Walrus* were stripping everything of value from the wreck, and piling the plunder of both vessels on shore, where Flint had a guard mounted over it day and night.

The loot was split into four piles – gold bars, silver bars, minted coins, and arms, and any one of those dumps looked a heap of money, Jim.

When it had all been counted and sorted, and the *Walrus* was beginning to look herself again, Flint called a mass meeting at low tide, and word went around that Silver was going to address us on the subject of divisions and future operations.

All the men liked Barbecue and respected his judgement. Too many times he'd been proved right, and the more impetuous among us dead wrong. Added to that none of the *Walrus* company had forgotten how it was Silver who put heart into us during that awful march over the swamp. The men respected Flint too, of course, he was too cool and too lucky to merit otherwise, but none of us liked him more than we feared him, the way we did Silver. If the crew had ever broken up, and gone separate ways, I reckon nine out of ten of us would have signed articles with Barbecue rather than with Flint.

Well, we sat down on the hot sand, more than two hundred of us, and Silver paddled ashore in a gig and talked to us like a fond father.

I can close my eyes and see that scene now, Jim.

The sun was shining above the trees and there was a fresh, wholesome smell about the anchorage, resin from the pines higher up the twin-pointed hill, and a whiff of wildflowers from the woods. The men, for the most part, were stripped to the buff, with gaudy handkerchiefs tied on their heads to keep off the sun, and their weapon belts and banderoles laid aside for comfort's sake.

Men of every nation there were, English, French, Dutch, Spanish, Levantines, Moors, woolly-headed niggers, and a power of half-breeds from every settlement on the Main; old men, with balding heads and grizzled whiskers, men in their prime, like Nick and Silver, and a sprinkling of beardless boys too young to be keeping such company, all with their eyes on Silver's gig, and maybe a covert glance or two at the far beach, just to satisfy themselves that nobody was fingering the loot.

Silver swept off his hat and beamed round at us. I can remember most every word he said on that occasion.

'Mates,' he began, 'I told some of you when we signed articles as you were born under lucky stars, every mother's son of you, and I reckon I was about right as you'll allow when you look yonder. You got such men as me and the Cap'n to do your thinking for you, and the time's arrived to admit it right out and above board, like true seamen every one, for we got a deal more thinking ahead of us if we're to get that blunt to places as we can spend it freely, as gentlemen o' fortune should!

'Now, mates, we ain't clear o' the woods yet, not by many a long sea-mile, and neither we won't be if you get ideas of your own, and won't be guided by me as have brought you so far with a king's ransom to split. The fact is, mates, we can't ship that blunt to Tortuga right off, we got to leave it here until the plate fleet is half-way to Spain, and the guard-ships along of it!'

There was a stir at this I can tell you. A sort of growl ran round that circle like a low roll of thunder. Some of the men sprang to their feet, and started to shout Silver down. They had been expecting a division there and then, and Silver's words were a bitter disappointment to them. However, he had enough sea room with them to make them hear him out, and only glared round, and waved his hat for silence. When he got it he went on:

'Do you reckon as the Dons take kindly to sacking a settlement, and sinking one o' their escort ships? Why, I tell you the Viceroy would as soon have you lot decorating his gibbets up and down the coast than he'd sit himself on the throne o' Spain in Madrid! Every armed vessel between here and the Gulf is out looking for you, aiming to get the stuff back, aye, and stretch your dirty necks into the bargain! To load it, and take it to Tortuga with a swollen ship's company as we'll have aboard would be as good as offloading it on the wharves of Cadiz, or walking slap into the main square o' Panama with ropes round our necks!

' "We got a fast ship and can run or fight for it," says you. Well, we have, but we've also got far more than that vessel

122

can carry in men and plunder. If we run into a fight what's to become of us, that's what I'd like to know? If we lose a spar, we're as good as taken and moreover men can't fight easy with that much stuff aboard! One broadside and we've lost a fortune, one reef and down goes the lot. "Well", says you, "we can't spend it here can we, we got to get it away sometime", and so we have, as I'd be a fool not to allow, but what I say is this – now's not the time to do it, when the sea is a-crawling with Spanish sail! Our best lay is to take our time, bury the stuff here where it's safe, and come back for it with two ships, or maybe four, for I was never a man to put all my eggs in one basket!'

This second part of the speech produced a notable effect. I could see by the way the men turned to one another and remarked on it. I don't say everyone agreed straight off, but the common sense John was talking set a few of the older hands thinking, and there was no more growling and muttering.

It was quite true what Silver was saying about a ship full of gold being unfit for a fight. With all that money and bullion aboard, the men would have been inclined to run for it every time, and the chance of getting to settlements where we were welcome, that is, any settlement where the Spaniards weren't, would double and treble as time went on, and the plate fleet and escort were safe out of the way on the voyage to Spain.

Then Job Anderson piped up and voiced a question that must have been troubling most of them.

'Suppose we go along with you, John, suppose we agrees that now ain't the time to venture out into deep water with the blunt, what I say is, who's to do the burying? Who's to know where it's cached?'

There was a chorus at this, and Silver beamed. He could see now the worst was over and he had everyone in hand.

'That's a simple question, Job, as deserves a simple answer!' he went on. 'We ain't in the line o' business to trust one another, I reckon, and I'd be the last man in the world to look for it, fore and aft as you might say. There's some as would trust me, but I'd take no offence if I run across others who didn't! But someone'll have to bury it and if you ask me the safest plan is to find who by ballot, same as everything else is decided, one ballot among the Lords, and another among the Commons. That way they'll have the weather-gauge of each other, so to speak!

' "What happens then?" you might ask. Well, after that it's plain sailing. Those as is chosen stays here and buries it, and the rest of us stand off and wait for a signal, telling as it's done. Then in we sail again and pick up the burying party, holding the lot of them hostage until we've sailed into French Tortuga, sold off the market trash, found ourselves vessels, and come back for the big shareout!'

'How many of 'em stay here?' bawls George Merry.

'As few as possible,' says Silver, straight off, 'the fewer there is, the fewer to watch, them's my sentiments!'

And so it turned out, for Silver's plan, once they'd discussed it, met with general approval. There were those who disliked it of course, and George Merry was one of them, and so was the new French captain Gaspard, but he was outvoted by his crew. It was finally agreed that the Lords should be represented by a single man and that the actual burying party should be made up of no more than six, and a main tiresome job they would have of it disposing of all that plunder.

For men of our sort this arrangement had much to recommend it, the general opinion among the buccaneers being that to allot the task to a stronger party would be dangerous, whereas a mere half-dozen would be easy enough to watch during the voyage to Tortuga. The plan had Silver's mark all over it.

The two ballots were held that very night, in the light of a dozen great fires ranged along the beach. A tally showed a total of ten reckoned as Lords, and one hundred and seventy-eight reckoned as Commoners. There were a score or so wounded who had to be left out, on account of their being unfit to perform the heavy labour ashore, and once this was settled Nick marked six crosses on six of the hundred and seventy-eight papers, and placed all of them in a big copper pot set midway between the two biggest fires.

It was decided to hold the Commons ballot first, and the Lords stood round the pot while every able-bodied man ashore stepped up and picked out a paper, before moving on to the far side of the Lord's party.

The first thirty or forty papers were blanks and excitement ran high when one of the Frenchmen drew the first cross, to be followed, almost immediately, by the second, drawn by a mulatto from our crew, a man we had recruited from one of the prizes.

That left four and after another score or so of blanks one of the West-country felons, a squat, broad-shouldered ex-smuggler drew a cross, then another Frenchman, and finally a Dutchman from our crew again, leaving but one for the dozen or so of us who were waiting our turn.

I tell you, Jim, but I was sweating pretty freely. I didn't want to have any part in the burying of the gold with that treacherous mob hemming me in, but I had to take the chance, same as everyone else, and when I hung back Nick noticed it and sang out:

'Come on, Ben lad, you're the only man among us as was paid to dig graves before you went on the account!'

I moved forward then amid general laughter for it was known I'd been a grave-digger, and put my hand down among the few scraps of paper at the bottom of the pot. I took hold of one and pulled it out. It was folded four ways, and my hands were trembling so much that I had to take hold of myself to flatten it out. When I did, and glanced at it in the light of the leaping flames, I almost fainted. It had a cross. I was the sixth hostage.

I don't recall exactly what happened after that. I reckon I must have edged out of the firelight, and gone up the beach to be by myself and think. All the others had crowded round the pot again for the Lord's ballot, and the next I knew there was a shout that could have been heard right across the island, and Nick came running to say Flint himself had drawn the single cross for the poop-deck party.

That was about the last thing I wanted to hear. To be set on shore with Flint, five desperadoes, and all that gold, was a prospect as would loosen the knees of a braver man than me, Jim, but there it was, there was no help for it, and the thought drove me to the rum bottle then and there. I drank sufficient before sunrise to put Flint and the future out of mind for a spell.

CHAPTER FIVE   THE RELUCTANT BUCCANEER

NEXT morning a strange thing happened. Along comes Silver to sort out the six who had picked crosses, and take us a little ways down the beach and tell us that from then on, till the *Walrus* sailed, we were to keep to ourselves, and take up quarters in the palm-leaf hut on the south side of the anchorage that had been Flint's place ashore.

It seemed that the men generally had decided on this as a precaution against any of us coming to some arrangement with special mates of either crew, and although I didn't take kindly to it at the time I reckon it was a good enough idea when I look back on it.

We tramped, the six of us, the two Frenchmen, the mulatto, the Dutchman, the English felon and me, and when we were cooking our junk over our own fire I got to thinking of a story one of the Indians had told me about a custom his heathen kinfolk had regarding folk singled out for sacrifice to some god or other, over in Peru. The Indian told us that young men and women about to be offered up for rain were always kept apart a spell before the ceremony, no one being allowed to talk to them, or even look at them. You can judge that remembering this didn't do much to raise my spirits.

Meantime the rest of the crew got busy stowing the gold, half the silver, the minted coin and the more valuable of the arms, into specially-made packing cases. The rest of the silver was going with us.

As each was ready it was branded by the armourer with the name *Walrus*. There were nine cases in all, four containing gold bars, two housing the bags of coin, one for the arms, and two for the silver. Only the arms chest was awkward to handle, the rest being squared and fitted with strong rope handles for carrying.

This done everyone except a few of the Lords went aboard, and come nightfall it was unnaturally quiet on the beach, though later, when the rum was passed round, we could hear the buccaneers singing further down the anchorage, their voices sounding mellow and pleasant across the still water.

Flint hadn't been near us six and we hunched round our solitary fire to eat supper. After the days of brawling and the press of men about the beach, it felt ghostly and lonesome having the beach to ourselves. The moon hadn't risen, and outside the circle of firelight the woods looked black and grim. We had rum of course, but somehow there didn't seem any power in it that night. We talked in half-whispers, and I remember the talk as a whole was different from the usual run of conversation among pirates. One of the Frenchmen, a young fellow called Bazaine, sang us a love ditty about his old home in the wine country, back of Bordeaux, and I remember his notes gave me a choking feeling in the throat. The English felon tried to cheer us a bit by spinning yarns of smuggling affrays he had been engaged in, along the Cornish coast, but soon enough the talk ran out, and we all six turned in to sleep.

The hut was too small for all of us and, seeing the night was close, I stretched out under my sea-cloak on the beach.

It must have been well after midnight when I started up to find someone jerking at my shoulder, and putting a light hand over my mouth.

I sat up to see the moon risen, and Nick was beside me, with someone else standing well back against the trees. Nick didn't say anything but motioned to me to get up and move back to the fringe. When I got there I saw that the other person was Silver, and even in the pale light I noticed his big face looked set and solemn. He turned off and we followed him a little way into the wood.

'Ben,' says Nick, when we were out of earshot of the hut, 'you got to go back to the ship along of John.'

'What about the cacheing,' I asked him, 'I was chosen fair and square, wasn't I?'

'You were,' said Nick, 'but Flint wasn't, and me and John mean to keep grapples on him. You just do as I say, and go along with John. When Flints starts out to find a place to bury us he'll have me to reckon with.'

'He'll suspect you rumbled him and kill you,' I told him.

'He might try,' says Nick, and winked at Silver, 'but he'll have no choice but to carry me with him, because the ship will have sailed. She's dropping down to open water at the turn of the tide. She'll be clear by sunrise. Here, drink this,' and he handed me a small flask containing something that smelled like camphor.

'What is it?' I asked him.

'Something to let on you're sick,' he told me, 'but it'll do you nothing but good, you can rely on that!'

I was about to ask him for more explanation. Inside me I was glad enough to escape even a few days' marooning alongside Flint, and the knowledge of where all that blunt was buried would have weighed on my mind like a net full of roundshot. All the same, the plain hint of treachery they were giving me didn't make me feel any too easy about Nick, for of all that motley company he was the only one whose life was precious to me.

I did ask one question however. 'Who knows about this change-over?' I asked Silver.

'Only we three, Ben,' he said bluntly.

'When the others find you aboard John'll give out you were ill, and I changed places last minute,' added Nick. 'There won't be any trouble on that score, they'd all as lief have me ashore as you.'

There didn't seem anything more to say so I took a long swig from the flask and handed it back to him. Silver was anxious to get to the gig that was moored further up the beach and growled out his impatience.

'So be it then, but you keep yours barkers primed and a dirk handy,' I warned him.

He grinned and held out his hand.

'We've seen a deal together, Ben,' he said, and they were the last words I ever heard him utter.

Silver and me went down the beach and climbed into the gig, John bending the oars down the Inlet towards the *Walrus* moorings. When I turned round in the sternsheets, and looked back to the spot where we'd talked, the beach was quite empty, there was just the night-sparkle of the wavelets on the silver sand, and the dark wall of woods beyond it.

*

We got aboard without incident. Everything had been made ready for sea and the buccaneers were sprawled everywhere, nine-tenths of them prone in the heavy sleep of drunkenness, and only the watch, with Bones' chunky figure aft, waiting for the tide to ebb. I wondered if Silver had told the truth, and whether Billy shared his suspicions about Flint. If he did he said nothing when he saw me go below, and two hours later we were all tumbled out to the capstan and were soon dropping down to the narrowest part of the channel and hauling to the north-west, with Foremast Hill on the port bow.

I don't know what was in the physic Nick gave me but it must have been something mighty drowsy, for all that day, and most of the next, I couldn't keep awake, and everyone thought I had the ague, or was sickening for something worse.

Because of the way I kept dropping off, or because of what Silver had spread around, nobody asked me any questions as to why I wasn't ashore. I was too hazy in mind, most of that time, to so much as ponder on Nick, and until my senses cleared I kept getting the strangest fancies, like my head was four times its normal size, and my fingers were thicker than tree trunks.

It was main hot weather and calm, so calm as to make cruising a tedious affair. We never let the island out of sight but drifted and tackled all the time, some two or three leagues from shore, and with Spyglass in view the whole time.

On the fifth morning, when we were a deal closer in than usual, there was a shot from the poop and a lot of running to and fro on deck.

My head was almost clear by now and I asked somebody what was happening. He said it was Flint's signal, and pointed to a long, thin column of smoke that was spiralling up from the lower slopes of Mizzenmast, at the western side of the Southern Anchorage.

We stood in then and had the linesmen out in the anchor-chains, nosing into the channel between Haulbowline and Skeleton Island, and finally dropping anchor in four fathoms.

No sooner had the anchor splashed down when every man aboard ran to the port bulwarks and a terrific hubbub broke out all over the ship. Being shorter than most I couldn't get

a glimpse of the shore, but I heard Israel shout: 'It's Flint, by thunder, and he's alone!'

This was enough to make me skip into the mizzen shrouds, and as soon as I hauled myself above the press of the bulwarks I saw that Israel was right. Flint, without his usual cocked hat, and his head wrapped round with a bright blue scarf, was pulling the heavy boat slowly towards the vessel. There was no one else with him and, as the boat approached, we could see he was far from his usual self, and drooped somewhat over his sculls.

'Ahoy there!' bellowed Pew, 'where's the others, Cap'n?'

Flint stopped pulling with his starboard oar, and eased round alongside, grabbing the line Anderson threw to him, and making fast to the painter.

He looked up at us and his face was even more ghastly than usual, for it was corpse white, with the cheeks sunk right in, and his eyes glowing like coals, red-rimmed and deeper-set than ever. He looked like a death's head, with a tight brown skin stretched over his skull.

'The others?' he growled out. 'They're below hatches, and be damned to 'em for a pack o' treacherous curs!'

He faltered on the ladder and Anderson had to climb down and half haul him aboard.

As he stepped down you could have heard a nail drop on that deck. The men stood round with their mouths open and he glared back at them, his thin lips drawn back, and his yellow teeth showing in a wolfish snarl.

'Well,' he said at long last, 'is there any among you as is spoiling to join 'em?' And as he said this his right hand dropped to the butt of the lowest slung of his four pistols.

Not a man among them moved. They just stared and stared, he looked so terrifying and awful.

'You're wounded, I see,' piped up Billy from the poop.

He didn't say Cap'n and I thought his voice sounded more harsh and grating than usual, rough as it was at the best of times.

'Aye,' said Flint slowly, 'I'm wounded, and it was that swab of a surgeon who did it, after I'd settled the others just afore they settled me! Who had the planning of it? That's what I mean to find out! Who had ...'

He didn't get any further. Suddenly he spun round and fell headlong to the deck, his scarf coming off in the tumble and showing a long red furrow like a great whip-mark beginning

131

near his left temple, and reaching back into the crown of his head. His thinning hair was all matted with dried blood. It was a wound, I reckon, as would have killed most men, and it came as near as matters to killing Flint.

'Well here's a howdedo,' exclaims Silver, calm as ever, 'Flint with his head wide open, and all six messmates gone below! Lend a hand, some of you, and get him to the cabin. If he crosses the line we're sunk, every lubber aboard here, for how in tarnation are we to know where he's buried the stuff?'

This struck the pirates like the first blast of a typhoon. I judged no one had thought of it before, but it was plain enough now. With Flint the last above board of the burying party we had the whole island, nine miles by five, to comb over when we called back for the dollars!

I don't reckon any man aboard was ever handled more tenderly than Flint when they carried him below, washed his wound, and stripped off his soiled clothes before settling him in his bunk. They fussed round him like two hundred nurse-maids, all falling over one another in their concern and each with a different remedy for bringing him to. Finally Silver and Bones took over, with Pew and Israel in close attendance, all four watching one another like tom-cats on the prowl, and everyone else cleared from the cabin by Silver's final injunction:

'There's nothing a-going to happen to the Cap'n mates, you can lay to that! Just leave him to John, and give him air!'

Young George Merry was the least trusting of the crowd Silver shooshed out on deck.

'Suppose Flint made a map of the place?' he wanted to know.

'We've been through his clothes and half the men aboard saw us do it,' said Pew. 'There wasn't no sign of a map about him, so it's all in his head, I reckon.'

Those among us who had seen Flint's clothes searched confirmed this melancholy news. Flint hadn't been out of sight since he came aboard, and it was plain he had committed nothing to paper or, if he had, it was well hidden ashore.

That same evening we stood out for Tortuga and the curtain went up on the last scene of the *Walrus* company as I knew it.

CHAPTER SIX   THE RELUCTANT BUCCANEER

WHAT happened after that is soon told, Jim. It was a tale, for
most of them, of battle and sudden death, and for some, like
Pew and Silver, of long drawn out misery and suffering. For me
and me only it was the beginning of the road back, after years
along the path to the Pit.

I said Flint's luck deserted him after the affair at Santalena.
Well, it had gone right enough, but we didn't know how far
away until we ran into a hurricane east of St Kitts, and got
blown far to the west into dangerous waters, south of Jamaica.

After that we were becalmed and having two hundred men
aboard ran perilously short of water, and were soon down to
a pannikin a day.

I ought to have told you that our haphazard sacking of all
manner of vessels shortly before the Santalena attack had run
us foul of the new Jamaican Governor, who had appealed
direct to the Home Government for naval support. Since we
had heard about this we had little cause to complain; all the
same, it was a bad area to be found in and made everyone
jumpy.

Flint kept to his bunk and the only ones who saw him, apart
from Darby, were the Lords. Darby, devoted as ever, tended
him night and day.

We knew he was still alive, for during the still nights we could
hear him raving, and singing snatches of sea-songs. There
was a sort of foretaste of doom about the ship that cruise, and

the men were unaccountably sullen and out of sorts. Maybe it was the uncertainty about the loot that preyed on their minds, or perhaps because we had drifted into an area where pirates weren't welcome.

When a light breeze did spring up we were able to make an island some leagues west of the Great Cayman, but we didn't linger here, as this part of the ocean was the area a frigate was most likely to patrol. We had lost touch with conditions this far west and hardly knew what to expect, one way or the other.

Billy tried to get the men to clear decks in case of an action, but the heat was too intense to get them to work long and the litter was everywhere, even round the guns, some of which had hammocks slung between them.

We didn't see a lot of Silver. He spent a deal of time in Flint's cabin and looking back I can guess why. He and the other three seemed to have come to an agreement to get Flint to fill in the blank spaces on the map Billy had drawn up of Kidd's Island. They admitted this much to the crew at large, after a mighty suspicious deputation had waited on the quartermaster.

The end of that sultry spell came on us with awful suddenness.

We had just cleared the last point but one of the island we had watered at, and were hauling round to the north-west, right into the sun, when a new-class frigate, flying the Union Jack, shot out from behind the last point, her canvas cracking under the land breeze, and driving her across our course at a speed nearly double that of the *Walrus*, which hadn't yet shaken out half her sheets.

The lookout screamed a warning from the crosstrees but we didn't need his yelling to make us jump to our action stations, and start tearing away the rubbish that was cluttering the guns. Everyone aboard could see it was a naval patrol ship, the one that had always been promised and never turned up, and all of us knew too that the Jamaican Council had sworn that once they did get naval backing they would wipe piracy from the seas round the Crown possessions. All who hadn't taken or had violated the pardon, they said, would hang within the year.

The next thing we knew the frigate had hauled round to starboard and let fly, with every gun she could train on us.

It was the worst broadside I'd ever witnessed, much less faced on a crowded deck. In one swathe it carried away foretop, mizzenmast, and an upper spar on the mainmast, piling thirty to forty dead in the waist, and maiming half as many again under the wreckage that came thundering down aft and forward with the mast and spars. The shredded canvas settled over the foredeck like a shroud.

All who could win clear rushed to the companionways driven below as much by the itch to get under cover as by Billy's hoarse shouting from the poop. The mate, I imagine, was urging us to clear away and return fire before the frigate could move in closer and rake us again.

I dived down the fore companion like a rabbit. I didn't feel the pain in my shoulder, where a splinter had lodged; it was to give me endless pain and trouble in the weeks ahead.

As it happened, crowding below was about the worst thing we could have done at that moment. Long before we could sort ourselves out, and run out so much as a single gun, the frigate's second broadside caught us at point-blank range, and clean a-line the gunports.

The execution was awful. If the deck volley accounted for fifty men the second broadside, that overturned guns, spun their carriages in all directions, and ploughed through whole knots of men working madly to clear away cordage and litter, was even more deadly. In the space of a quarter-minute that gundeck was an inferno.

Right against the bulkhead, where Nick and me had once crouched watching him hatch his plot with Pew and Hands, John Silver lay pinned under a ten-pounder. The gun had been hurled from its carriage by the sudden heeling over of the shattered vessel and he lay there screaming like a child, and no one to help him, they were all too occupied with their own hurts and terrors.

Under a pall of smoke men rushed pointlessly this way and that, stumbling over the dead and such wounded as were trying to crawl out of the way, calling to one another to fire guns that lay this way and that, one upon the other, and not one, it seemed, capable of answering fire.

One man and one only kept his head – the Chief Gunner, Israel Hands. It shows how you can never really judge a man, Jim. Ashore or afloat, Hands was a stupid, sour-tempered drunkard, good for nothing except maybe a brawl, or a shanty-chorus, and only that when pickled in rum. With a linstock in his hand, and a gun to lay, he was a living marvel, cool-headed, steady-handed, and brave as a gladiator.

I shall always remember Israel as I saw him at that moment, leaping from dismantled gun to gun, and peering at each with the slow-match burning in his great fist ready to touch off the first serviceable weapon he found.

I ran to him with a kind of instinct as the one man in that shambles likely to do something before a third broadside sent such as us as had survived to feed the fishes.

In the angle between the afterdeck bulkhead and the extreme end of the stern galley he found what he was looking for, a twelve-pounder still positioned to fire through its port and ready laid, with powder-bucket and two balls to hand, the rest having rolled out through the ports.

The gun had no business to be there. It was a stern-chaser and belonged on the after-deck, but it had never been set up again after careening, and some freak of the two impacts had tumbled its carriage to starboard so that the muzzle was pointing square through the last port on that side of the ship.

Israel squinted along its length and gave a low growl of satisfaction. Over his shoulder I could see what pleased him. The frigate was less than half a cable's length away and in a half-turn as she hauled around to windward, either to let her reloaded starboard guns play on us, or to position herself for boarding. Her stern presented a target like a church wall and Israel, after a tug or two at the elevator, touched her off with his match.

The single explosion sounded foolish in all that clamour, but the shot went home, smack into the frigate's rudder which it shattered at a blow, leaving the vessel at the mercy of our wash, and the ever strengthening land breeze.

Turning our backs on the uproar behind us, Israel and me reloaded unaided, sponging her out, ramming in the charge, then hauling her forward from the bulkhead that had shortened her recoil. This time he aimed a point higher and the ball struck splinters from the stern bulwarks and ploughed forward, cutting a lane through her crowded deck and spilling men in every direction.

Those two shots were as good as a broadside and it was them as saved us, for if the frigate had run alongside the *Walrus* would have been overwhelmed in the first rush, and those of us taken alive would have sun-dried on the nearest gibbet inside a month.

I told you the sun was setting when the engagement began. Well, mercifully for us, the Caribbean twilight is brief and in ten minutes it was dusk. The sea between us turned violet, then purple, then black, with the two of us drifting ever further apart as the frigate bore off before the wind, unable to do more than shorten sail, and losing leeway all the time she was doing it.

Bones, for our part, sailed due north-west, making skilful use of all the canvas left to him, and standing at the wheel all that night while the rest of us hacked away the wreckage, and rigged jury-masts fore and aft.

My shoulder was beginning to pain me now, but there was not time to attend to it. It was almost dawn when I went below, weak from the loss of blood, and with my right arm as stiff as a bilboe.

Two men, Israel and Billy, had won us clear, but there was one other, below decks, who had distinguished himself in that action, and but for him not one in three of the wounded would have made Savannah, the port for which Billy was now running.

Between decks was a scene as would have turned the strongest stomach on the Main.

Silver, his left leg crushed and shattered, was lying alongside the gun that had maimed him. Pew, sightless and moaning, was among the mob of injured men under the foredeck, his fingers clawing at the rough bandages wrapped round the upper part of his head, and him blaspheming fit to call forked lightning down the hatchways.

Big Prosper, the negro, lay stone dead, beside a port gun, his iron-shod mallet still clasped in his hands as he must have grabbed it the minute he ran below to be cut down by the second broadside.

Gaspard, the new French captain, was dead, and so were two score others, apart from those killed above board. In addition there was hardly a man who hadn't received some hurt, most of them injuries from which they seemed unlikely to recover. Altogether we had ninety-two dead, and almost as many out of action, the killed including some of the best men aboard, carpenters, sail-makers and armourers, whom we could most ill afford to lose.

George Merry, of course, came through unscathed and so, fortunately for us, did Billy and Israel, but in all that company there wasn't a score fit to go aloft, and if we ran into heavy weather we were done for and knew it.

Silver bore his pain pretty well. I fetched him some brandy and went aft to look in the locker that Nick had used for a medical store. He had his salves and saws in there, and as I cast around, searching for them, I couldn't help thinking that many of those aboard were going to curse Flint for killing the surgeon before we dropped anchor. There were many in that crew who already owed their lives to his patchwork.

The medicines and instruments were nowhere to be found and while I was ferreting for them along comes the old half-mad psalm-singer, Jabez Patmore, the man who had stuck with us ever since he refused to be parted from his irons when the ship was taken in Royal Port Harbour.

Jabez had appointed himself master-surgeon and the curious thing was he didn't seem mad any more, but strong, and kind of saintly, as he padded to and fro on that hell-deck, giving drinks, sewing up gashes, drawing out grape-pellets and splinters from raw wounds, and altogether handling Nick's instruments as if he'd been born to the use of them.

It was Jabez who patched up Silver's leg, cleaning it and splinting it while Silver bit on a plug of baccy, his face running with sweat, and his great hands wrapped around ringbolts to keep from wincing against the probe. It was Jabez who had bandaged Pew's eye-sockets and tended two score more of those rapscallions, and when he could give his time to it he had a dozen of the lightly wounded, such as me, scouring below decks, tearing up bandages, and rigging up hammocks over the gun ports.

Later on, when we had shaken down a bit, I asked him if he reckoned the men he was tending were worth saving, and if so why he hadn't got busy with surgery long before this and helped Nick in his rounds after other engagements. He looked at me, solemn as an owl, and then reached into his ragged shirt and pulled out his Testament which he handed to me to examine.

It was hardly worth calling a Bible any more. The binding was split, and half the pages were missing, but as I looked at it I saw that a sharp splinter of angle-iron had driven it way clean through the centre of the print and stuck there, with a bit protruding back and front.

'I carry it over my heart, Ben,' said Jabez, 'and I reckon this was a sign from the Lord of Hosts as I was worth sparing. It came to me that if He saw fit to send his own Son to patch up sinners, then who was I to stand idle between decks?'

I reckon Jabez was right. It was as clear a sign as ever I saw, before or since, and when my shoulder eased a little I set to and gave him all the help I could, which was considerable, seeing as I'd watched Nick at his work many a time since we left home.

Billy had good friends in Government House at Savannah, and that was what caused him to head there. Some of the Southern Governors were hand in glove with us, like the dago juntas on the outlying islands, and if they could get goods without paying import revenue to King George they were ready and willing to give us sanctuary, just so long as we behaved ourselves off their towns.

When we sailed in and dropped anchor the first thing we saw was Davis's corsair, the *Revenge*, berthed in the middle of all the legitimate shipping.

Davis was a well-known pirate and still had some of Robert's old men serving under him. He and Flint weren't particularly friendly but Silver knew him well and, as a general rule, dog didn't eat dog in those waters. There was plenty enough for all of us.

As soon as Davis saw our condition he came aboard and with him his surgeon, a gentle-bred youngster out of Boston, who, like Nick I reckon, had seen fit, God forgive him, to exchange college for adventure afloat.

This man had a look at our wounded, particularly Silver, and soon as Jabez took off the splints, and exposed the leg, he said it would have to come off unless Silver preferred to die of gangrene.

Silver took the news well. 'So be it,' he grunted, 'just so as I can still go a-looking for that frigate and the Jamaicans, burn 'em!'

They took it off there and then, and for the rest of my time aboard Silver hovered between life and death. It was years later, when I was back trading, that I heard he made a final recovery and was, by all accounts, as spry on one leg as he had been on two. Taken all round, Jim, Long John was head and shoulders above most men afloat. I never saw the like of him, not once, in all my wanderings.

Pew made a good recovery, but his blindness brought out even more bile in him if that was possible. He was reduced to beggary, of course, and I heard no more of him until I ran up against you.

Flint neither got better or worse, but still stayed on in his cabin, seeing only Billy and McGraw. It was then that the chart must have been drawn out, and Billy made up his mind to pull out with the key to the treasure, for one morning, a few days after I'd quitted the ship, his cabin was found empty, and his things gone, how or when nobody knew, for none saw the going of him, and most aboard were too sick and sorry to care until they had time to put two and two together.

As for me, I had other things on my mind just then and most urgent of them, once my shoulder wound healed, was to find out what happened to Nick, even if it meant holding a dirk to Flint's throat, and finishing him off as soon as I was satisfied one way or the other. Even before I left, Billy was ashore most of the time, hobnobbing with his friends in Government House.

Billy's quitting of the poop was a great help to me. All I had to do now was to keep a close watch on the cabin and wait until Darby was out of the way, leaving me a clear field.

All this time Flint had never left his bunk, and seemingly knew nothing of the fight we had had, for when he wasn't rambling on account of his wound he was dead drunk on the rum. He might have recovered, and taken over command once again, but Darby was either too stupid to realise this, or as set on killing him one way as I was another, for he gave him as much liquor as he wanted, and every so often we heard him bawling for Darby and the bottle at the top of his voice.

My chance came about a week after we'd berthed, and most of the men were ashore selling off the stuff that hadn't been damaged in the fight. Such of the silver as we hadn't buried had disappeared piecemeal, for there was no order or discipline aboard after those two broadsides. It was a plain case of every man for himself.

Darby had slipped ashore to get fruit, and Jabez asked me to keep an eye on the Captain while he was gone. I said I would and I meant to, but it was a different sort of watch from the one Jabez intended. I went below and got a dirk and then aft to Flint's little cabin under the poop-deck. It was a sultry afternoon and most everyone aboard was sound asleep.

As I went down the poop-companion I heard Flint raving, and then, as I took a last look around outside the sliding door, a rattling sort of cough, like a rusty anchor chain fouling the windlass.

I went in and across to the open port under which Flint's bunk was situated. Not until then I reckon, did I realise how much I hated him, and had always hated him. I was trembling from head to foot, but not with fear, for there was nothing about him to fear any more, he just looked small, and pitiful, under his coarse blanket, with his ugly head lolling on the cushion and his head thrown back with chin pointing at the scuttle.

I pulled out my dirk and moved forward.

'Cap'n,' I said, 'I come to find out about Allardyce and I reckon you'd best out and tell me afore I cut your throat!'

He neither answered nor looked at me, but lay quite still, staring up at the open scuttle. The only sound in the stuffy cabin was that of flies buzzing in hundreds round the necks of a stand of rum bottles on the locker beside him.

I moved a step nearer and looked down on him. Then I started to laugh aloud, as well I might. He was stone dead, and that rattle I heard had been his final gasp. I stood there dirk in hand laughing fit to burst. Perhaps I was a little mad, or overweak from my half-healed wound. At all events, mad or sane, I knew then as I'd never discover how Nick Allardyce met his end among all those dollars.

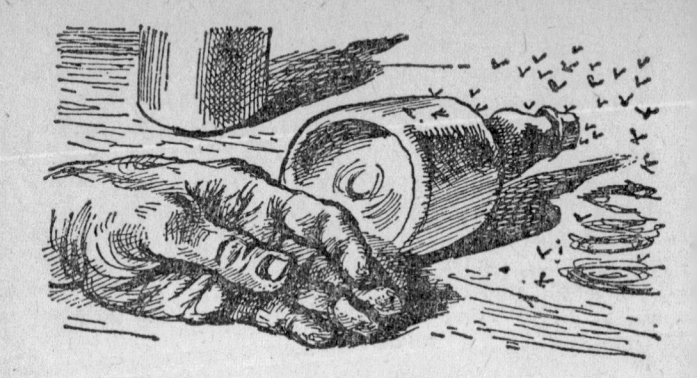

I DON'T know how long I stood there laughing, whether it was a few seconds or an hour, but suddenly I stopped laughing as the thought struck me that perhaps this was intended as plain a sign to me as the Bible shield was to old Jabez Patmore.

The more I thought about it, the clearer it became, that God had reached out in the last minute, as it were, to prevent me from committing a cold-blooded murder. I had gone in there with a knife to kill Flint, and here he was dead, when I was within a few yards of him. How could this be anything else than the hand of the Almighty reaching out to show me how wrong I had been to try and take the law into my own hands, and collect my own rental, so to speak, for a mere one of all the bloody crimes that had been committed by the ugly pirate? Why, at this very moment, I reckoned he was coming up for judgement before a far more important judge than me!

This, I'm persuaded, was the first hesitating step I took on the road back, and it left me weak and trembling, so much so that I had to get out of that cabin like the devil was after me, and find someone I could talk to, and get advice from.

There was only one such person aboard that ill-starred vessel and I went in search of old Jabez, who had stayed aboard all the time we had been in harbour and was still carrying out his duties of nurse to the sick.

He had just come from tending Silver, who was in high fever that afternoon, and seemed likely to follow his captain over the line at any moment. I told Jabez I had something

important to say to him and took him forward to my berth under the foredeck. It wasn't any use to make half a confession so I told him everything, holding nothing back, from the moment Nick and me had to run for it, to the moment I'd walked into Flint's cabin with murder in my heart.

He heard me out to the last and when I'd finished he said:

'It's plain enough, Ben, you've been singled out by the Lord for redemption, and you stand at the parting of the ways. It's a matter for you to decide which road you're treading from now on.'

'What choice have I got but to continue aboard the *Walrus*?' I asked him. 'I'm as guilty as any one of 'em, and it's too late to start afresh.'

'It can't be too late, Ben,' says Patmore, 'or the Lord wouldn't have intervened to take Flint before you took him. My advice to you is to slip ashore now, at this moment, while the mood of repentance is on you.'

'I got nothing but the clothes I stand up in,' I argued, which was true, seeing not one of us had had a share-out since long before the affair at Santalena.

'You came into the world with nothing, Ben and you'll go out of it the same,' said Jabez. 'What's money got to do with it, seeing that your soul is crying out for a drink? You don't belong with us no more and that's plain. You just leave go, and let your Redeemer take a turn at the wheel. It's your one chance o' getting safe to port.'

'Why don't we both go?' I begged him. I badly needed someone to claw hold of just then, but Jabez only shook his grey head.

'My place is here,' he said quietly, 'I've known that a long time. I was at hand to read your heart when you come to me and, God willing, there might be others as the Lord thinks is worth saving.'

At this moment we heard somebody calling aft – one of the wounded wailing for water – so he stood up, gave me his blessing, and moved off with a pannikin.

That was the last time I ever saw or heard of Jabez Patmore, and he must have gone to his rest these thirty years or more, but if I need someone to speak up for me, Jim, when it comes to my final reckoning it's him I shall call on, for he's numbered among the Saints, mark my words, and it wouldn't surprise me if St Peter hadn't long since roped him in as a sort of special pleader for doubtful cases such as mine, when good, bad and indifferent is being balanced up by the Recording Angel.

I felt a deal better after that talk with Jabez and I was minded just how I felt only the other day, when Parson read out that bit from *Pilgrim's Progress* about Christian's bundle tumbling from his back, and leaving him free to continue his journey without a dead-weight of sin dragging him down. I don't mean to say, mind you, that I was able to cast off the past like an old coat, but at least I'd made a start, and was uplifted, you might say, by the fact that a man like Jabez, who had already made his peace with God, was sure I had a chance, however slight.

I packed a few things in a bundle and going on deck, hailed one of the dago scows that was always ferrying round us for trade, and asked to be set ashore in the town. I said no good-byes to such as were aboard, and I didn't so much as bring a knife ashore with me. I wanted to be free from all that in future.

I set my face to the north and began the long tramp up the Eastern Seaboard, reckoning that, at one port or another, I could find a berth with a seagoing trader, and earn the first honest money that had come my way since I dug graves in the East Budleigh Churchyard.

In less than a week I was a foretopman aboard a three-masted schooner out of Charleston, and from then on I thought I had turned my back on piracy for good and all. I was to find, however, that a man can't change the course of his life as he might switch from a tired horse to a fresh one at a posting station, and that the guilty past, no matter how much or how genuinely it is regretted, has a habit of lying in wait for a man just when he least expects it. It was that way with me, Jim, and mine came face to face with me more than four years later, when I reckoned I was nine-tenths of the way along the road back to honest citizenship. It was a shock, Jim, to realise that in those four years I'd barely travelled half-way.

PART THREE

THE ROAD HOME

CHAPTER ONE   THE ROAD HOME

Iт's curious how I struck the island again, quite by accident, as you might say, and right out of the run of a normal voyage.

I always chose the fastest ships when I was looking for a berth, and I never stayed on one ship more than a single voyage on account of my fear of its luck running out.

My knowledge of piracy in those waters stood me in mighty good stead. I knew what ships buccaneers went for, and where they were likely to be at various times of the year. Consequently I was never once boarded, in all that time, and if it did so happen we saw what I judged to be the topsails of a corsair on the horizon, then I gave the master due warning, and we were off on a fresh tack as soon as we could fetch the wheel round.

I made two or three long trips and did a deal of coasting, sometimes up as far north as New Amsterdam, or south to the Plate. This time I was aboard a smallish ship, a brig out of Philadelphia, called *Swallow*, and she was rightly named, for a better-found vessel I never struck, not for speed or handling.

The skipper was a hard man but just, and strong on religion. We had prayers every morning and evening, and the crew abided by this on account of the food being better than the tack served out on the majority of coasters.

There were fourteen of us on the *Swallow*, including the skipper and mate, and at least half the forecastle party were dagoes. The bo'sun was a Yankee and him and me were pretty close, having sailed together before. He was called Oxley and I reckon he was my second evil genius after Silver.

We were heading south-west, with a cargo of hogs for some of the islands in the Grenadines, but had sailed into long spells of calm and were soon short of water. On account of the live-stock aboard we used as much water as we could carry, and had counted on replenishing barrels two or three times during the outward trip.

We weathered out the calms but it was dry going, and when the wind freshened at last we crammed on sail and headed south with all speed, but a series of heavy squalls carried us off course, and one morning what should I see on coming on watch but the peak of Spyglass, breaking the skyline to the south-east.

If there was one place I was anxious to keep clear of it was Kidd's island, and not only because we might run into trouble with buccaneers in the latitude. I got a sinking feeling in my stomach as the outline of the island began to show up, and I realised that we were heading direct for the southern anchorage.

'What's the skipper thinking of?' I asked Oxley, 'that's a careening haven for buccaneers!'

The mate heard me say it, and gave me a sidelong look.

'How come you know that?' he asked me.

'I been there,' I admitted, 'we ran into trouble there years since, and only just got off with our lives. We wouldn't have done that if they could have put to sea after us but their vessel was high and dry for a refit,' I added. I was pretty glib with my tongue by this time, and usually had a yarn pat. I don't suppose the mate believed me but he pretended to.

'Buccaneers or no we're bound to run in,' he said, 'we're down to our last barrel, and we shall lose half our cargo if we don't water. However, keep a sharp look-out, all of you!'

As soon as he was gone aft I told Oxley about the treasure and you can imagine he was mighty interested in what I had to say. As a general rule I was as close as a clam about my time with Flint, but Oxley I trusted, foolishly as it turned out, for inside the hour he had blabbed everything to the other hands, and when I came off watch there was greed shining in every-one's eyes, and a deal of speculation about our chances of strik-ing something more rewarding than fresh water soon as we set foot ashore.

'Ben,' says Oxley, voicing the opinion of every man in the forecastle, 'you ought to go aft and tell the skipper what you told me. Maybe he'll heave to, and set us all looking for it. If it was Flint's cache there's enough to make all of us rich.'

Up to that minute it hadn't struck me as a possibility that

149

we might start looking for the stuff. We had no map, no single clue where to start searching, and I knew the skipper was more anxious than any of us to water those hogs, and set them ashore where they would show him a good profit. He was part owner of the brig, and therefore more concerned with its profits than most skippers. When I pointed this out Oxley only laughed.

'Why man, there's a bigger haul in one of 'hem chests you tell about than in all the hogs in the islands,' he said. 'Get along aft, and he'll thank you for it!'

I let myself be persuaded but as it turned out I was right and Oxley was wrong. The skipper was the sort of man who believed two hundred hogs in the hold was worth more than a fortune under the rainbow, particularly as I had to admit I hadn't a notion where the stuff was buried.

'We'll refill and leave it at that,' he said sharplike, and sent me back to my duty, with a flea in my ear as the Doctor used to say.

His decision to leave without a search provoked what amounted to a mutiny. This was a chance in a million of getting rich beyond a man's wildest dreams, the crew said, and they weren't going to miss it on account of a few thirsty hogs. They sent a deputation to the skipper and even the mate sided with them, until at last the skipper, seeing no course to the contrary, agreed to send a search party inland and give them the chance of finding the gold.

I'm sorry to say, Jim, that by this time I was as eager to look as any one of them, and after we'd coasted around a bit, just to make sure the island was deserted, I piloted the *Swallow* into the southern anchorage without a thought for anything but how lucky I was to be sharing that fortune with thirteen instead of two hundred as was intended.

You see what fools this gold-worship makes of men, Jim? There wasn't one of us aboard save the skipper that wasn't certain sure we as good as had that blunt under hatches, and were sailing off to enjoy it, together with a life of ease and plenty.

We dropped anchor close to the spot where Anderson had hauled the wounded Flint aboard. It was more than four years since I had looked on that spot and I'm ashamed to say I had hardly a thought for poor Nick, but for whom my bones would have been whitening there. All my good resolutions went by the board, every blessed one of them. In spirit I was just a seathief again, and ready to knock anyone on the head who stood between me and the bullion.

While we were hoisting out the longboat the skipper strolled up and watched us, and I noticed a twisted smile playing round his mouth.

'Ben Gunn,' he says to me, casual-like, 'how comes it you know so much about Flint and his jolly dollars?'

I'd been expecting this and had an answer ready for him.

'I was pressed aboard the *Walrus* afore they buried the stuff,' I told him, 'we were boarded and sunk not far from here, after the buccaneers had sacked Santalena that time.'

'Oh!' he says, still smiling, 'that must have been a blessing in disguise for all aboard, Gunn,' and strolled away, humming a tune, while the rest of us, mate and all, piled into the longboat and pulled ashore as if the Devil was chasing us.

We didn't give a thought to those hogs. We spent day after day, in pitiless heat, tramping the length and breadth of that blessed island, loaded with picks and shovels, and combing the sandhills and gullies like scavenger-beetles.

All we found was the skeleton of one of the Frenchmen – I recognised him by a crucifix he wore round his neck – and had remarked upon that last evening we spent together round the fire in North Inlet.

He was lying in the open, far to the north, under Foremast Hill, and his cutlass was rusted in its sheath. I reckon Flint must have shot him in the back from some distance off before he went back to settle with the others.

We dug all round him but the only treasure we came off with was his crucifix trinket and there was a quarrel and blows over that.

On the twelfth day we trekked back to Southern Anchorage, no nearer finding the treasure than we had been the day we landed, and the men were in a dangerous temper. Standing on the beach near the boat was the skipper. He still had that crooked smile on his face.

'Well,' he drawled, seeing us come trailing out from under the trees, still shouldering the picks and spades we'd taken ashore, 'have we stowage room on the *Swallow* for all the treasure you've digged up?'

'Not a dollar,' said the mate with an oath, 'and we reckon as Ben Gunn dreamed it, burn him!'

'Ah,' said the skipper, 'but that's a pity, for we've room to

151

carry all you could find seeing as the hogs have died for lack o' water!'

They had, too, every last one of em, for the skipper had been alone on the brig, and was quite unequal to the task of hoisting out and refilling the casks unaided. As far as he was concerned the voyage had resulted in dead loss, and the crew knew they could expect no pay-off at the home port.

The mate was the readiest to admit his mistakes, and ask for forgiveness. After he had said his piece up piped my mate Oxley, who had been the prime mover in the search.

'It was Ben as talked us into it,' he said, 'and I reckon we're all ready to admit we were blamed fools to listen to him!'

'Ah,' said the skipper, in a sharper tone of voice, 'I reckon you were that, and if justice was done I'd put the lot of you in irons, and have you tried for mutiny the minute we drop anchor in Philadelphia, but seeing as how I can't sail the ship home unaided, any more than I could keep the cargo alive without help, I'll have to make the best of a bad job, and overlook it this once, providing you're all back aboard and we're out of here on the tide! Look sharp, fill those barrels, and man the capstan before I change my mind and put a bullet in one of you.'

My word, but we moved smartly enough to please any skipper. In three hours every water-barrel was full and shipped, and the last man was jumping into the longboat and shoving off.

All the time the skipper remained sitting on the gunwale, and as I was about to wade out he held up his hand.

'Not you, Ben,' he said, 'you're the most favoured of all of 'em, you can stop here and keep right on looking for that treasure, and if you find it I'll call back here in five years' time and claim my share of it to offset them hogs as you've lost me!'

I stood knee deep in the surf staring at him. I couldn't believe that a seaman who wasn't an out and out buccaneer, and a man as conducted a prayer-meeting aft night and morning, would abandon me alone in a place like that. Someone in the longboat laughed but the skipper cut in:

'It's no joke, Ben, I'm marooning you, same as your old friends the pirate would, only I take leave to doubt as they'd see fit to give you the means to keep body and soul together after they'd put off. You'll find a musket, powder and shot, a barrel of pork, and some other useful odds and ends up in that old blockhouse. As for picks and shovels, well, there's plenty at your feet, and I only hope as you have cause to use them as time goes on. You got plenty o' time, Ben, a lifetime one might say, so long as your old shipmates don't put in again for careening!'

With that he jumped aboard and signalled to Oxley to push off, drawing and cocking a pistol in case I tried to rush forward before they were out of the shallows.

'Cap'n,' I shouted, 'have mercy on me!'

'Mercy?' he called back, as they pulled clear of the surf, 'you're getting a sight more mercy than you gave my hogs.'

I stood there, water up to my knees, and watched that boat draw away towards the mooring. Not one of that crew ventured to reason with him, or attempt to make him relent. They hoisted up the barrels and the longboat, and within two hours were slipping out with the tide, and hauling north-west.

By sunset the *Swallow* was hull down on the horizon, and I was alone with the goats and ghosts on Kidd's Island.

EVEN then I couldn't believe the skipper was going to do more than teach me a lesson.

I hung round that pestilential anchorage for the better part of a week, straining my eyes out to sea, half-expecting all the time to see the *Swallow*'s topsails show above the horizon. Nothing showed up, not the suspicion of a sail, and when I was certain I was abandoned I broke down and wept, hour after hour, and day by day.

It was some days before I so much as went up to the block-house to pick over what had been left for me. During those first days I lived on turtle eggs, and berries, and some of the time I must have been rambling, for I once fancied I saw men on Skeleton Island opposite, and at low tide waded over calling on them for help.

When I got there, however, it was nothing but a few sea-lions, like those that live off the Cape of the Woods, and then I knew I was well and truly alone, and had best do what I could about finding a place to live, and a means of getting some flesh to eat.

Up in the blockhouse I found the captain had been as good as his word. There was a musket, powder and shot as would last me a long time if I was careful, and lots of other things, including a spare sail, some rope, the barrel of pork, a knife and a blanket, already green with mildew.

I can't recall much about the first month or two I spent

there, living in the blockhouse, and feeding mostly off the pork and a turtle or two. I only remember I was well enough by day, when the sun was shining, but pitifully weak and afraid o' nights, waking up suddenly from a dream in which Flint was after me, waving his cutlass, and shouting out oaths. Once I saw Nick in a dream, as plain as I see you now. He stood by the door smiling down at me and beckoning and another time I saw Flint bludgeoning him to death, and woke up in a sweat, screaming and cursing.

One way and another those first nights were full of wretchedness, but after a spell I got my bearings, as it were, and came round to thinking more of old Jabez, and his final words to me about me being the one man aboard the *Walrus* who had been singled out for redemption.

That made me a little easier, not much at first, but more as time rattled on, and I'd been alone the best part of three months. By this time I had explored every corner of the island which I knew pretty well already after our old hunting trips on Spyglass, and my trampings to and fro with the crew of the *Swallow*.

It was on one of these trips that I found the old cemetery, the place where Kidd had buried his dead after some fighting ashore, or an outbreak of fever maybe the time the stockade was first built.

We'd buried a score or so of Frenchmen up in North Inlet soon after we came ashore that last time, but Kidd's burial-ground was older, and I reckoned it was consequently more hallowed, so I chose it as the best place to go and pray, and try and confess what a rapscallion I'd been, and ask for forgiveness.

It did me a power of good, Jim, did that first prayer. The words didn't come easy, for I hadn't offered up a prayer since I'd left home, but maybe the Almighty made allowances for soul-rust, and after a time or two I found that the prayers I'd learned as a boy in Devon came back to me, like a brook finding its way into an old, dried-up channel, and washing away the silt that was stuck there.

After that I found a sort of peace, and slept easier. I moved out of the blockhouse, recalling what Nick had said about its nearness to the swamp and bad air, and cast around for a cave where I could dump my few belongings, and keep dry during the rains, which came down like a cataract during one part of the year, and had the blockhouse awash during the first hour.

I found what I was looking for above Rum Cove, and besides

being dry, and cool in the afternoons, its entrance provided a good lookout for ships, for I hadn't then given up hope of being rescued by a vessel that put in for water, the same as we had.

I kept a sharp lookout for buccaneers too but I never saw any. I had made up my mind to avoid them if they did land, for I preferred staying on the island alone to getting back among that sort of company. The reason none of them put in, I suppose, was that none of our old crew, save only Bones and Silver, knew the true location of the place, and that Flint had kept it a close secret from the rest of the Brethren and that was the reason he judged it safe to leave the gold there. As I said, it was right off the track of traders, and yours was the first vessel I sighted in the three years I was stranded there.

How did I put in the time? Hunting mostly, and being sparing with powder. The goats were plentiful enough and I soon stalked sufficient to lay up a stock in some casks I found and mended along the shores of North Inlet. I salted the flesh with brine as I panned myself down in Rum Cove, and I lived well enough, although sometimes I found the diet mighty monotonous, and longed, as you know, for a savoury, especially cheese as I've always been partial to.

I also took some time making the boat as was so useful to you, and it called for a deal of patience, Jim, seeing as I was without an adze, or anything in the way of nails and tallow. I tried using the goat fat to make a sort of glue but it was no use for caulking, and I finally used it to make dips, so as to have a light in the cave after sundown.

There was the old wreck too, *La Panne.* I went over her pretty thoroughly, and salvaged a number of useful things, a tinder box that I was in sore need of, and bolts that I ground down into fish-spears. You recall what I said to you that first afternoon we met, Jim – wherever a man is there a man can do – and it was about right, for when there's no soul to turn to a body has no help but to consult himself and, having done it, go about his problems the best way he can.

Most of the day, that is, from dawn to noon, I was occupied in keeping myself going so to speak, and in the afternoons I generally took a nap. It was between the time of waking and sundown that I got to thinking, and you can judge, Jim, what it was that I thought most about – no, you'd be wrong, for it wasn't where the treasure was buried, but *how* that old devil had buried it, and accounted for six strong seamen in the process.

As time went on this puzzled me more and more. It was like having a few fragments of a torn-up map, and knowing that the rest was around somewhere, and not far off. It just meant finding them, and piecing them together, and the more I pondered it the more determined I was to do just this, for in some strange way I reckoned I owed it to Nick and that this was the real reason God had placed me in the circumstances I found myself in.

It may seem odd to you, Jim, but I got to feeling that I was meant to solve that puzzle once and for all.

Well, I set about it in earnest the second spring I was marooned. Spring was the best time for tramping. It was usually coolish from first light until shortly before noon, so I laid in a stock of food, and set off on a yard by yard comb-out of that island, not looking for disturbed ground particularly, but with all senses alert to discover any signs laying around as would help me to piece together what happened after we sailed the *Walrus* out of North Inlet, and stood offshore until Flint came back alone.

I had one clue, the dead Frenchman we found up on the lower slopes of Foremast, so I started from there, and took a closer look at the bones before burying them. It didn't seem right to leave them to bleach out there alone and they had, of course, been picked by the birds long before I discovered them.

As I said, this Frenchman was the one who had sung that song about his homeland the night we six had that solemn carouse round the fire after the ballot. It looked to me as if he had been shot in the head from behind, for the back part of his skull was shattered and I even found the ball that killed him.

After thinking it over I decided that the only way Flint could have won out against such odds was to have contrived to split the party into three groups, and ambush them one at a time. This seemed all the more likely because I remembered there had been three caches, the gold, the silver, and the arms. The minted money, I reckoned, would be carried along with the gold, and the silver and arms buried in different places, for Flint was far too careful a man to put everything into one hole.

As it turned out, of course, I was right – the chart showed that. He had buried the silver in the north cache, the arms in the sandhill north-east of North Inlet, and the bulk of the treasure on the slopes of Spyglass far to the south, but all this I didn't know at that time, and was working in the dark.

The Frenchman I found had seemingly been killed by someone firing from cover and at longish range. He was close to
where the arms were buried. Flint had probably kept all six
together until the chests were dumped at the three different
points, and then doubled back to pick the party off one by one,
leaving the others to guard their chests until their turn to be
killed came round.

This was borne out by my second discovery, the skeletons
of the other Frenchman and the mulatto, far to the north, at
the extreme end of the east hummock. Here I found the black
crag, mentioned in the chart as having a face on it.

Whether the face had been carved there by Kidd's party
years back, or whether it was the work of Indians who had
inhabited the island generations ago, I had no means of telling.
It was neatly done, and reminded me of some of the rock carv-
ings I'd seen in the islands much further west on the other side
of Panama.

These two men, also skeletons picked clean, were lying half-
buried in brush about a fathom apart. The mulatto – I recognised him by the curiously carved knife he had clutched in his
hand – must have tried to make some sort of a fight for it, but
the Frenchman had died without drawing a weapon. His cutlass
was sheathed and his pistols still charged, being slung in his
bandolier, but too far rusted to be of any use to me.

I had a good look round the hummock, and all about the
area, to see if I could spot Nick's remains, or the least sign of
the ground having been disturbed, but Flint must have covered
his tracks very carefully. There was nothing else to be found
up there so I buried the two men and struck south, towards the
centre of the island.

One by the sandhill, two by the hummock. There were still
three to account for and I spent whole weeks sifting through
the centre swamp and along the East coast to the Cape of the
Woods. I found goats a-plenty, all manner of curious trees and
flowering shrubs, but no more bones, nor any sign that man
had ever trod the thickets before.

By the time the rainy season was on me there was only one
section of the island left to explore, the biggish knob of high
ground that flanks the southern anchorage to the west, and is
bounded by Haulbowline Head.

It was at the very top of this knob, on the plateau rising
to Spyglass Hill, that the principal object of the search was
hidden and I should have saved myself a deal of trouble if I

hadn't spent so much time in the swamp and the woods.

After the rains had dried up I started again, sometimes combining the search with a hunting expedition, for the goats knew me by this time, and stayed over that side of the island.

If I needed one – and I was using their skins for most everything, my clothes having long since dropped off me and my bedding rotted – I had to resign myself to an hour's stalk and run one down, finishing it off with a club or the mulatto's knife. They were far too spry to let me get within easy musket range, and, anyway, I liked to be sparing with powder, for it now looked to me as if I was going to spend the rest of my life on the island.

Almost the first day of my second search I found the bones of the Dutchman and the English smuggler, lying close together in the grove, right at the foot of the giant tree that marked the principal cache. I must have walked over the treasure to find them and here, it seems, there had been an out and out fight, for both men held drawn cutlasses and about ten yards down the slope I came across an old musket that had been dropped down in the underbrush.

I went at it all ways and finally came to the conclusion that Flint had circled this party after disposing of the others up north, and fired on them from cover as they stood beside the gold.

He had probably discharged the musket, dropped it, and then weighed in with pistols, of which he was never without four.

The men had had time to draw but had been shot down in their tracks long before they could reach their attacker, a little lower down the slope.

The mystery was – what had happened to Nick? Here I was, with five of the party accounted for, but still no sign of the only one I was interested in. Had he been with this couple, or had he been off somewhere on his own? If he had been attacked along with the other two, where was his body? Again, if not one man among the five I'd already found had been able to discharge a firearm (and such it would seem from the fact that three had drawn a cutlass or knife, and the other two carried loaded pistols) how did Flint come by that terrible head wound as finally accounted for him at Savannah?

Thinking don't come easily to me, Jim, but I sat down on that spot and went at it, hour after hour, until my head fairly spun with the effort. I finally concluded that Nick had dashed off while Flint was firing at the others, and maybe come at him later, in another part of the island, probably down nearer the anchorage.

Sitting there in the shade of that giant tree I pictured the dreadful days and nights these two must have spent stalking one another, creeping to and fro in the thickets and starting up at the first crackle of undergrowth in expectation of a sudden crack from the bushes as would settle it one way or the other.

As it turned out I was wrong. Nothing like this had happened, as I was to find out a day or two later.

I had more or less given up the search by then. I had been over almost every inch of the island and not found what I was looking for, neither the treasure nor Nick's bones, and with them any certainty as to how he met his end.

That week, however, I thought I might as well finish the job by combing the lower slopes of the plateau between the tops of Mizzenmast. I went at it lazylike, not expecting to find anything important.

This, as you know, was one of the most pleasant places on the island, covered with scented broom, and pretty, flowering shrubs, and dotted all over with little nutmeg thickets growing under the redwood trees and the whispering pines.

One day, about noon, I sat down in the shelter of a biggish tree to have a bite to eat, and a draught from the gourd I always carried. I had satisfied hunger and thirst, and was leaning back against the bole of the tree when my eye caught something shining within a yard or so of my feet.

I looked at it some time without taking much note. Maybe I judged it was a piece of quartz, or a bead of moisture. Finally, with my curiosity aroused, I got up and went over to discover it was a gilt button. The next instant I'd jumped as though Flint had reared up at me out of the creeper. I was looking down on the clothed skeleton of Nick Allardyce.

I leapt back as if I'd been stung by a rattler, and leaned against the tree, my heart pounding away fit to burst out of my ribs.

There he was, just as you and the others found him, with his long arms stretched above his head like a diver, his feet pointing down to the anchorage, his clasped hands right in line with the plateau where the final struggle had been.

In a second or so it was clear, everything that had happened. He must have been shot dead with the others, and hauled down here by Flint who was just such a man to relish the joke, particularly as he had always hated the surgeon, ever since

they had that quarrel about Flint's defiance of the carousal regulations.

But why? That was what nagged at me. I could understand him doing it, and doing it to Nick, but what purpose was there in a wounded man going to that much labour? And why had he gone to further trouble by lacing the hands, and stretching Nick's arms like a signpost?

Then it came to me, with the word 'signpost', and I reckon the shock was nearly as sharp as the one I got discovering the body. It was in the nature of a signpost that Nick had been used, and his hands now pointed to the spot where the major part of the gold was lying!

My heart, Jim, but there's no cure for gold-fever, not this side of the grave. All that time I'd been looking for Nick's bones, and hoping maybe to pray beside them, and then give them Christian burial as I had the other five, but the knowledge of all that money lying within a few cables' length of me put every other thought clean out of my head, and I went chasing up that woody slope like a goat, never pausing until I was atop of the new dug graves of the Dutchman and the smuggler.

I went down on my hands and knees and sniffed over the ground like a spaniel. When I came to a spot on the edge of the shadow, that looked to me as if it sprouted younger vegetation than that growing around, I began to scrabble with my bare hands until my nails were broken and bleeding, and I was bathed head to foot in sweat under that sweltering sun.

Later I calmed a little and took a rest, judging I should have to go back to the cave for a pick and a shovel, and this I did, crossing the island and returning when the evening chill was beginning to strike into me, but still I wouldn't give up – me, with all the time in the world, I had to start digging that instant, and I didn't pause until I felt the spade strike wood and it was too dark to see what I was at!

Then, and only then, I climbed out and tottered back to my cave, but I couldn't sleep, I was in too much of a sweat that someone might find the hole before I could get to it in the daylight. I reckon as Almighty God put gold in the world in order to discover for Himself what follies men were capable of committing for it. Here was me, more than two years alone on a desert island, yet unable to sleep for fear of having to share six hundred thousand pounds with goats and parrots.

I didn't go out there that day, however, I was too weak and ill. The frenzied digging in that blazing sun, and the chill of the night air striking my overheated body, had set up a fever, and I lay alone in my cave for the best part of a week, too feeble to do more than crawl out and replenish my water gourd, and raving, I don't doubt, about the fortune that was awaiting me on the slopes of Spyglass.

WHEN at last I was able to cross the island, and climb the shoulder of Spyglass, I found what you might expect – the pit was just as I'd left it, with the corner of one case just showing about a fathom below the surface. I was still very weak, but that didn't prevent me from scrambling down and prising off the lid on the instant.

It was just as I'd surmised, the chest contained gold bars, and alongside, when I'd scraped away more soil, was the chest containing the minted coin.

I knelt there in that pit and laughed aloud, Jim. Here was a fortune, as had taken hundreds of men to gather, and of all that crowd only one – a grave-digger's son from far-off Devon – was able to get his hands on it, yet what use was it to me, here on a desert island, where a keg of powder was worth more to a man than all the money in the world?

I suppose you might say this reflection sobered me. It didn't make me think any the less of the gold – all the rest of the time I was marooned there I thought of little else – but at least it made me go about things in a more seamanlike manner, instead of acting, as I had been, like a nigger with a pot of silver dollars.

I sat down before doing any more digging and made a plan, and the first thing that struck me was that I should lose no more time in finding a new hiding-place for the stuff. I told you I'd resigned myself to staying on the island for good, but that doesn't mean I discounted the possibility of having visitors from time to time. Over a hundred men knew there was a fortune buried on Kidd's Island, and sooner or later some of them, Silver and Bones in the lead most probably, would be back to dig for it. If that happened, then I had made up my mind to stay hidden until they sailed off again, with or without the gold, for gold-hungry or no I was still resolved to stay finished with buccaneering. Apart from this I knew the men I had sailed with too well to reckon my life was worth a minute's purchase once they found me cheek by jowl with that much money. Once the gold was raised I knew without a doubt that the killing would start all over again.

By this time I was too familiar with the island to lose sleep over being run to earth on it. Not all the buccaneers in the Main could have laid me by the heels in that place. Meantime, my best lay was to stack the treasure in some place where any map Flint might have drawn up would be useless to whoever had it, and as things turned out I took the best course open to me.

There was another problem as had to be settled right away and that was, how was I to move the chests with but one pair of arms.

I could have inched them out of the pit with a hoisting tackle, rigged from pulleys and cordage I found aboard the French wreck, but even so this wouldn't serve my purpose, for once they were on level ground I had no means of transporting them through the brush, and over the swampy ground to my side of the island.

There was nothing for it, I decided, the boxes would have to be split open where they lay and the blunt shifted bar by bar, and bag by bag, until there was nothing in Flint's pit but broken boxes.

I rigged up a goatskin tent under the big tree and more or less lived on the spot. The truth was, I could hardly bear to be parted from the money. Looking back on the days I'd lived there alone, before I discovered the cache, seemed part of another and free life, but that's the price a man pays for wealth, Jim, whether come by honestly, or the way I'd come by mine. Maybe you've discovered this for yourself by now.

All that spring and early summer I dug gold. I didn't stop to carry any clear away, but lugged it, piece by piece, to a small clearing in the thicket a few hundred yards east of the pit, and only when the last bar was above ground did I load it into some new goatskin sacks I'd prepared and begin taking it over to my cave above Rum Cove.

I found I could carry either two bars, or four bags at a time, and this meant scores of journeys. Many of them were longer than they need have been, for I soon discovered I was beating out a track that led from the edge of the pit to the path leading to my cave, and this was as good as a signpost pointing to the new cache.

On account of this I set about varying my routes, sometimes dropping down south, and crossing the swamp near Southern Anchorage, and sometimes striking north up the cliffs of the Cape of the Woods inlet, and then turning sharp right-handed to approach the cave from the north-east.

Vegetation springs up quickly in that climate and soon enough the beaten track was grown over, and there was a maze of half-concealed footpaths leading all ways from Spyglass shoulder, I reckoned these would pass easily enough as goat tracks.

You might think as the cave I lived in wasn't much of a hiding place, but it was, for all that, and here's something I never told Squire. I had a false wall to that cave, and the treasure was stacked right at the back of it, where it was darkest. I spent whole days piling rocks inside the cavity, and kept a pile of stream-bed clay handy for use as mortar. I could have sealed off that cave in a matter of hours and was, in fact, just about to start on it when I met you ashore that day after the *Hispaniola* dropped anchor. If Silver and his party had gained control nobody would have set eyes on me, much less the treasure, and I reckon there would have been some glum faces among those mutineers when they finally gave up looking for a new cache, or sailed off having decided there was no blunt left on the island.

Well, as I say, before the rains came on again I had it all safe, every last dollar of it, and then I took a long spell of hunting, and laid up my food stocks as were low. During the times I'd been treasure-lifting I hadn't so much as seen a goat and I reckon they was beginning to think I was gone and would soon have returned to their usual pastures.

All this time I hadn't been near Nick's bones, and although I put them out of mind, time and again the thought of them lying out there above ground kept returning to me, whether I liked it or no, so at last I decided to go and take a second look at them and to think about getting them decently buried.

The reason I hadn't been near them was not simply because I was too much occupied with the gold, it was more on account of the strange fact that they frightened me. No other bones ever had, I was a gravedigger born and bred and accustomed, you might say, to bones from babyhood upwards. Besides that, all as I'd seen since I took to buccaneering had made me as callous as a beast in a jungle, and small wonder, seeing as I'd stepped over more dead men than there are pods on a bean-row at gathering time.

But with Nick's pitiful remains it was different. He had been my friend, and the one man I looked to for comfort over the long years of fine weather and foul since we shipped west. He was more than that even, being the last link I had with home and family, and somehow I could never really get it into my head that he was below hatches. I did bring myself to search what remained of the shreds of clothing around him, and took away his buttons, and a few odds and ends as had been in his pockets when he was cut down. Even so, it was more than I could do to bring myself to touch his long bones, and every time I came at them I seemed to see him looking at me, and hear his voice protesting. As I saw it we were two lost souls marooned side by side, and unable to do anything to aid one another. I had gold as was no use to me, and he had death without peace or forgiveness.

I said more than one prayer over him but that didn't seem to alter it much, and finally I thought it might help to set the pair of us at peace if I got the burying over with and put up a proper headstone for him, with his name and age carved on it the proper way.

I would have liked to have added a verse or two of the Bible, as I thought I might remember if I scratched my head hard enough, but this was beyond my powers. Still, I thought, if I set about this job in a Christian manner, and dig a proper grave for him on that side of the island looking down on the Anchorage, then maybe I shall find the strength of purpose to carry him to it, and give him the Christian burial he merited, at least as far as I was concerned. I tried and tried to recall the words of the burial service, as I once knew by heart, but hardly a word of it came back to me and small wonder, as I hadn't thought on it for years. This troubled me no end but I put it by meantime, bending myself to the practical side of the job and hoping the proper words would come back at the moment of committal.

So I went at the task straight off, as soon as I thought of it, and down on the slopes of Mizzenmast I rooted up a flat slab of granite as I thought would serve my purpose.

Nick had taught me to spell out my name, and to letter and figure a little during one of our long spells in Tortuga, and I thought if I tried hard enough I could just about carve his name, and perhaps his age, which was thirty by my reckoning when he was killed.

Of all the tasks I set myself on that island this was the most heartbreaking. I had a hammer made from a stone with a hole in it, and I used a home-made chisel, cut from a rubbed-down cable link, but it was the spelling that fogged me and I was soon looking for my third headstone, having spoiled the first two on the 'K' in 'Nick' (It was you, Jim, as first told me there was a letter 'C' in the spelling of it!)

By the time I'd chipped out those three letters I had long since decided I would have to leave it at that. To spell 'Allardyce' was way beyond my powers, and so was the fashioning of the figure '3', though I had a notion I could have managed the nought.

I dug the grave on a little shelf, about a cable's length from where he lay, and then hauled the big stone, inch by inch, up the long slope from the beach. That part of the job alone cost me near a week's labour.

One might suppose that all that work would have brought me peace of mind for a spell, but it didn't, not so much as a wisp of it.

The grave was there and the headstone, and close by the bones to go under it, but still I couldn't bring myself to finish the work.

I went over to the slope where Nick lay and fell once again to racking my worn-out wits for that burial service, but not one word could I lay hold of, and fit into its proper place, no matter how hard I tried.

Finally, and I recall I was weeping like a child from the fury and disappointment of it, I gave up and turned for home.

I didn't make straight back to the cave. It was mid-afternoon and I had time on my hands, time as I'd rather not spend sitting and brooding, so I took the long way back round the shoulder of Haulbowline Head, and along the tall cliffs where Mizzenmast falls sheer to the rockbound coast.

This stretch of shore had a special attraction for me, largely on account of the steady roar of the breakers immediately below. I've always liked the sound of breakers and sometimes, in this part of the island, it seemed to me that the suck and bellow of the long rollers took on the sound of organ music and choir chant, they were that regular, and awesome.

This particular afternoon they sounded holier than ever, and as I fetched up a point or two below the Cape of the Woods the boom of the tide began to chant like a sevenfold Amen, so clearly, and so unmistakably, that I was brought up short, and let my tools and firelock fall to the ground while I stood listening.

Then the strangest thing happened. From far away, out beyond the horizon it seemed, I heard a gull scream out my name – 'Benn . . . Ben . . . Ben!' three times, and as clear a hail as I ever heard.

I went down on my knees and then on the instant, the chant began, not merely organ chords, and descanting, but actual words, the words of the hundred and fortieth psalm as begins: 'Deliver me O Lord from the evil man, preserve me from the violent man . . . '

Believe me, Jim, it was a wonderful thing to have happened at that moment, and I don't reckon the Almighty could have picked on a more harmonious piece from the Book. That message fitted me skin-tight, and it passed over me like a cooling breeze on an airless day.

Kneeling there on the cliff the words of the hundred and fortieth came back to me clear as clear from the time I was a boy, standing alongside my father in the Sexton's pew near the main door of East Budleigh church, and listening to him trolling out the verses he knew by heart; every word, you might say, had a special bearing on my particular case.

The proud have hid a snare for me and cords, they have spread a net by the wayside, they have set gins for me . . . Let burning coals fall upon them, let them be cast into the fire, into deep pits, that they raise not up again . . . '

It was all there, every last word of it, in the chant of the breakers and as it finished, and I picked up my traps again to turn inland across the island, I felt new life flow back into me, and my steps and bearing were light as a boy's.

It came to me then how near-sighted I'd been to pester myself over Nick's bones when I should have sat quiet and looked for closer communion with his soul, as must have been closer to me on that island than his flesh had been all the time we were together in the past. For I was persuaded, without a doubt, that it was he who had cried out to me through the gull's mouth, and he who had prevailed upon the choir to send me that hundred and fortieth as set me once and for all on the real road home.

Here I was, worrying myself dizzy over graves, and headstones, and committal prayers, on account of a pile of old bones as had no more to do with Nick, as he then was, than an old jacket, worn out and discarded years back. I'd give him burial, I was resolved on that, but the real Nick, the man I'd followed out into this desolate place, the friend who had died in my stead, and given me a second chance to let daylight into my soul, was free now, and had long since squared himself before God, for how else could he have positioned himself to ask for that psalm?

I got home tired but happier than I'd ever been since I was left alone in that place. I had supper and went to bed early, having pleasant dreams of my mother, the first I'd had since setting foot on the island.

I woke up refreshed in body and spirit and went out for a swim as I always took in the Cove at first light when the weather was dry.

Then I fetched up at the cave mouth like a man struck with apoplexy. A full-rigged schooner was cruising slowly down the east coast of the island, right past my front door, so to speak. She was so close in I could see the men aboard her, scurrying to and fro as the captain brought her about to enter the Southern Anchorage.

I was that thunderstruck and dumbfounded I stood there in full view, mouth wide open and knees a-tremble. I tried to cry out but found I couldn't, my tongue seemed stuck to the roof of my mouth, and as I watched the *Hispaniola* passed out of sight beyond the headland, with me still rooted to the spot, and a cloud of birds rose screaming over the woods opposite Skeleton Island as the creak of your tackle, coming clear across the water, told me you were already lowering boats to warp into the channel.

CHAPTER FOUR   THE ROAD HOME

I STILL can't make out how it was you didn't see me from the first.

I stood stock still in the cave mouth, and anyone sailing close up along the eastern coast could spot the cave – that was partly why I chose it for quarters. I reckon you were all too much occupied, the captain's party with their desperate situation, and the mutineers with the thought of all those riches as they felt sure lay waiting ashore for them. At all events you didn't, and soon as I recovered from the shock I nipped back into the cave, and sat down to think what I should do for the best.

You see, Jim, I made sure you were pirates. You were flying the Union Jack, of course, but to a man who has sailed along of buccaneers, flags don't mean very much. They use any flag as comes handy, or the one as suits their purpose at any particular time, and as for the rig of the schooner, well, pirates use any vessel they happen to board if their own is in bad shape, and pirates were about all I was expecting since I'd stumbled on the treasure.

After I'd calmed down my courage began to flow back. After all, I had the gold safe, and the means to wall it up. It was lucky for me, I thought, that the schooner didn't arrive a month or two earlier, when I was camping on the far side of the island, and shifting the bullion, or carving the headstone. If that had happened I might have been caught napping, and lost my freedom of movement to and fro.

As it was, I knew none of you were ashore, or likely to be

171

until afternoon with the tide running the way it was, and this being so I loaded up with musket, powder and shot and thought I'd take a good look around before I set about walling up the blunt. There was no sense in going to all that labour if it wasn't necessary – you might have been merely watering, down at the Southern Anchorage.

I skipped out and stayed close to cover. I was accustomed to this on account of the goat-stalking, and I reckoned there was no one could do it better. I moved down the eastern shore and took station in the brush, between the stockade and the anchorage. There was a monstrous tall pine near the water's edge and I climbed it; from the crow's nest I had a good, though distant, view of the schooner being towed in to its moorings opposite.

I stayed up that tree all morning, and only shinned down when I saw the two boat parties pulling for the tidemark. Then I crawled closer in, trusting the thick foliage, and to my knowledge of the runs through it, to stay out of sight when the men came ashore.

The first thing I remarked on was your jump from the bows of the leading boat, and quick disappearance inland. I put that down to boyish excitement, and forgot all about you, for as the men of the leading boat spilled out I got the second big shock of the day. One of the first men ashore was Job Anderson, whom I recognised in a flash, although he was a lot thicker round the middle than when I had last seen him in Savannah.

That was enough for me, I doubled back inland on all fours, without waiting for the second boat to pull in. If I hadn't been in such a hurry I should have seen Silver then, an hour or so before I was able to get true bearings by talking to you up by the gravel slide.

The sight of Anderson convinced me I was right about the ship's purpose offshore. Anderson was a dyed-in-the-wool buccaneer, and never did an honest day's sea-toil in his life. I hadn't recognised anyone else in the first boat, but Anderson was plenty enough for one shipment, and I was sure then that the schooner had put in for the treasure and nothing else.

I guessed the party would come inshore by the river line, for the going was much easier along the channel, and the underbrush, on each side, gave me plenty of chance to keep out of sight.

Silver, as you know, took that poor seaman Tom off on his own, to a tract higher up and nearer the coast, but the main party did just what I thought they would do, that is, wade up the channel towards the centre of the island, and I kept close watch on them from the thick foliage on the west.

It was thiswise I saw Anderson murder the last but one of the loyal men, the one you knew as Alan, and it was a little before Silver, maybe a quarter-mile off, settled with the other one, Tom, as you witnessed.

From where I was situated, about fifty yards or more west of the group, I recognised another old shipmate, the carpenter Tom Morgan, who had been the other survivor of Silver's crew, when they were adrift in the ocean the time the *Walrus* took them aboard and started all the trouble.

I was surprised to see he was still alive, for he was middle-aged when I first came up with him, and he didn't look much different, I thought. George Merry, who I would also have recognised, of course, was still aboard that afternoon, being one of those five who turned the gun on the Captain's party when it was pulling for the stockade. I saw him later and he was changed a lot, being broad and fully-grown by that time, and that much deeper in villainy.

As I watched, the party – there were nine of them in all – stopped at a little clearing where the river widened. Anderson seemed to be in command for he sang out:

'This is as good a place as any and it's time each of us knew where he stood, mates!'

Most of the others murmured agreement, but there was one, the seaman Alan, who hung back, and seemed mighty put out about something.

'Lookee here, Job,' he said, stopping beside one of the live oaks as had its roots in the stream, 'it's high time you played square, and come out on deck as it were. What's at the back of this whispering and shilly-shallying? Do you mean to desert ship? Do you reckon as to get the whole ship's company stranded in this lonesome spot on account o' Cap'n Smollett hazing those backward in dooty? I want the truth, Job, and you'd best give it me, here and now, or I don't budge another step!'

Anderson looked at him, kind of sneeringly, with his eyes screwed up against the sun.

'Alan,' he said, 'you've asked for the truth and you'll have it, nothing less. We're here for treasure, and we don't go 'till we get it, as John's told you plain enough a'ready or I'm much mistook!'

'Well,' says Alan, 'that's common knowledge aboard. We've

known that, the lowest among us, since we shipped out of Bristol, but how's defying the Cap'n going to increase our shares, that's what I'd like to know?'

Morgan laughed outright at this.

'Why, you blamed fool,' he says, 'we mean to have the whole of it! Who's resting content with the two-hundred or so hush money that blubberly Squire is likely to dole out to us? Not me for one, nor John either if I know him!'

This must have been the first hint that the poor devil had of the real character of messmates he'd been berthing alongside. Horror and surprise showed all over his stupid face.

'You mean you're aiming to go for 'em?' he gasped out, 'go for 'em and snatch the whole of it?'

'Aye,' said Anderson, 'that's about it, Alan, and you can make your choice here and now, are you standing with them or with us?'

His only course at that moment was to pretend he was joining them but he was like the one you saw murdered, Jim, not very quick at making decisions, or playing along with scoundrels like Job and Tom Morgan. He looked from one to the other with his mouth agape and then, without a split second's hesitation, he turned and ran for it, back towards the boats.

Morgan must have been half-expecting this, for he let out a shout as did Anderson, and stuck his foot out just in time to send Alan sprawling into the bushes. The next instant Job was on top of him, and the man's death-yell, as you heard clearly from higher upstream, rang through the woods.

When Anderson stood up he was wiping a long dirk and Alan was dead, stabbed to the heart. As for me, I was snaking back out of it, as fast as I could scramble, and intending to make straight for the cave and seal off that treasure. I had a goodish idea by that time what was happening aboard the *Hispaniola*.

It must have been less than ten minutes later when I first spotted you and I'll own it, you puzzled me for a spell, for I couldn't settle my mind whether you was one of the pirates, acting as a scout, or was being hunted down by them to share the fate of the man I'd seen Anderson murder.

In any case, you were making straight for my cave, though you didn't know it, and I had to head you off, even if it meant being seen by you.

I had a good look at you from the gravel pit and it was then I decided you were a fugitive and so might prove an ally, so I stepped right out and made myself known to you, and mighty surprised you looked, Jim, if you don't mind my saying so, and that drawn about the face, and a-trembling in the hand, that the pistol you had would have been no more use to you than a hoopstick.

It was fortunate for all of us that you saw fit to tell me the whole story, and give me a chance to get things straight and make up my mind on the spot to part with the bulk of the treasure in exchange for a passage home, and a fresh start ashore.

I took to you from the first, Jim, on account of you being so frank and friendly-like, though I couldn't help thinking that, to judge by the wary look in your eye, you reckoned you was dealing with a crazy man, and maybe you were, after a fashion, for you were the first human I'd talked with since the captain of the *Swallow* left me to my fate on the shore of the Anchorage. I reckon my tongue was as rusty as a slipped anchor chain.

Howsoever, my head was clear enough by the time you'd done talking, and I learned as Silver was in command. I knew then as we should have a fight for it and I was relieved to hear that your party had the chart, and would keep Silver dancing round you 'till he got it and set out looking for pig-nuts.

When I saw the Union Jack float out from the blockhouse I knew Silver had his work cut out, and that made me kind of comfortable, for it also meant he wouldn't be likely to stray over to my side of the island. The minute the cannonade began, and we ran for cover in different directions, I moved higher up the coast, then settled down to watch points from the brush above the white rock where my boat was hid. Taken all round I was feeling pretty satisfied with the events of the day and, knowing all I did, I had more cause than you to look comfortably at the future.

From now on, Jim, I'll tell my story from my own point of view. You've set down your side of it pretty shipshape, but there are stray ends as you must still be curious about, and I'll try and remember everything that happened between the minute we parted and the time I stepped out from the ambush alongside the treasure pit, and saved you and that one-legged seathief from being carved up by Merry and his mates.

I reckoned my best lay was to keep hidden, watch over the counsels of the mutineers, and maybe pick off one or two if I got the chance, without letting them know I was loose on the island.

First I did a bit of figuring, putting two and two together, as it were, and matching the result with what you'd told me.

The first thing I studied was the strength of the two parties. Nineteen against six you had said, not counting yourself. Abe Gray had gone over to you and two others were already dead, leaving sixteen. Another had been shot outside the stockade that night, leaving nine ashore and six afloat.

One of those afloat, you recall, was mortally wounded by the Squire's shot, fired from the jolly-boat, but neither you nor I knew this at the time, and I had to reckon on fifteen to six and a boy from then on.

I knew about the one killed in the stockade skirmish, for I saw, a few minutes before sunset, two mutineers come out of the trees, and drag his body clear. They did this not out of a desire to get him decently buried but because they needed his powder and shot. When he'd been rifled they left him to the carrion-birds, who were mighty well fed on that island during the next few days.

When night fell I was able to creep in close and watch the carousal of the mutineers round their camp-fire in the swamp. It was there, in the flickering firelight, that I saw Silver again, and with him Blackbeard's old gunner, Israel Hands, as lean and surly as ever. The last time I'd seen Barbecue, remember, was at Savannah, when he was shorn of his leg, and running a high fever in his hammock. Well, here he was, as lively as ever and I couldn't but be astonished at his nimbleness as he hopped to and fro round the fire. He was even doing the cooking for the able-bodied and was seemingly quite his old self in cheerfulness and patter. The gunner's team had come ashore by then, and your party was slow in not sallying out, and making an attempt to recapture the schooner, for there was no one aboard her that night. I toyed with the idea of paddling out myself but I thought better of it, reasoning that I alone couldn't handle her, even if I did manage to cut her loose without being seen. Besides, I knew the ebb scour in the Anchorage a deal better than you did, and that ship was my one chance to get out of my situation with clean hands. I didn't want anything to happen to it.

The pirates had brought rum ashore and, as you'd expect, before midnight Silver was the only sober man round the fire. They made such an uproar singing and shouting and quarrelling among themselves that I couldn't overhear any discussion of their plans. Finally they rolled themselves in their blankets and slept like hogs, without so much as posting a sentry, and if your party had crept up on them then you could have killed more than half at a blow, and put the others to flight.

However, it looked to me as if you were sticking close to your blockhouse, so I thought it was time I took a hand. I had with me a knotty club as I used to stun goats, and with this handy I crept into the circle, an inch at a time, till I fetched up alongside a snoring buccaneer and handed him a crack as I knew would put paid to him.

The next second I was out of it, just as Silver started up with an oath, and his parrot began squawking blue murder. None of them so much as saw who was attacking them, least of all the man I accounted for, and I won free and slipped back up the coast to my cave, pleased enough with the day's happenings, and reckoning the odds were now a little more even in your favour.

I was dog-tired when I reached home but too confident of the outcome of the struggle to waste what little of the night remained in walling up gold. Silver and party I wasn't afraid of, now that I'd had a crack at them, and your party I knew would play fair with me, once I could come to terms with them. All in all it was the most satisfactory day I'd had since I struck the treasure.

CHAPTER FIVE   THE ROAD HOME

THE next morning I was up at sunrise, and after a hurried breakfast, and a cooling wash in the Cove, I took musket, ammunition and club and went down to reconnoitre the mutineers' camp.

This time I got in close enough to overhear something of what was being said. I counted the group, just to make sure none would surprise me from behind, and everyone was all present, including the dead one I'd brained in the night.

When I arrived they had just finished breakfasting off the stores they salvaged from the jolly-boat and were already lapping at the brandy-keg, whipping up their courage as had been badly tested by my night attack.

Silver, it seems, was already having trouble with some of the older men, notably Anderson, Hands and George Merry. These three were talking as if they were already dissatisfied with the way things were going, and they were blackguarding Silver for bad leadership, and even threatening him with the black spot.

Silver, however, was getting the best of it, for he was a sea-mile ahead of that precious trio when it came to fighting, or talking, and he still held the confidence of the others, who ranged themselves alongside him and back-answered the mutineers.

'I tell you,' Silver was saying, 'we'll get a sight more by

treaty at this stage than ever we can hope for by running in under their fire! Them as can't see that is fools who deserve to have holes drilled in their thick skulls! Here they are, snug behind cover, a score of muskets between them, and men enough to load while the good shots is picking us off. "Rush 'em!" – that's Job's notion, and right he may be when he says we'll have settled with em before they've winged more than half of us. Well, mates, have it that way if you've a mind to. If some of us have got to go, then there's more left for those who come out of it, and that's one way of looking at it. Here's another, however, suppose the attack don't succeed, suppose that blamed Squire, as could shoot Dirk through the head from a rocking boat yesterday, takes three or four more shots at us before we come up with 'em, and the Doctor, and Cap'n, and that Abe Gray, as I mean to spit and roast before the week's out, suppose between 'em they shoot down six of us, as is likely, mind you, before we get to grips with 'em? Ah, then it's a more even toss isn't it, them against us, whereas now we outnumber 'em more than two to one, and should make good use of it or I'm no sort of a general! Suppose some of you is only wounded, how do you reckon you'll attend to your wounds, and check mortification in this pesky climate while the others is off digging for treasure? Is that swab of a doctor coming down with his ointments? Is that what you're counting on? Now you listen to me, every blamed one of you, since I was elected cap'n o' this here crew, and have yet to be deposed according to rules. My lay is to get hands on that chart, first and foremost, and as for what happens after, that can take care of itself and you can trust me to leave none of 'em above ground when the time comes, and we got the dollars aboard.'

This speech had a notable effect on the main body and, although it far from convinced the grumblers, they saw the majority was against them and gave in. Silver was to be allowed to carry his flag of truce up to the blockhouse, and to promise the captain's party their lives in exchange for the chart. If this failed the stockade was to be stormed within the hour.

The mutineers' camp was well situated from my point of view. They had made their fire in a dell, overlooked by a long, wooded ridge, with thick undergrowth growing right to the edge of a little escarpment. In these bushes I was snug enough and mostly within earshot, particularly when they raised their voices. I could come and go as I wished, just so long as I moved stealthily and, as I said, I was well used to this sort of thing having depended on stalking for food over a period of three years or more.

The pirates crowded to the fringe of the woods to watch Silver and I stayed where I was, expecting them back before long. Sure enough, in less than an hour, back they came, and this time it was Silver who was doing the raving. In all the time I knew him I never saw him in such a rage, and you can be sure that Israel and the other two didn't help him to cool down, but kept telling him it was just what they'd expected and he should have taken account of them in the first place.

My word, Jim, but there was a bustling to and fro as they got ready to attack, so much so that I could hear practically nothing of their plans but was driven to guessing from their scurrying round how they aimed to go about staving in the blockhouse, and putting everyone in it to the sword.

It was fortunate for you Silver was in such a rip-roaring rage. If he hadn't been he would have sat down and thought out something more sensible than a frontal attack on a fortified post. As it was he was in such a hurry to be at your party's throats that he never so much as thought of using a mine, such as we'd used at Santalena, and which Israel could have made in a matter of hours. With a bucket of powder and ballast iron they could have blown a gap in the stockade large enough to let everyone into the enclosure in a body. Furthermore, Israel could have made up a few fire-baskets, such as we had used time and again on the Main, and if but one of these had landed on the blockhouse roof it would have gone up like tinder, and your people would have been smoked out in no time, and shot down like partridges from the woods.

All that Silver did remember from his drill book was to give plenty of covering fire, but even then he spread his thin forces on too wide a front, having men stationed on all sides of the blockhouse. This, however, made things difficult for me, as I had some hopes of taking them in the rear while they were fully occupied with you. With men coming and going it was difficult to position myself without being spotted.

I finally worked round to the west side and took up position but a minute or two before the attack opened. There was only one man there, a mere boy, and him I could have shot dead if I had reckoned him worth it. As it was I was after one of the boarders, for this, I reckoned, would serve the double purpose of weakening the attack, and concealing my presence from the mutineers, who would be certain to think my target had been hit by a ball from the house.

I barely had time to find a hole in the undergrowth to poke my musket through when a party of seven men stormed out of the trees from the north side, and made straight for the fence.

I aimed at the nearest, a lean fellow naked to the waist, and I bowled him over just as one of your party killed the man alongside him.

It was a snap shot on my part, and I only wounded him, for he was on his feet again in a second and back in the woods. I was disappointed, having no time to reload and fire again, but I reckon my shot served its purpose, having reduced the number of men who did make a footing inside the enclosure to five. In skirmishes like this an odd blade can often turn the balance between victory and defeat.

Your people made short work of the five who did get aboard, and even while I was ramming home a second charge out came the last of them, running like a hare, and I soon saw it was all over, and the pirates had bitten off a sight more than they could chew.

Israel ran forward into the open, cursing and shouting at them to make a second try, but he was the only one who showed any more fight that day, the others just piled back into the woods and gathered to take stock of themselves round the fire.

The youngster near me – young Dick as we marooned, it must have been – joined in the general panic, and ran past within yards of me, sobbing and carrying on in a frenzy of fear and disappointment. He was new to it, I reckon, and was beginning to wonder if he had picked the wrong side. I had a mind to shoot him then and there but somehow I thought better of it; looking back I'm glad I hung fire, for Dick had his punishment ahead of him.

It was some time before I could work my way back to my vantage point above the camp fire and when I did I saw that the mutineers were sadly reduced in numbers. There was a mere eight of them and one, the man I'd winged, was out of action with a head wound as had come within a hairsbreadth of splitting his skull.

I never saw such a dispirited lot. They went for the rum bottle there and then and sat around, bewailing their luck, like a crowd of boys cheated of rifling a hen-roost, and nursing the welts the farmer had given them into the bargain.

I had a real good look at them this time. There was Silver,

his face like a thundercloud; Israel, already half gone in liquor; a big red-capped Irisher, the one Hands knifed aboard the schooner, and you tossed to the sharks as was all his carcase was fit for; the scared boy Dick, who ran past me in the woods; old Tom Morgan, glum and cast-down; George Merry explaining over and over again why the attack would have succeeded if Silver had given an ear to his plan of campaign; the man with the head wound trying to bandage himself, and not succeeding very well, and two others, one middle-aged and grizzled, and the other a red-headed deckhand Silver had talked into treachery – altogether about as good-for-nothing a crew as ever I clapped eyes on, and not worth two pennyworth of cold gin, neither as seamen nor true gentlemen o' fortune.

It came into my head then to shoot Silver and be done with it. I could easily have downed him from where I crouched, and I went so far as to draw a bead on him. Then the thought came into my head that if I did the most likely course the rest of them would follow would be to sail off with the schooner, and maroon the whole boiling of us. That didn't suit my book any more than it would have suited yours, so I thought I would leave them be for a spell, and snake round to see how your party was getting along, and maybe pay you a friendly call if I could get over the stockade without being shot at as a buccaneer.

Well, I made a wide circuit, and came at the blockhouse from the west. Just as I was casting round for something to use as a flag of truce out comes the Doctor, cool as a Cuban melon, and armed to the teeth. I said to myself: 'Ben, here's another embassy, and one as looks a good deal more promising than the last!' and I watched him tramp into the woods to the north-east.

The moment I saw the way he was heading I knew he was out looking for me, and a rank piece of foolishness it was, as I told him many a time since, for if any of the pirates had spotted him he would have been shot down in his tracks from the brush, and not one of you inside a penny the wiser!

He made clean away across the island, however, and I dogged him, flitting from tree to tree, the way I shadowed you the afternoon before. When I judged we were far enough from the camp I hailed him and he stopped, looking this way and that. Even then he didn't see me, for my goatskins matched up with the landscape and were a great help to a man set on stalking.

He unslung a musket and stood, legs apart, in a little clearing.

'Doctor,' I sang out, for I judged it was him, you having told me the Squire and the Captain were all of six feet, 'you stand where you are, and we'll come to terms from a distance!'

He laughed at that and clapped his firelock on his shoulder.

'Jim told us about you, Ben Gunn,' he calls back, 'and you've nothing to fear from any one of us. Why, man, I'm risking my life to step out and talk to you like this!'

It was true enough, so I stepped out of the trees and told him to follow me across the marsh to my cave.

He did as I bid and along we went in Indian file, until we climbed Two-pointed Hill and fetched up in the cave.

I judged he would be bowled over when he saw the amount of coin and bullion I had stacked there, but he wasn't. He was always a cool one was Doctor and seemed to expect nothing else.

'Well, Ben,' he said, when we had examined the treasure, and taken a seat at the cave mouth, 'it seems as you got there ahead of us and it'll suit the two of us to make treaty. What do you say to a passage home, no questions asked, and a thousand pounds at the end of it?'

It was a good deal more than I'd hoped for. Maybe a thousand out of all that money might seem little enough to a man who had the whole of it under his hand, so to speak, but it was no use to me where it lay, and I was willing to trade every last dollar of it for a clean break with the past, and a chance to see home again.

We made our bargain there and then, and fell to talking what course we'd best take with the remaining mutineers. At first he tried to persuade me to load up with goat's flesh, and sign articles with the captain in the stockade, but I soon talked him out of that, pointing out that I was more use to the loyal party loose on the island, and I would be serving them better by getting them clear than by watching a loophole in case Silver attacked again.

Our chief anxiety at that time was the ship. Doctor Livesey told me that a consort would show up in time, but I didn't have as much faith in the consort as I had in a vessel I could see close-reefed in Southern Anchorage, and I was in a fever to feel her decks under my feet, and the wind in my face as we shook out for home.

I didn't tell him much about my life on the Main but passed it over by saying I'd been pressed aboard Flint's ship whilst serving as a servant to Nick on an out-bound schooner. Later on, when I knew him better, I told him the facts about the

Custer murder and he said he'd go bail for me when we fetched up in Devon and I've no doubt he would have done too had it been necessary. That, however, was before we found out about Nick's confession, as cleared me of the whole unlucky business.

Well, the upshot of that talk was that I undertook to hail the blockhouse night and morning, and give the captain's party full details of what Silver and his men were up to, and with this settled I escorted him as far as the stockade, and after a last look at the buccaneers, six of whom were ashore and singing round the fire, I slipped off up the coast to the cave. It looked to me as things were shaping very well.

At first light that third day I went out to watch the camp, at least, I had every intention of so doing, and was making my way over the cliff top above White Rock, when I happened to glance over towards the Anchorage, and found the ship gone.

I tell you, Jim, I sat down there and wept like a baby, and fell to cursing myself for not keeping a closer watch on the defeated mutineers, and raising the alarm the minute I saw them shaking out sail, for I naturally judged it was Silver who had gone off with her.

When I got my breath back I thought I'd take a quick look at the camp, and then carry the black news to the blockhouse. You can judge my surprise then when, on slipping along the escarpment, I found myself looking down on a group of men as dumbfounded and castdown as myself. Silver and his crew had discovered their loss about the same time as me, and all six of them were cursing up and down the swamp fit to shame the devil.

I thought at the time the schooner must have dragged her anchor, and drifted out with the ebb though how, in those moorings, I couldn't imagine. I didn't waste any more time with the buccaneers but went out through the wood and hailed the blockhouse.

I found the Captain's party had something else to worry about.

'Young Jim's gone,' said the Doctor, straight off, 'been gone since yesterday afternoon, and no sign of him!'

They did you the credit, Jim, of allowing you had gone off on fresh mischief, and not to join up with Silver, but what with one thing and another, we reckoned your chances of seeing the next day's sunrise were about as slim as could be, and the Squire fell to blaming himself for ever bringing a boy of your age on such a wild-goose chase in the first place. He told the Captain as how he could never face your mother, and tell her the rights of things. I felt right down sorry for him, for he was wretched enough on account of the three servants he'd lost in the siege, and was already faced with the news of telling their wives they were widows.

The fact of the matter was the whole lot of us were in a dreadful fix, Squire, Doctor, Silver, and all. It never occurred to any one of us that the ship could be safe somewhere. She was clean gone, and that was the end of it.

Presently, however, the Captain pipes up. He was weak, and in some pain from the two wounds he'd got during the attack, but he still had more common sense than the rest of us put together, and he pointed out that the loss of the ship called for a change of plans regarding our present quarters. With Silver at large on the island, he said, it was of prime importance to set a guard on the treasure but the problem was, of course, how to leave the blockhouse, and get ourselves settled in the cave?

It was plain as the Captain couldn't set foot to ground, and would have to be carried. If two men were saddled with this job it left but the two remaining to fight their way to the cave. We were stuck fast on this reef when the Doctor reminded us of our best card – the old and now quite useless chart. He asked me if I reckoned Silver would barter a two-hour truce for that map, and if so he would, could he be trusted to keep the terms?

This was a ticklish question. I said John would certainly promise anything to lay hands on that scrap of paper, but as to being trusted, I wouldn't trust his oath pledged on a pile of Bibles higher than Spyglass. Abe Gray, who heard me say it, growled hearty agreement.

'There's a little more to it than that,' says the Captain, 'for once he gets the chart his only chance is to set off after the gold, and if I know that precious crew they won't waste a minute shouldering picks and spades to do it! If they were once safe over Spyglass shoulder, then I've a notion we could get as far as the cave unhindered.'

There was good sense in that, and after talking it over, we all agreed it was our best chance. It turned out, of course, that we were wrong in a sense, for Silver never let on he had the chart for at least another twelve hours, and then only when his situation, along with yours, Jim, was about desperate. However, the ruse served to get us safe out of the blockhouse, and alongside the treasure, so it was a good idea for all that, and after giving me time to get into position, and watch points from the escarpment, out goes Doctor and Gray with a flag of truce to set about making a bargain with the mutineers.

I had orders to fire into the mob the moment I saw any one of them make a treacherous move, but they were so cast down about the loss of the schooner, that Silver had little or no difficulty in persuading them to allow him to talk terms.

Under the agreement the mutineers were to get the Doctor's services, the blockhouse stores, of which they were already in sore need, together with the chart, whereas we were to gain nothing but a free passage over to the north of the island.

Silver and Doctor did their parlying out of earshot of the other five, and even Gray stood well back, although both parties kept arms in their hands, and eyed one another like gamecocks while the wagers were being laid by their owners.

As soon as the Doctor disappeared into the woods, and Silver had hopped back to the camp fire, he was surrounded by the men who demanded to know what they were gaining by such an arrangement.

'Meat and drink, such as none of us can do without, not even you, George Merry,' he announced pretty shortly. 'With the ship gone how do you reckon we're going to keep going at all? Can any one of you lubbers answer me that?'

'They're snug enough there, what makes 'em want to come out?' asked Morgan.

'North of the island,' chimes in Merry, before Silver could reply, 'how come they want to go north of the island? Mebbe that's where the treasure's hid, and they aim to keep us occupied with a barrel o' pork while they go after it?'

Silver looked at him slantwise, the way I'd seen him look at men before when he was itching to kill them for crossing him.

'George,' he said slowly, 'maybe you've got a better plan. If so, then out with it, and we'll study it, as men in our situation is bound to or starve to death around this here camp-fire!'

'We can go for 'em on the march,' says George, 'and finish with every last one of 'em. That way we'll have treasure, pork, brandy and blockhouse all in one, or I'm no gentleman o' fortune, nor never was!'

'True,' said Silver, still keeping his voice low, 'you never was, and you ain't now, or you wouldn't come out with a blamed silly scheme as would do credit to a chuckle-headed nigger knocked on the cranium as a babby! Listen to me, you lumbering baboon,' he went on, raising his voice high enough to set the birds squawking above the pines, 'how do we know as the Doctor don't know where the ship is, and how soon that rum-soaked Hands, and the Irisher with him, has arranged with the Captain to sail back and take 'em off, treasure and all? For mark you, that's what's happened, and that's what they're a'planning to do, and our sole hope lies in keeping a gauge on 'em until Hands has sailed back again, and reported for dooty at the rendezvous as they've agreed on! Kill 'em you say, and if you do we're sunk, the lot of us, for Hands won't get the all-clear signal that brings him in, and we won't get the treasure nor a passage to a place where we can spend it! That's all I'm saying for now because I'm fair sick of reasoning with you, the same as I wore out my tongue a' reasoning with Anderson, who's dead, burn him, and Hands, who's turned traitor, and left us in such a fix!'

This said, Silver flung himself round and began loading himself with arms, preparatory to marching up to the blockhouse, his great back a study of disgust, you might say, on account of finding himself in harness with such a company of dolts.

Placed as I was, almost on top of them, I had hard work to keep from laughing at the expressions of the five other men around the fire.

George said nothing in reply – there was nothing he could say – but after a long silence, during which all were digesting what Silver had said, Morgan spoke up boldly.

'Well, John,' he said, taking his pipe out of his mouth and spitting into the fire, 'I reckon you got it about right, and me for one'll stand by you as being the longest-headed among us!'

There was a murmur of agreement from the other four and it was plain Silver had carried the day once more. The very fact that he had never so much as told them he had the chart in his pocket made me more certain than ever that it was all up with the mutineers and that, from now on, Silver would prove more of an ally than an enemy to the rest of us ashore.

As for Hands, and Silver's reference to the gunner and a rendezvous, I couldn't imagine how John had gammoned them that far, for what chance had any of the Captain's party been given of getting aboard the schooner during the night, and talking the gunner into such a fantastic arrangement?

Still, they swallowed it, trusting so little among themselves, I suppose, that it was easy for them to imagine two of their number had turned backs on their shipmates. With a broadside of oaths in the general direction they supposed the schooner to have sailed, they picked up their weapons, and such truck as they had about them, and moved off sullenly enough through the woods towards the stockade.

I followed them at a safe distance and, after seeing them enter, slipped off across the island to overtake the Squire's party that was now making slow progress through the swamp in the general direction of my cave.

We had the Devil's own job to get through those thickets, with two of us guarding the flank, and the other two carrying captain in a sort of litter-chair Abe Gray had rigged up.

The flies tormented us every step of the way and the ground was often so soft that we often sank into it shin deep. All the time we half-expected Silver and his crew to fall on us, cutlass in hand, and a sorry fight we should have made of it in those circumstances.

However, we got there without incident, and I made them as comfortable as I could in the cave, bedding down the captain on a thick pile of goatskins, and laying up water supplies in case of a second siege.

We speculated a good deal that day, Jim, as to what had become of you, and towards later afternoon, when we might have seen the *Hispaniola* come sailing into North Inlet, with you at the helm, and Hands balancing his dirk to put paid to you the moment you beached, the Doctor, Gray and me were all down in the thickets at the foot of the Two-pointed hill, waiting and watching against a surprise attack by Silver.

Only the Squire was up in the cave with the captain and he must have been inside making him comfortable when you coasted up the little bit of Inlet as can be glimpsed from my quarters.

Soon as it was dark the Doctor and Gray went back up the hill, and I went over to see what the pirates were doing. I saw them through a chink in the palisade, sitting round the fire, singing and three-parts gone on the brandy you'd left them.

I saw we had nothing to worry about from them for the night, and went home before moonrise. Another half-hour mayt e and I would have heard you coming through the woods, and stopped you from walking slap into them the way you did after settling Hands' hash, and crossing the island.

Well, as soon as the sun rose off goes the Doctor to tend the sick, as by arrangement, and two hours later, sweating like a pig from crossing the swamp at the double, back he comes gasping out the news that you were a prisoner in the mutineers' hands, and that your life wouldn't be worth a clipped groat after they'd stumbled on that empty treasure-pit.

There was only one thing for it, to get there first and lay up an ambush, and we set out on the instant, the Doctor, Abe Gray and me, and moved as fast as ever we were able along one of the tracks I'd beaten out when I was crossing and recrossing the island with the gold.

Fast as we moved, though, it wasn't fast enough. I was well accustomed to the ground, and could have got there soon enough, but the Doctor, who had already covered ten to twelve miles that morning, was soon lagging behind, and Abe Gray, who had been on shipboard for weeks, and was flabby about the calves, wasn't in much better case. We soon saw that I should have to go ahead, and do what I could on my own.

I gave the Doctor careful directions as to where the pit was and ran on, looking to my priming as I trotted, and when I finally gained the breast of the long slope that leads up to the big tree I spotted you all, gathered round the bones of poor Nick, and doubtless speculating on them. You didn't cross my headstone in your line of march, the grave I had dug being too far to the east.

I had to think of something to keep you down there for a spell, so as to give the Doctor and Gray time to come up and get hidden. It was then I had the notion to play Flint, and sing out like his spirit pleading for rum, the way I heard him call McGraw oftentimes back in Savannah, years before.

It was a good job for you that sailormen, even the worst of them, are superstitious souls, Jim. I reckon that first hail of mine gave every man jack of them the gallows' shakes, and set their teeth rattling in their heads like Spanish castanets.

Anyway, the ruse served its purpose, and they hung back long enough to give Doctor and Gray time to come up, and we settled down to wait in the thicket, about half a musket-shot from the pit.

It was interesting to study their expressions, Silver's particularly, when they came running, and found nothing but one guinea, my broken pick-shaft, and the old packing cases. I reckon George Merry nearly choked with the disappointment of it all, and if my first shot hadn't brought him down he would have buried his knife twenty times in the first carcase as presented itself, be it yours or Silver's.

190

The doctor was still so breathless with his run that he missed, even at that range, and it was Abe's shot that finished off the wounded man with the bandage, as I'd come near killing in the attack two days before.

Well, I reckon you know the rest of it, Jim, leastways the greatest part of it, but you've yet to hear how I saved the lot of you once again by getting rid of Silver on the voyage home.

You may not believe it, Jim, but that was about the best turn I ever did your party. Long John was that wily, and smooth-tongued, as I could see he would have won the confidence of every man aboard long before we sighted the Bristol Channel and got all that treasure unshipped. Once he'd succeeded in doing that, it was watch out for fresh squalls.

Me he couldn't fool, not any longer, and that because I reckon I'd known him too long, and seen too much. You could have put him in irons if I'd have warned you he was plotting fresh mischief, but he'd have slipped out of them somehow, and bested you one way or the other. There was only two ways to thwart him. One was to kill him in cold blood, as I knew neither one of you would agree to, and the other was to connive at his getting ashore on the Main which I did, and have never been sorry for.

How was it done? Well, I'll tell you, and that'll about finish the yarn as you've promised to keep to yourself until I'm adrift on wider seas, and sore in need of a pilot.

CHAPTER SIX

THE circumstances as kept me on the jump during the early part of that homeward journey, Jim, was the fact that Long John was allowed the freedom of the ship.

I admit we were shorthanded, and that a mere seven, one of them a boy, was called upon to do the work of two dozen or more, still – it was flying in the face of a Providence that had been uncommon merciful to every mother's son of us, and when I saw old John, propped up against his galley, and a-whistling away as if he hadn't a care in the world, I set myself to keep an eye cocked for all our sakes.

It was as well I did, for it was asking a deal of John to expect him to sail home to a hairsbreadth escape from the gibbet, when there was close on six hundred thousand Jimmy o' Goblins under hatches.

I knew it wouldn't be long before he fell to sounding me and I was right, for it happened the third day out, when I was fetching pots from the cabin aft into his galley for scouring.

'Ben,' he says to me in the voice of a mating dove, 'Ben, me old shipmate, and how much is this here Cap'n Smollett settling on you out of all that gold you digged up from Flint's cache? Five thousand would you say, or ten mebbe?'

I told him our articles called for a thousand pounds and a free passage home.

He sucked in his cheeks at that, and made clicking noises with his tongue.

'Well, now,' he says, 'that's not what you might call fair and above board, is it, not seeing as you're working your passage home, same as the rest of us, and have been the means of pouring all that blunt into the Squire's lap? A thousand, you say? Why, it ain't even a hundredth part of the treasure to my figuring, Ben!'

'John,' I told him, 'I long since made up my mind that a guinea honestly come by is worth a thousand snatched from the steps as leads down to Execution Dock!'

'And right you are, Ben, right you are,' murmured the old rogue, 'as is crystal clear to anyone in my situation! Still, there's those as would reckon you did come by this honestly, for it was you as found it, and transported it, and you who fouled them bad men at every bend in the channel!'

From the moment of rejoining the Captain's party, Silver had referred to his former messmates in terms of the strictest censure, forgetting, it seemed, that it was him, and him alone, who had led the greater part of them into mutiny. If you could forget the villainy of the man for a spell his attitude was downright comical.

'Maybe,' I told him, 'but don't go forgetting that I was one of those who helped to collect that gold aboard the *Walrus*, so no amount o' preaching is going to persuade me that one copper of it was come by without bloodshed and piracy!'

He laughed at that, and clapped me on the shoulder in his old familiar manner.

'Ah, Ben,' he says, heartylike, 'money's a strange thing to be sure, for split me if I can ever see how any of it is honestly earned in the first place! Now you take them gold bars below, as is worth mebbe two or three hundred guineas apiece. Where did we get 'em? From the Spaniards, says you. And where did the Spanish get 'em? From the mines, says you. And who digged 'em from the mines? The Indians, say we, and died a-doing of it, and most of 'em under the whip! Well now, that being so, who has the more right to 'em? The Indians, the Spanish or you?'

He was at it again and I knew if I stayed long enough in that galley he would have talked me into believing as the only honest trade afloat was that of a common pirate, and that we were doing people favours by boarding and sinking them, so I skipped out, and took a turn forward, where I could puzzle over in my mind how to make sure it didn't start all over again, and I didn't come up on deck one morning to find every honest throat cut, Silver on the poop deck, and me for his crew.

I was so certain sure that this would happen that I set about thinking how to get rid of him then and there, without wasting another moment.

I went at it three ways. I could have pretended to go along with him until I learned enough to warn the captain, and get him clapped in irons, but what good would that have done? With gentlemen aboard who respected the law, and didn't seem inclined to set it aside, not even for men as treacherous and as dangerous as Silver, it would have been a waste of time, besides the irons weren't made as could keep Silver harmless for two watches together. I could have killed him I suppose, though I didn't fancy the job overmuch, for he wasn't the man as you could catch off his guard, not even when you judged him sound asleep, and beyond that I reckoned I'd done with killing from now on, even men who deserved nothing better.

The third lay was to get him ashore somewhere simply by conniving at his escape. I was pondering along these lines when Abe Gray hails me, and says as we were making for the Main to pick up crew for the eastward voyage. Right off I saw my chance. I could get Silver away then and make a clean breast of it afterwards.

It was a deal easier than I bargained for. The night we dropped anchor off Surinam, what does your party do but go aboard the British man-o'-war you were lucky enough to find, and stay there half the night, leaving but me and Abe Gray to guard a fortune in gold? True, you did take the precaution of locking Silver in the forecastle, but, my heart, I came near to laughing out loud when I saw how much reliance you placed on that man's promise to reform, and how much faith you had in a bolt and staple, and two sailormen, each of whom had been talked round by Long John in the past.

I reckon you owe both fortune and schooner to the fact that Abe is a sound sleeper, and was fair worn out with all the maintop work he had done since leaving the island, and also, maybe, to my knowledge of Silver over the years.

An hour before moonrise I went forward and hailed John. There was no answer and I saw the door swinging free. I flashed a lantern inside and the forecastle was empty. Silver had slipped the bolt with a piece of wire, bent like a shepherd's crook.

'Well,' I said to myself, 'he's gone, and that saves me the trouble.'

I went aft to where Abe was supposed to be on guard outside the poop cabin, and sure enough there he sprawled, snoring like a hog, with his pistols and firelock laid by ready for anyone to pick up or step over, whichever they preferred.

I was about to wake him, and let on we were being attacked just for the fun of seeing him jump up and make a wild grab at his weapons, when I heard a faint scraping noise, like a hawser being dragged over timber, and it seemed to come from close under my feet.

I was puzzled for a minute and then it came to me in a flash. Silver was still aboard, and already coming to grips with the doubloons as we'd been considerate enough to stow aboard for him.

It didn't take me long to make up my mind to that, or as to where he was at work. He was breaking in from the sailroom, slap under the cabin, and I reckoned I could catch him red-handed if I went about it the right way.

I took off my shoes and went forward again, slipping down the forecastle ladder, and along the sparred gallery to the after companion, just the way you did when you were keeping a weather eye on the wounded Hands. Here I stood listening and the scraping sounds were louder and came, as I'd suspected, from the far side of the sailroom bulkhead.

I had a pistol but I didn't intend to use it so I laid it by and called softly from the companion.

'John!' I said, 'it's Ben, and I'm here after my share!'

There was silence as he stopped work. A moment later he showed up at the sailroom hatch. He was sweating and half covered in sawdust. A carpenter's handsaw was swinging from his crutch lanyard and he didn't seem that much surprised to see me.

'Ah, Ben,' he said finally, 'I judged you'd be along, so you was aboard, and it's main glad I am that you showed up, for it's beyond my powers to haul up more than the price of a bumboat ride with this timber leg o' mine. Jump down and lend a hand, shipmate!'

There it was; he had long since made up his mind that I was beyond changing, and took it for granted I was still as much a sea-thief as he was himself.

I dropped into the sailroom and took a look at his work. In the light of a masked lantern he had sawn a square hole in the cabin floor, and had been on the point of lifting out the trap, and struggling through to help himself when I hailed.

'John,' I said softly, for if Abe had awakened he would have pistolled the pair of us, I reckon, 'how much do you reckon to take, and how do you plan to haul it ashore?'

'As to that,' he said, 'as much as I can carry, and I've a nigger waiting under the stern with a boat as'll ferry the pair of us.'

How he had managed to get hold of that nigger and arrange to be picked up is more than I can say, but he had and the boat was there waiting, moored to our stern hawser, with a nigger sitting like a statue in the thwarts.

'John,' I said, still speaking in a whisper, 'I'm not coming and as for you, you can take one sack of minted coin as I'll go so far as to carry aloft for you. If you want more you must fight for it, not only against Abe Gray, as I can wake with a sharp hail, but against me too, I reckon, and there's my terms, take them or leave them!'

He looked at me hard for a minute, his big face blank with astonishment. Then he let out a stifled guffaw and clapped his free hand to his stomach.

'Why, sink me if you don't mean it, Ben!' he exclaimed, 'and me all the time trying to guess the private game you was up to!'

'Well,' I said, 'which is it to be, John? A clean pair of heels, and a few pocketsful of doubloons, or a fight with the pair of us, a trip in irons, and a noose to fit your thick neck at the finish of it?'

He saw he was beaten and was quick enough to own it.

'Ben, Ben,' he said, for the second time since we re-met, 'to think as you've done me!'

I didn't waste any further time in talk but slipped in through the hole he had made and hauled out one of the smallest sacks of coin. I carried it out for him and he jingled it down into the boat before turning to hoist himself on to the ladder that swung from the poop rail.

Just then the moon sailed out from behind a bank of cloud and shone full on his big face.

'Ben, boy,' he said by way of a parting shot, 'don't you go forgetting all as I've said to you about the ways men come by their money! It's been a notion o' mine these twenty years that Providence helps those as forage for themselves, and as to the contrary, well, let them who wants to pull forelocks for bread go to pulling 'em, until they goes grey or bald in the doing of it! As for me, I'm a lone wolf, Ben, and one who has had his

fill of pack-hunting. From now on I hunts singlehanded, or burn me fcr a chicken-hearted seacook!'

And with a sort of mocking sea-salute he slipped down the ladder, and pushed off into the bay.

I leaned on the rail watching him until his boat was a blur against the shore lights, and I fell to thinking, for the hundredth time maybe, what a strange manner of man he was, and whether, in all creation, there had ever been another like him.

Then I went forward and broke the news to Abe against the captain's return.

CHAPTER SEVEN THE ROAD HOME

There's little more you don't know already, Jim.

Captain and Squire said little or nothing about the part I had in Silver's escape. Maybe I was wrong about them, and they were as glad to be quit of him as I was. Howsoever, they stood by me like Britons when we got home, and both Squire and Doctor, being magistrates, travelled up to Exeter, and brought about the cancellation of the warrant that was still laying up at the Castle charging me with a share in the Custer murder.

I think things were made a deal easier for them by a letter the Doctor got from Miss Dulcie, Nick's sister. It had come to her four or five years since, and had been written by Nick during one of our spells in Tortuga. He must have handed it to the skipper of a Plymouth or Bristol-bound ship as we rifled and let go.

I never set eyes on that letter itself, but the Doctor told me what was in it. Nick had set down that he alone was responsible for killing Basil Custer, though in self-defence, and that I had found him injured the following morning, and had merely obeyed his orders in getting him conveyed by post-chaise to Plymouth. He said further as I knew nothing of the murder until I was afloat, and was then not placed to do much about it. I don't know how much of this the Sheriff believed, but it was enough to get me clear of the Law, and enable me to go back home once Old Man Custer had died, and the estates had passed into the hands of strangers.

By that time, of course, my old mother and father had long since passed to their rest, and all I could do was to pipe an eye over the grave that they shared not a stone's-throw from our cottage, the same as you've given your affydavy to lay me in when my time comes. The hardest job of that homecoming was the call I paid on Miss Dulcie, who was still living up at the parsonage, paler and greyer than I remember, but still sweet of voice and disposition. She made me tell her everything I recalled of Nick, what he said, how he looked, how often he'd spoken of her, and finally how he had come to die.

I told my fill of lies that day, Jim, and I don't regret them. If she had known the truth I reckon it would have about finished her. She sent me away with a guinea, as I didn't feel called upon to refuse, and I hope I left her comforted by the story I thought up on the instant, of how poor brother Nick had died of blackwater fever on his plantation in Virginny long years ago.

You'll stand witness, I reckon, that since coming ashore I've tried to make such amends as came handy, and if I did go for the rum now and again it was because I've never ceased to have doubts as to whether I hadn't started in too late.

The best comfort I've had latterly is to hear you read over that bit of the Scriptures that says there's more joy in heaven over one sinner who repents than in the ninety-and-nine as have nothing to repent on.

If that's true, and we've read it aright, Jim, then I reckon I have got a chance. More I don't ask, or expect, and there's an end to it!

*

Narrative continued by Jim Hawkins,
in the year 1811.

It is more than six years since I carried out Ben's final wish and laid the old buccaneer where he asked to be laid, alongside his mother in the churchyard.

More than four years have passed since I wrote 'finis' to my account of his story and, with the writing of it, thought to complete at last the curious story of Flint's treasure, and all that befell us in bringing it home.

The last of my companions, Captain Abe Gray, died a year or so back, father of a large family, a man of some substance, and the owner of several tall vessels pursuing a thriving Indian trade.

When Abe died I thought of myself as the last member of the *Hispaniola*'s company above ground, but I was wrong, as you shall see from the following pages.

It was about a year ago on a gusty March evening, that one of my outdoor servants came in to me and said he had detained an elderly man whom he had found prowling in the dusk on the big lawn that fronts my study windows.

I thought at first that it must be a poacher and long friendship with Ben had made me unusually tolerant of such intruders. I never yet arrested one or sought to, for I can never forget the fate of Ben's uncle, or the miseries the Custers occasioned by their harsh application of the game laws fifty years ago.

My servant, however, declared that this man was no poacher,

201

but a seaman and a poor one at that, for he was approaching his seventies, woefully undernourished and clad in nothing but tarry rags. The man, it appeared, had actually asked my keeper to conduct him into my presence as he stated he had something to say to me.

Curious to discover what such a beggar could demand of me other than alms, I gave orders that he was to be fed and brought in. This was done, and with log fire blazing, and curtains drawn, I settled down to receive my visitor.

He came in with a timid, one might almost say a servile air. He was about middle height, but bent and emaciated. Such hair as he possessed was iron grey, and fell in sparse ringlets about his bent shoulders, reminding me a little of Ben Gunn as he first appeared to me on the island. His clothes, as I had been warned, were little more than rags, but he wore a seaman's belt and had a seaman's gait when he crossed the floor, mumbling apologies and hunched up, as though expecting a blow from the nearest quarter. His face was burned a deep mahogany, and his voice was cracked and wheezing. Altogether I had seldom looked upon such a pitiable object, and I bade him sit down and say what he had to say, dismissing my servant, and ordering up punch and pipes.

As soon as my servant had gone the stranger subjected me to a long and steady scrutiny, so long and severe indeed as to cause me some embarrassment.

Finally he said: 'Mr Hawkins, sir? Mr Jim Hawkins, once of Black Cove?'

I told him shortly that such was my name and he had best declare his business.

'Ah,' he said, with a deep sigh, 'but I wanted to be sure, for it'd do me no good to go blabbing to the wrong man, and such I might well ha' done, seeing as it's forty years since I looked on you!'

'You know me?' I demanded. 'But how and when?'

He fell to coughing and it was some time before he could speak. I ladled him punch and he thanked me, over and over again, as he raised it to his trembling lips.

'I'm Dick!' he said simply, 'Dick as cut the Bible, and paid dearly for it, as dear as a man can pay and still breathe!'

I started up with an exclamation. No matter how hard I looked at him I could see nothing in this broken old man that reminded me in the least degree of the young seaman who had fought against us in the stockade, and had been marooned, with two companions, when we finally sailed off with the treasure.

'Dick!' I exclaimed. 'You!'

He dribbled his punch and, now that he had made his confession, a look of renewed fear showed in his eyes.

'What I done has been paid for,' he quavered. 'You're the only man as is likely to recall me and I reckon I'm here after such mercy as I can get from you, Mr Hawkins!'

I saw that what he needed most, after food, drink and clothing, was my reassurance, and that I was ready to give him, for I could not find it in me to see him further punished for the crime of mutiny, and that after a lapse of two score years. Besides, I found myself thirsting for his story. Many a time when Ben and I had fallen to talking over old times, we had wondered what had happened to the mutineers on the island, and how long they had been able to survive.

The poor wretch responded to my promise of an amnesty in a manner that was pathetic to regard. Warmed by the fire, and the food and drink he had taken, he told me everything he could recall of his sojourn on the island, and of his wretched experiences since leaving it. It was not a long narrative but for me at least it was full of interest and not untouched by pity.

You will recall that the last survivor of Flint's original crew (apart from Silver himself) had been old Tom Morgan, who was all of sixty when he was marooned. The other member of that wretched trio was a young seaman called Jim Fowler, a tall, redheaded mutineer, whom Silver had succeeded in wooing from his duty on the voyage out.

Tom Morgan and Dick, it seemed, had settled down to make the best of things once they had recovered from the horrid shock of being abandoned. Morgan was ever silent, dependable pirate, clever with his hands, and loyal after his fashion. He was not slow to realise that only the gallows awaited him in England, and he set about using his homely crafts to the best advantage of himself and his companions.

Dick was young enough to shake off his attack of fever once the little party had belatedly taken the doctor's advice and moved out of the bad air of the swamp. It was he who, being the most active, did most of the hunting, and with an unlimited supply of goat's flesh, together with the stores we had left for them, the trio lived well enough in a shanty they built for themselves on the southern shoulder of Spyglass. Dick said they preferred this to the more cramped quarters of Ben's cave, on the other side of the island.

The redheaded man, however, made little or no attempt to acclimatise himself, and the loneliness of the place, or perhaps his guilty memories, gradually affected his reason. After several attempts to restrain him the others were obliged to drive him out of the camp and he lived wild for a time, subsisting on berries and turtles, the flesh of which he appears to have eaten raw, like the wild beast he ultimately became.

Dick glimpsed him once or twice during his hunting trips. He was stark naked, and covered with long, reddish hair, that made him look more like a dangerous animal than a man. And dangerous he proved as time went on, once rolling a rock from Foremast Hill that came near to killing Tom Morgan, and another time creeping into the camp while his shipmates were asleep and using the embers of their fire to burn down the cabin.

Finally Morgan and Dick agreed that their lives depended on hunting him down and killing him out of hand, and this was eventually done, Dick creeping upon the madman in the old camp by the Anchorage, and shooting him through the head as he tore at his uncooked meat.

I think the killing of that poor wretch did more towards sobering Dick than anything else that had occurred, including our act in marooning him.

From then on he went hard at his mutilated Bible until he got a great deal of it by heart, and he told me that when Old Tom died, and he was as lonely as Ben Gunn had been, his knowledge of the Scriptures proved a source of great comfort to him. In all conscience he needed comfort, isolated as he was, and surrounded by the bones of men he had helped to murder.

Eight years he was there by his own reckoning, and not once during that time did it occur to him to look for the silver or the arms in the northern caches. Long John, it seemed, had never returned for what remained of the treasure although, from the markings on the chart the Doctor had given him, he must have known pretty well where they were buried.

In the ninth year, however, a ship did put in, a Spanish vessel engaged in charting that section of the ocean, and it was to the captain of this ship that the unfortunate Dick presented himself as a castaway.

He would have done better to take to the woods.

The Spaniard was from Europe, and consequently a very different type of Spaniard from those who had been raised in the western isles, and had learned to wink at the King of Spain's decrees regarding foreign seamen. Having satisfied himself that Dick was an Englishman and being far from satisfied with his rambling account of how he came to be alone on such a place, the captain took Dick for a runaway slave, and sold him ashore to work out the rest of his life in the plantations.

Here he remained tending sugar cane for more than twenty years, longing, no doubt, for the solitary bliss of Kidd's Island. At the end of that time, during a naval sally by the British Governor of Jamaica, the poor wretch was rescued by his fellow countrymen and given work aboard ships until, old and broken, he managed to work his passage home.

The day he landed he began to tramp along the coast, having made discreet enquiries about the Squire's party and ultimately met someone in Plymouth who had spoken of me as a man unlikely to nurse a grudge for half a century. Now, having quitted the sea, all he sought was a menial task about my house, that he might die on the soil of his native land from which he had set out, with such high hopes, as a sailor-lad so long ago.

I did what I could for him but as events turned out it was little enough.

Dick's body was racked with fevers of the island, and further undermined by the brutal treatment he had received from the Spanish. He lived with my servants less than a year and then passed quietly away in his sleep, happy I hope, to have died a free man, and not a bondsman in the squalid cabins of the plantation slaves.

February snow fell as I buried him near Ben, whose experiences he had in some senses shared. As the parson intoned the burial service over his coffin my mind travelled swiftly back to that soft night so long ago, when I had crouched in the apple barrel, and heard Silver beguile the boy with tales of piracies past and fabulous riches ahead.

What had Dick said when Silver pointed out that most pirates ended their lives in beggary? 'Well, it ain't much use after all?' And Silver had replied: "Tain't much use for fools!' How prophetic this question and answer had proved, for here was Dick, a fool if there was one, ending a life of misery. As for Silver, where was he?

Did his bones lie on some desolate headland like Nick's, or on the floor of a wandering sea like Hands'? Had his huge frame dried in the sun on some tidemark gibbet, as he once feared, or had it been lightly tossed to the sharks in some half-forgotten affray among the cays and shoals of the Spanish Main?

It seemed to me at that moment that not one of these predictable fates had overtaken him, for I do not think Divine Justice would be so conventionally served. I believed, as I turned from Dick's grave on which the thin snow was already gathering, that John Silver had gone to his long home not less pitied, not less poor and despised than Dick, the least of his victims, and perhaps, without a single fellow-man to wish him well on his dark journey.

If this seems hard and unforgiving to a man of Silver's parts, then let it be recalled that, unlike the rough and ignorant seamen he led, Silver had within him the capacity to be big and free and generous, yet, not once, but many times, had he turned his broad back on the gifts God had given him, and deliberately ranged himself alongside the forces of evil.

That, to my mind at all events, was the greatest sin of all, and when he faced the Court where glibness is of no avail, he was probably ranked high in the hierarchy of villainy, far higher than Ben, or Dick, or any of the men who went singing and shouting about their trade among the island of the Golden West.

For with Silver, as with none of these others, there was promise that was lamentably unfulfilled.

THE END

NEL BESTSELLERS

Crime

T012 484	FIVE RED HERRINGS	*Dorothy L. Sayers* 40p
T015 556	MURDER MUST ADVERTISE	*Dorothy L. Sayers* 40p
T014 398	STRIDING FOLLY	*Dorothy L. Sayers* 30p

Fiction

T015 386	THE NORTHERN LIGHT	*A. J. Cronin* 50p
T016 544	THE CITADEL	*A. J. Cronin* 75p
T015 130	THE MONEY MAKER	*John J. McNamara Jr.* 50p
T013 820	THE DREAM MERCHANTS	*Harold Robbins* 75p
T018 105	THE CARPETBAGGERS	*Harold Robbins* 95p
T016 560	WHERE LOVE HAS GONE	*Harold Robbins* 75p
T013 707	THE ADVENTURERS	*Harold Robbins* 80p
T006 743	THE INHERITORS	*Harold Robbins* 60p
T009 467	STILETTO	*Harold Robbins* 30p
T015 289	NEVER LEAVE ME	*Harold Robbins* 40p
T016 579	NEVER LOVE A STRANGER	*Harold Robbins* 75p
T011 798	A STONE FOR DANNY FISHER	*Harold Robbins* 60p
T015 874	79 PARK AVENUE	*Harold Robbins* 60p
T011 461	THE BETSY	*Harold Robbins* 75p
T013 340	SUMMER OF THE RED WOLF	*Morris West* 50p

Historical

T013 758	THE LADY FOR RANSOM	*Alfred Duggan* 40p
T015 297	COUNT BOHEMOND	*Alfred Duggan* 50p
T010 279	MASK OF APOLLO	*Mary Renault* 50p
T014 045	TREASURE OF PLEASANT VALLEY	*Frank Yerby* 35p
T015 602	GILLIAN	*Frank Yerby* 50p

Science Fiction

T015 017	EQUATOR	*Brian Aldiss* 30p
T014 347	SPACE RANGER	*Isaac Asimov* 30p
T015 491	PIRATES OF THE ASTEROIDS	*Isaac Asimov* 30p
T016 331	THE CHESSMEN OF MARS	*Edgar Rice Burroughs* 40p
T013 537	WIZARD OF VENUS	*Edgar Rice Burroughs* 30p
T009 696	GLORY ROAD	*Robert Heinlein* 40p
T016 900	STRANGER IN A STRANGE LAND	*Robert Heinlein* 75p
T011 844	DUNE	*Frank Herbert* 75p
T012 298	DUNE MESSIAH	*Frank Herbert* 40p
T015 211	THE GREEN BRAIN	*Frank Herbert* 30p

War

T013 367	DEVIL'S GUARD	*Robert Elford* 50p
T015 505	THE LAST VOYAGE OF GRAF SPEE	*Michael Powell* 30p
T015 661	JACKALS OF THE REICH	*Ronald Seth* 30p
T012 263	FLEET WITHOUT A FRIEND	*John Vader* 30p

Western

T016 994	No. 1 EDGE – THE LONER	*George G. Gilman* 30p
T016 536	No. 5 EDGE – BLOOD ON SILVER	*George G. Gilman* 30p
T017 621	No. 6 EDGE – THE BLUE, THE GREY AND THE RED	
		George G. Gilman 30p
T014 479	No. 7 EDGE – CALIFORNIA KILLING	*George G. Gilman* 30p
T015 254	No. 8 EDGE – SEVEN OUT OF HELL	*George G. Gilman* 30p
T015 475	No. 9 EDGE – BLOODY SUMMER	*George G. Gilman* 30p

General

T011 763	SEX MANNERS FOR MEN	*Robert Chartham* 30p
W002 531	SEX MANNERS FOR ADVANCED LOVERS	*Robert Chartham* 25p
W002 835	SEX AND THE OVER FORTIES	*Robert Chartham* 30p
T010 732	THE SENSUOUS COUPLE	*Dr. 'C'* 25p

NEL P.O. BOX 11, FALMOUTH, TR10 9EN, CORNWALL

Please send cheque or postal order. Allow 10p to cover postage and packing on one book plus 4p for each additional book.

Name ....

Address...

....

Title ....
(SEPTEMBER)